The Mystery
of
"A Yellow Sleuth"

The Mystery of "A Yellow Sleuth"

Detective Sergeant Nor Nalla,
Federated Malay States Police

Ronald Allan

*With a Foreword by Paul Kratoska
and an Introduction by Philip Holden*

RIDGE BOOKS
SINGAPORE

Published under the Ridge Books imprint by:

NUS Press
National University of Singapore
AS3-01-02
3 Arts Link
Singapore 117569

Fax: (65) 6774-0652
E-mail: nusbooks@nus.edu.sg
Website: http://nuspress.nus.edu.sg

ISBN 978-981-4722-64-3 (paper)

National Library Board, Singapore Cataloguing in Publication Data

Name(s): Allan, Ronald. | Kratoska, Paul H., author of foreword. | Holden, Philip, 1962- author of introduction.
Title: The mystery of "A yellow sleuth": detective sergeant Nor Nalla, Federated Malay States police / Ronald Allan; with a foreword by Paul H. Kratoska and an introduction by Philip Holden.
Description: Singapore: Ridge Books, [2018]
Identifier(s): OCN 986890936 | ISBN 978-981-4722-64-3 (paperback)
Subject(s): LCSH: Crime--Malaysia--Malaya--History--20th century. | Criminals--Malaysia--Malaya--History--20th century. | Detectives--Malaysia--Malaya--Biography.
Classification: DDC 363.2092--dc23

First published in London in 1931 by Hutchinson & Co. (Publishers), Ltd.

Typeset by: Ogma Solutions Pvt Ltd
Printed by: Markono Print Media Pte Ltd

Dedicated
(*by permission*)

TO

CAPTAIN LINDSAY VEARS
(*A.D.C. to his Highness the Sultan of Perak, K.C.M.G., K.C.V.O.*),
WHO HAS STOOD MY GOOD FRIEND IN PEACE AND WAR

By

THE AUTHOR

THE AUTHOR — AND A FRIEND.
(*It is interesting to note the difference in stature between the native Malay and his European friend.*)

Foreword

I suppose it was "the Chinaman getting his throat cut on my bed" which really brought things to a point. Captain Ferguson had often spoken to me about it, and so, for that matter, had Mr. MacDonald; but, after what they chose to call my narrow escape, they both became insistent. As Mr. MacDonald cheerfully said, "Suppose it had been your throat that was slit from ear to ear, all your stories would have been lost." Superintendent O'Brien joined them in insisting that I must write my autobiography forthwith, as I "might be killed any minute".

They were so insistent that they even supplied me with a library of autobiographies "to show me how it was done", and, in one way and another, gave me no peace till I sat down to write this account.

My readers must not blame me, therefore, for inflicting my story on them, but they must blame these two police officers and the civil servant, mentioned above. I find, from my studies of autobiographies, that the names of living people should be suppressed, so the names of those offenders, together with all other names which I will doubtless have to mention during my story, are not those of the actual people concerned. Following my models, I will also from time to time alter, where necessary, the names of the places where the incidents occurred, in order that those not directly concerned in them may not recognize the individuals under their new names.

Strangely enough, my friends also insisted that my own name should be similarly disguised, for, as they pointed out, there are many criminals who do not know that it was owing to my efforts that either they or their friends suffered punishment, and as this story will honestly recount the part I have played in the detection of crime, it would be foolish of me to advertise my identity thus widely.

So there you have it! An autobiography! A true history! And, for a start, you learn that it is largely untrue, and that not even the author's name is genuine! If I am to listen to my advisers, such deceit seems to be essential, I am sorry to say. I suppose that I had better, now, really start on my autobiography.

The author

Foreword to the New Edition

In September 1931, the British publishing house Hutchinson & Co. published a book entitled *A Yellow Sleuth, Being the Autobiography of "Nor Nalla"* (*Detective-Sergeant Federated Malay States Police*). The book described police cases from British Malaya and the accounts were full of harrowing situations and narrow escapes leading to the capture or sometimes the death of many criminals. The author identified himself as a police detective with a Malay father and Sakai mother. He wrote excellent if somewhat flowery English, and claimed to be sufficiently fluent in the languages of his parents along with Chinese, Javanese and Tamil to pass as a native speaker. Contemporary reviewers accepted these claims more or less at face value. A writer in the *Spectator* commented that some of the stories in the book "appear so far-fetched as to be impossible" and thought it "remarkable to find an Oriental native of the humblest origin writing a book in English", but nevertheless concluded "we believe it is entirely true".[1] In Singapore a reviewer for *The Straits Times* had doubts about whether a Malay detective could have written a passage describing "the eldritch shrieks of the attackers", but noted that it was possible because such language could be found in secondary school magazines in Malaya. This reviewer was even more sceptical about the contents of the book, saying that it presented "an interesting problem of distinguishing between fact and fiction".[2]

I first encountered Nor Nalla in a second-hand bookstore in Paris, where a battered copy of a French translation of *A Yellow Sleuth* was languishing in the basement. At the time I was a lecturer at Universiti Sains Malaysia, and once back in Malaysia I found a photocopy of the original English edition in the university library. I read it but there

---

1   *Spectator*, 19 Dec. 1931, p. 22.
2   *The Straits Times*, 6 Nov. 1931, p. 14.

matters rested until NUS Press decided to re-issue the book, and I set out to learn more about Nor Nalla.

Neither the French nor the English version had any information about the author apart from a photograph captioned "The Author— and a Friend", and an internet search proved fruitless. As a last resort I published an appeal in the Notes & Queries section of the *Journal of the Malaysian Branch of the Royal Asiatic Society*, a very old fashioned thing to do in an era of social media. Shortly after the issue appeared, a reader sent me an entry from the US Library of Congress catalogue that attributed the book to a Ronald Allan. Some two weeks later, a letter arrived from a man named David Allan saying that he had come across my note while looking online for a copy of "my great uncle's book 'The Yellow Sleuth'". The ensuing correspondence cleared up many, but not quite all, of the mysteries surrounding Nor Nalla.

David Allan told me that Ronald Allan was the tall European in the photograph and that Nor Nalla is an anagram for Ron Allan. He referred me to his cousin, Richard Torrance, who provided further details. Ronald Allan was born on 25 February 1886, the youngest child of Sir William Allan MP and Jean Beattie, and died in 1945. He grew up in Sunderland, where the family lived in Scotland House near Mowbray Park, and was educated at Sunderland High School, Durham School and Armstrong College. He subsequently worked at S.P. Austin's shipbuilding yard, and at McKenzie & Torrance, an Edinburgh engineering firm.

The next phase of his life is germane to *A Yellow Sleuth*. He was in Aden around 1909, apparently on his way to Malaya where he was employed on Castlewood Estate, a relatively large (2,055-acre) rubber plantation located near Kuala Lumpur.[3] Around 1912 his name appeared in a newspaper report after he became involved in an imbroglio with a group of estate workers. Allan was fined $5 for causing hurt to a labourer whom he struck with a rattan cane. He in turn prosecuted ten labourers who had retaliated by attacking him, breaking his finger and causing heavy bruising, and seven of them received prison sentences. This episode aside, his time in Malaya seems to have been uneventful, and in 1914 he was back in the United Kingdom as a probationary 2nd Lieutenant in the Army. During the First World War he served in Europe

---

3   *The Directory & Chronicle for China, Japan, Corea, Indo-China, Straits Settlements, Malay States, Siam, Netherlands India, Borneo, The Philippines, &c. ... for the Year 1912* (Hong Kong: The Hongkong Daily Press Office, 1912), p. 1386.

and presumably encountered the Chinese Labour Corps, which figures in *A Yellow Sleuth*.[4]

Ronald Allan married in 1918, and from 1920 through 1940 worked as the London representative for the marine department of Richardsons Westgarth, a business involved in shipbuilding and marine engineering. Family lore suggests that he lived beyond his means and developed a reputation for a bohemian lifestyle. Joyce Grenfell's book *Darling Ma* mentions him briefly in an account of concerning a supper Grenfell attended along with one of Allan's nieces.

> The uncle is very Scotch about fifty-five, retired from rubber planting out east and is now in some City job. They warned me that he was Bohemian; that he might not be wearing socks! The flat was high in an old-fashioned block. The uncle wore a black velvet smoking jacket, open-silk shirt, and *no* socks![5]

Ronald Allan may have written *A Yellow Sleuth* to qualify for membership in the Savage Club in London, where his father had been a member. According to a history of the club published in 1867 by its then president, Andrew Halliday, it was founded in 1857 as "a meeting of gentlemen connected with literature and the fine arts, and warmly interested in the promotion of Christian knowledge, and the sale of exciseable liquors". Named for Richard Savage, an eighteenth-century poet who was the subject of Samuel Johnson's *Life of Savage*, the club was, and is, self-proclaimed as "one of the leading Bohemian Gentleman's Clubs in London".[6]

Allan had been absent from Malaya for nearly 20 years when *A Yellow Sleuth* appeared, so the failure of reviewers to identify him from his photograph is not altogether surprising. However, a number of questions remain unanswered. The review in *The Straits Times* stated that "there is no doubt that 'Nor Nalla' knows this country thoroughly and has lived in it many years, for he speaks of the disturbances in Kuala Lumpur which followed the inauguration of the Chinese Republic

---

4 For a short account of Chinese labourers sent to Europe during the war, see Mark O'Neill, *The Chinese Labour Corps: The Forgotten Chinese Labourers of the First World War* (London: Penguin Books, 2014). The labourers were poor working-class men from northern China, making it unlikely that "Nor Nalla" could have communicated with them, let along pass unnoticed.

5 Joyce Grenfell, *Darling Ma: Letters to Her Mother, 1932–44* (London: Coronet Books, 1999), p. 71.

6 Andrew Halliday (ed.), *The Savage-club papers* (London: Tinsley Brothers, 1867), p. x; http://www.savageclub.com/.

in 1911, the Singapore Mutiny of 1915, and other events which date his career". The reviewer said the book gave rise to "a mixture of admiration and incredulity", but reiterated the point that "the authentic street-life of Malayan towns is here".[7]

It is far from clear how someone who left Malaya before the First World War and apparently never returned could write such a book. A clue to the answer may lie in its dedication to Captain Lindsay Vears, "who has stood my good friend in peace and war". Born in 1882, Vears like Allan worked on a rubber estate in Malaya prior to the war, and the two men may have met then. During the First World War he served as an officer with the Royal Field Artillery, and Allan's dedication suggests further contact. Unlike Allan, Vears returned to Malaya, and during the 1930s served as Aide de Camp to the Sultan of Perak. He was interned during the Japanese Occupation and stayed after the war, retiring in Penang where he died on 21 February 1963.[8] Whether he had a role in the writing of A Yellow Sleuth can only be a matter of conjecture, but he would have had the sort of local knowledge displayed in the book, and through his connection with the Sultan of Perak could have had access to information about police cases.

Whether fact or fiction or some of both, the book is unquestionably engaging. The author ends his Foreword with this warning: "So there you have it! An autobiography! A true history! And, for a start, you learn that it is largely untrue, and that not even the author's name is genuine!" The secret of his identity survived for three quarters of a century, and Richard Torrance said, "If Ron were alive today he would be revelling in the attention and be delighted that it has taken so long for his identity to be revealed."

Paul Kratoska
NUS Press

7   Review of A Yellow Sleuth, The Straits Times, 6 Nov. 1931, p. 14.
8   http://www.gloucesterrugbyheritage.org.uk/page_id_767.aspx.

Introduction to the New Edition

"Joining the crowd at funerals, at the races, at weddings. Listening, listening, listening, and reports, reports, reports," complains Sergeant Nalla, the fictional protagonist of Ronald Allan's *A Yellow Sleuth*. "How wearisome it all can be, when one returns from a mission on which one has been entirely one's own master!" (p. 154). Nalla's complaint dramatizes one of the central conflicts of colonial detective fiction. In one respect, the colonial detective might be seen as an embodiment of imperial power, "the Panopticon's central tower with legs" in Caroline Reitz's memorable phrase (p. xxii), his inquiries penetrating into all areas of society, and succeeding through the application of Enlightenment rationality associated with Europe. Yet the detective in the colonies, just like his metropolitan counterpart Sherlock Holmes, is often his "own master" as a marginal figure, alienated from the bureaucracy of the state apparatus, and only achieving success in solving crimes and bringing criminals to justice by crossing societal boundaries and moving outside juridical norms.

In Nalla, Ronald Allan creates such a figure, an impossible fantasy of hybridity. The sleuth is Malay, and yet loyal to British colonial power. A potential source of conflict with colonialism, Islam, is never mentioned in the novel, and an early reference to "that heaven in which my new religion has taught me to believe" (p. 10) suggests that Allan's protagonist may have converted to Christianity. Nalla's Malay identity draws on British fascination with the Malay population of Malaya as nature's gentlemen, enacting a form of feudal manliness that had been lost, it was felt, in rapidly industrializing Britain. His claims to indigeneity are bolstered by the fact that his mother's grandfather was Sakai, one of the indigenous peoples of the Malayan Peninsula: he has learned the language from her, and can pass as a Sakai when necessary. Yet he is also at ease in the many languages of other groups, originally migrants, who have made Malaya their home. The pretext of his father being the house servant of a European employee on what is likely a rubber estate means that Nalla learns Hailam (Hainanese), the regional language of Chinese servants commonly employed as domestic helpers and cooks. The estate's proximity to a tin mine means that he picks up Hokkien from the children of the Chinese workers there, thereby gaining knowledge of the most common Chinese regional language spoken in Malaya. The presence of Indian workers on the estate gives him proficiency in Tamil, and his father insists that he also learn English. As he moves into detective work, he learns Cantonese, Kheh (Hakka), Hindustani—"thrust upon me by my association with the many Indian boys who had been brought over with their officers" (p. 19) in a British military mess in Singapore—and then Dutch and Javanese in rapid succession. Later, in his travels, he acquires other regional Southeast Asian languages such as Vietnamese.

Nalla's appearance, which approximates to what we might now call "pan-Asian", also enables him to move across community boundaries. Aided by "the unusually light colour" of his skin (p. 44), he can pass as Malay, Sakai, Chinese, or Eurasian, as well as Burmese. There are, indeed, only two places in the colonial order of things that he cannot enter. He cannot, he notes late in his narrative, pass as Indian. More crucially, as his difficulties in carrying out regular surveillance duties when seconded to duty with the Metropolitan Police in London show, he cannot pass as White.

Despite Nalla's own liminality, however the narrative economy of the novel paradoxically requires that racial and linguistic divisions be kept firmly in place. A Yellow Sleuth illustrates the project of governance in British Malaya, in historian J.S. Furnivall's terms a "plural society" in which different racialized communities were allowed a degree of internal self-government but kept separate, and encouraged to meet only at the marketplace (p. 303). The novel thus makes substantial use of racial stereotypes, and indeed racist language such as "Kling" for Indians and "Chinamen". Political organization that attempts to cross racial boundaries—here represented by the concluding episode of the novel where Nalla infiltrates the "motley throng" (pp. 120, 135) of Asian "Bolsheviks" (p. 127) in a camp near the Siamese (Thai) border with Malaya—is shown to be motivated by bad faith. In linguistic terms, too, the frisson of the text is provided by the fact that Nalla can transgress boundaries of language that are marked by race or ethnicity as others cannot. He often overhears conversations that speakers think he will not understand, so much so that he confesses that "the practice of exhibiting ignorance of conversations which I thoroughly comprehend has become almost second nature to me" (p. 84). In performing his work of infiltration, Nalla thus indicates what Rachel Leow has characterized as the difficulties faced by the efforts of a colonial "monoglot state" in governing "a polyglot society" (p. 3). In British Malaya, Leow notes, "language diversity ... appeared to the state as something to be managed and mourned as a terrible confusion and a source of crisis" rather than being seen as an asset (p. 3). Nalla's exceptional linguistic transgressions, paradoxically, only serve the ultimate project of keeping a racialized linguistic order in place.

A Yellow Sleuth has an impressive geographical range, beginning with the protagonist's rural childhood, and then moving to his formal and informal education in spying and surveillance work in Kuala Lumpur, Singapore, Surabaya, and Borneo. After many anecdotes of his activities in Malaya in the early years of the twentieth century, Allan's protagonist moves first to the East End of London, and then to battle lines in France during the First World War. After a further excursion to the Welsh seaport of Cardiff, Nalla returns to Malaya to continue his work. As the narrative progresses, it changes structurally. The early part of the text consists of short, self-contained stories, very much in the mode of the fictional "autobiography" that Nalla presents to us in his Foreword. The later sections in England, France, Wales, and especially after the return to Malaya, are less episodic, and much more like a conventional novel in form.

It is a novel, indeed, that is clearly the greatest literary influence on Allan's writing practice. Rudyard Kipling's Kim (1901) is set in India, and follows the fortunes of Kimball O'Hara, the orphaned son of an Irish soldier, who is recruited by an intelligence operative working for the British, and becomes a key actor in the "Great Game" played out by clashing British and Russian empires in the Himalayas. A Yellow Sleuth's beginning has several parallels to Kim. Just as Kim is recruited first by the horse dealer Mahbub Ali, and only then is brought to the attention of his superior Colonel Creighton, so Nalla is put through his paces by a distant relative, Mat, in Kuala Lumpur, and impresses him enough to attract the interest of the civil servant Mr Ogilvy and the police department's Colonel Munroe. Nalla's first disguise, prowling the streets of Kuala Lumpur as a "street urchin" (p. 5), very much parallels Kim's peregrinations on the streets of Lahore. Both Nalla and Kim, furthermore, are sent by their sponsors to Catholic schools for European-style education: Kim to St Xavier's School in Lucknow, and Nalla to an unnamed Roman Catholic school in Surabaya. Both continue to have a remote but also filial relationship to their English superiors. Nalla tours Borneo with Ogilvy, and later, on his trip to England, is welcomed by a now retired Munroe, causing him to praise his superior's "invariable kindness and justice to me [that] taught me what a perfect being a man can be" (p. 78).

A Yellow Sleuth, however, was published some thirty years later than *Kim*, in a much-changed world. The twin shocks of the First World War and the beginning of the Great Depression had challenged both notions of as European civilising mission and the sustainability of colonial economies such as Malaya's that were based on plantation labour and resource extraction. Kipling's confidence and manly deeds of derring-do on the frontier had been replaced by an altogether different form of English colonial fiction, the writings of Somerset Maugham. Maugham arrived in Malaya and other locations of his "exotic fiction" as a tourist and professional writer, and he had little cultural knowledge of the Asian societies in which he moved. Yet he was a keen observer of colonial domesticity, and an astringent critic of the hypocrisies that it embodied. Most of his stories of Malaya were based on real incidents recounted to him or his partner Gerald Haxton: members of colonial society recognized themselves in them, but realized that any law suit would simply attract additional attention to scandals best kept secret. Like most colonial officials and his fellow unofficials, Allan was no doubt incensed by Maugham's portrayals, and Nalla indeed makes reference to Maugham's short story "The Letter", and the stage play and first film based on it, noting in particular that the movie represented "a farcical travesty of either the play or the truth" (p. 41). In this aspect, at least, *A Yellow Sleuth* seems to attempt a nostalgic return to an earlier style of narrative. Short stories such as Maugham's "The Force of Circumstance" explored the hypocrisy of the English planter who had a relationship and often children with a young Malay woman, and then attempted to pay her off when he married a European wife. Allan, like Maugham, explores crimes of passion arising from similar circumstances, but his description of the process as the replacement of a "housekeeper by a legitimate wife" (p. 44) leaves no doubt about where his, and his protagonist's, sympathies lie.

A Yellow Sleuth can perhaps best be understood by placing it in two more precise contexts: first, the intersection of detective fiction and stories of colonial adventure, and secondly the historical and literary context of Malaya in the 1930s. As the introductory paragraph to this essay suggests, in scholarly work influenced by the writings of Michel Foucault, both detective fiction and the colonial adventure story have been seen as expressions of modern forms of power. Foucault's *Discipline and Punish* draws on British philosopher Jeremy Bentham's vision of a Panopticon, a new form of incarceration in which prisoners, placed under continual surveillance, undertake projects of self-reformation, in order to make an argument about the manner in which power becomes internalized in modern societies. Foucault's insights were taken up in D.A. Miller's *The Novel and the Police*, which argued that the novel, far from being a subversive genre, actually incited readers to police themselves and conform to social norms. Miller's study, despite its title, is not centrally concerned with detective fiction, and yet studies of detective fiction inspired by Miller have proliferated. The detective, in these readings, appears to embody surveillance, using the light of rationality and scientific discovery to penetrate the fog of criminal activity in metropolitan society. The detective novel, in classifying and eliminating criminality, would thus appear to encourage a self-policing mind set in the reader.

Foucault's vision of a disciplinary society, and in particular societal uses of discourses, or regimes of truth, also profoundly influenced analyses of colonial adventure fiction. Edward Said's *Orientalism* famously explored a Western "discourse" of the Orient in which a series of discursive binarisms privileged Europe as Asia's opposite, modern and rational in opposition to primitive irrationality (p. 3). Said extended this analysis from *Orientalism*'s concern with what we call the Middle East to a famous reading of *Kim* that initially served as an introduction to a new Penguin edition of Kipling's novel, and was later included in the essay collection *Culture and Imperialism*. For all the mutability of its protagonist, Said argued, *Kim* kept Orientalist binarisms firmly in place. The novel, he argued, was marked by "political surveillance and control" in which all fantasises of "going native" were ultimately based on "the rock-like foundations of European power" (Said, *Culture and Imperialism*, p. 161). Interestingly, Said brought into his analysis a direct reference to the metropolitan detective story, comparing *Kim*'s superior Colonel Creighton to Sherlock Holmes, and noting that both were men "whose approach to life includes a healthy respect for, and protection of, the law allied with a superior, specialized intellect inclining to science.... Colonial rule and crime detection almost gain the respectability and order of the classics or chemistry" (p. 152).

Said's critique of the colonial detective novel is important, but it can be questioned in two areas. The first is from the perspective of metropolitan readers, "the peoples of Europe" (p. 76) for whom Nalla as narrator and Allan as author claim to write in *A Yellow Sleuth*. As Harish Trivedi notes, Said's concern with surveillance means that he focuses on Creighton in *Kim*, despite the fact that the British officer has only a small role in the novel, and neglects other aspects of the text (Trivedi, p. 132). In a more comprehensive discussion, Caroline Reitz explores the parallels between the emergence of the colonial adventure narrative and detective fiction in the nineteenth century. Both were connected to, and perhaps played a part in, changing notions of English identity. In the early 1800s, Empire and the police were both peripheral to Englishness. The American colonies had been lost, and the police were associated with an over-intrusive state exemplified by the excesses of the French Revolution. By the end of the century this had changed: Imperialism was central to British and English identities, and the presence of the police in society had become fully normalized. Detective fiction and colonial narratives of adventure played a part in this, not simply through the construction of Orientalist binaries, but rather in a "chiasmatic logic of identity formation" expressed by the "construction and deconstruction of opposing categories" (p. xix). The detective, the colonial adventurer, and by extension the colonial detective are all protected by the apparatus of colonial surveillance and knowledge, and yet they "chafe against social boundaries as much as they defend them" (p. 65).

A further critique of Said's reading of *Kim* can be made from a different perspective deriving from recent research interest in a world literature that transgresses national boundaries. Colonial detective fiction did not just exist for readers in the colonial metropolis, but was actively written and translated for various audiences in the colonies themselves. Doyle's Sherlock Homes stories were translated into languages such as Bengali only a few years after their initial publication (Pernau, p. 191). Moving closer to Malaya, Elizabeth Chandra has researched the emergence of detective fiction in the Dutch East Indies. Many such works were translated into Malay from both Dutch and Chinese and their ultimate sources—stories published in Europe, Australia, and the United States—were truly global (p. 40). By the 1920s, translated detective fiction in Malay had become very popular. Its publishers were largely ethnic Chinese, and the translations were part of a growing popular literature that served an important function of cultural brokerage, spreading the reach of the Romanized Malay that would develop into Indonesia's national language. As translations increased, they were increasingly supplemented by indigenous writing. Original stories composed in the Indies emerged, featuring ethnic Chinese detectives and set in cosmopolitan environments such as Shanghai, New York, Tianjin or Harbin. Finally, during nationalist studies in the 1940s, detective stories set in the Indies—or the nation of Indonesia in waiting—emerged.

This background enables us to consider the situation in Malaya in the 1920s and 1930s. British Malaya at that time was not a unified colony, but a complex series of different colonial and semi-colonial polities. The port cities of Penang, Malacca, and Singapore were united as the Crown Colony of the Straits Settlements, while the rest of the peninsula was occupied by the twin groupings of Federated and Unfederated Malay States, each individual state nominally independent, but with a British Resident or Advisor who wielded political power over all areas apart from customary and religious governance. In the Straits Settlements and Kuala Lumpur, the federal capital, publishing in Malay, Chinese, and to a lesser extent Tamil was vibrant, and was supplemented by English-language writing that was addressed not simply to colonial power but to a growing audience of Anglophone Asians. Historian Chua Ai Lin's work has illuminated the growth of this community, its struggle for political influence under a colonial regime that gave Malays precedence and saw other communities merely as immigrants and sojourners, and its creation of an "embryonic sense of shared Malayan identity" that began to be recognized by the British (p. 16).

Detective and colonial adventure fiction thus became a part of a contested field of colonial power. Adventure fiction by colonial officials such as Hugh Clifford was published in *The Straits Times*, while fiction written by Anglophone Asian writers appeared in publications such as *The Straits Chinese Magazine*. The latter publication featured detective fiction which wrote back to colonial power. In Wee Tong Poh's story "Is Revenge Sweet?", the bumbling and inefficient Englishman Inspector Catspaw of the Gambling Suppression Department must rely on the local knowledge of an urbane Straits Chinese doctor to solve his case. The cultural terrain that the detective story occupied was complex. An early article in the *Malaya Tribune*, a popular daily newspaper set up in 1914 with the explicit intention of representing the interest of Asians in Malaya, made use of the figure of a Malay detective as a "local Sherlock Holmes" in order to grant Asians agency ("Bicycle Thieves"). *The Singapore Free Press and Mercantile Advertiser*, more closely aligned with colonial authorities, had a contrasting vision. The newspaper reserved the title "Local Sherlock Holmes" for a Justice of the Peace who exceeded his authority, creeping into a house and using "criminal force" against a man he was sent to arrest ("Local Sherlock Holmes").

A Yellow Sleuth may be viewed in the context of this environment as an unconscious effort to manage social contradictions developing both within Malaya and the British Empire as a whole. For the colonial official, bureaucracy and the process of development had replaced any sense of adventure on the frontier. This new reality was recorded in Hugh Clifford's short story "Our Trusty and Well-Beloved" in which the Governor Philip Hanbury-Erskine disguises himself and escapes the "ironbound realities that hem in the life of a high Colonial official" for a single night's immersion "into the secret wells of native life" in Singapore's Kampong Glam reliving the excitement of his youth (pp. 15, 17). The first part of *A Yellow Sleuth* attempts to counter such ennui by devising a detective who, through his Sakai heritage, can still access the primitive. While many of the crimes Nalla investigates take place in cities, towns, or on plantations, his pursuit of the criminals who committed them often takes him into the central jungles of the peninsula, and up to the border with Siam. The jungle offers adventure, encounters with dangerous animals, woodcraft, and hand-to-hand combat. Nalla frequently returns from successful assignments there with the worry that he has, like the local Holmes of *The Singapore Free Press and Mercantile Advertiser*, exceeded his authority. Munroe, through bureaucratic sleight of hand, makes sure that everything is regularized.

The motif of pursuit to the frontier continues in the part of the text that is set in France, when Nalla pursues a suspected spy away from the Western Front to a remote border area. When action moves to England, however, it is superseded by a new concern familiar to its metropolitan readers—the stereotypes of "yellow peril" that condensed around London's first Chinatown in Limehouse, East London. The title of the book itself may have been influenced by Sax Rohmer's *The Yellow Claw* (1915), and in particular *Yellow Shadows* (1925), which featured a racist portrait of the restauranteur and cocaine dealer Brilliant Chang, whose antics received sensational coverage in the London press in the early 1920s. Nalla's discovery that the substance his drug dealers are selling is not opium but cocaine marks a transition from the Orientalist tradition of the opium den to a more contemporary figuration of the perils of interracial mixing in the 1920s London nightlife scene. Nalla's identity as a sleuth who can pass as Chinese but is committed to service of the police enables him to manage this threat. At times the narrative descends into bathos. When the sleuth moves to Cardiff it seems that he again faces stereotypes of transnational criminality, overcoming an "international gang of sycophants" (p. 121) run by an immigrant from West Africa, and then penetrating what appears to be another drug ring centred on a Chinese laundry. The substance traded, however, is ultimately revealed to be butter from Ireland, smuggled in to counter the rationing of dairy products.

Allan's text, indeed, at times challenges stereotypes of Chinese criminality even as it enacts them. While stationed in France watching over the Chinese labourers whose presence on First World War battlefields has been forgotten in most popular historical accounts, Nalla notes how often they are scapegoated (p. 115):

> It is a strange thing, but nevertheless true, that if there is a labour battalion of Chinese billeted in a district, all … misdemeanours entirely cease amongst the other units in the area! Any crime which is reported is one which has been committed by the Chinks. If there is a hundredweight of corrugated iron missing from a goods yard—the

Chinks have got it! If there are eighty standards of four-by-four timber short on the waybill—the Chinks have got it! These same malefactors will also have stolen bags of cement, loads of gravel, planks, coils of barbed wire, wheels, bandages, and even motor lorries!

If these reports were all true, the Chinks had collected enough material in my area alone to build a second Pekin in northern France.

As in other parts of the text, there is a contradiction between such moments of debunking of stereotypes and an overall narrative momentum that reinforces them.

Nalla's eventual return to Malaya returns us to a third concern, that of the growth of a community of Anglophone Asians and the challenge that they posed to colonial governance. A Yellow Sleuth's last section revolves mostly around an expedition that Nalla makes to a training school for "Bolshevik agents" (p. 128) located across the border in the jungles of Siam. The leader of this encampment, who styles himself Mohamed Abdulla, is revealed not to be Malay but Chinese, and the school is full of a "motley throng" of "all the races of the East [who] seemed to have supplied their outlaw recruits to swell the ranks" (p. 135). English is the shared language of both the hut to which the sleuth is assigned in his disguise as a cleaner, and in which lectures are given to the whole camp. Indeed, the sleuth notes of English that the camp's inhabitants "would even address their fellow nationals in it rather than in their mother tongue" (p. 136). Nalla dismisses the content of the lectures as "nonsense" (p. 137), and the Marxist rhetoric of equality is undermined by the governance of the camp. Abdulla here appears as an oriental potentate, maintaining a private underground and "luxuriously furnished sitting-room, the walls and ceiling of which were formed by Indian or Persian carpets,... a chamber which would not have disgraced a palace" (p. 146). Marxism, and by extension any progressive attempt to devise modern multicultural polities through the use of English as a lingua franca, is doomed to lapse into oriental despotism: the only path to modernity is through the supervision of the colonial state.

Reading A Yellow Sleuth in this way does not detract from the fact that its criminal cases are entertaining, and are crafted with both considerable skill and—as Paul Kratoska suggests in his introductory note—insider knowledge. Yet as with all popular fiction, the novel manages social contradictions for its readers, and provides both a space of transgression and imaginary solutions to them through the actions of a hybrid polyglot detective committed to serving colonial power. The legacy of colonial linguistic divisions and racialization would be taken up and transformed, but stubbornly persist in the very different modes of governance in the independent states Singapore and Malaysia after their separation in 1965. Fiction in the two countries, indeed, continues to respond to social realities. Nearly ninety years after the publication of *A Yellow Sleuth*, a new wave of Singapore speculative fiction published in the second decade of the twenty-first century continues to feature hybrid protagonists who have ambiguous relationships to governmental power.

Philip Holden
National University of Singapore

References

"Bicycle Thieves." *Malaya Tribune*, 26 June 1914, p. 10.

Chandra, Elizabeth. "The Chinese Holmes: Translating Detective Fiction in Colonial Indonesia." *Keio Communication Review* no. 38 (2016): 39–63.

Clifford, Hugh Charles. "Our Trusty and Well-Beloved." *Malayan Monochromes*. E.P. Dutton, 1913, pp. 12–32.

Chua Ai Lin. "Imperial Subjects, Straits Citizens: Anglophone Asians and the Struggle for Political Rights in Inter-War Singapore." In *Paths Not Taken: Political Pluralism in Post-War Singapore*, ed. Michael D. Barr and Carl A. Trocki. Singapore: NUS Press, 2008, pp. 16–36.

Furnivall, J.S. *Colonial Policy and Practice: A Comparative Study of Burma and Netherlands India*. New York: New York University Press, 1956.

Leow, Rachel. *Taming Babel: Language in the Making of Malaysia*. Cambridge: Cambridge University Press, 2016.

"Local Sherlock Holmes." *The Singapore Free Press and Mercantile Advertiser*, 28 Mar. 1911, p. 5.

Miller, D.A. *The Novel and the Police*. Berkeley: University of California Press, 1988.

Pernau, Margrit. "Rationalizing the World: British Detective Stories and the Orient." In *Empires and Boundaries: Rethinking Race, Class, and Gender in Colonial Settings*, ed. H. Fischer-Tiné, H. and S. Gehrmann. New York: Routledge, 2009, pp. 179–94.

Reitz, Caroline. *Detecting the Nation. Fictions of Detection and the Imperial Venture*. Columbus: Ohio State University Press, 2004.

Said, Edward. *Culture and Imperialism*. New York: Knopf, 1994.

_____. *Orientalism*. London: Peregrine, 1985.

Trivedi, Harish. "'Arguing with the Himalayas'? Edward Said on Rudyard Kipling." In *Kipling and Beyond: Patriotism, Globalisation and Postcolonialism*, ed. Caroline Rooney and Kaori Nagai. Hampshire: Palgrave Macmillan, 2010, pp. 120–43.

Wee Tong Poh. "Is Revenge Sweet?" *The Straits Chinese Magazine* 4 (1900–01): 100–2.

Chapter 1

IF YOU HAD BEEN WALKING along the road from Kuala Lumpur to Mana you would, in time, have come to a little clearing on your right-hand side largely overgrown with rough grasses. Looking through between the stems of the coconut palms, you would have noticed some eight or nine wooden houses, irregularly scattered about, and, beyond them, an intervening patch of cultivated ground, a patch of bananas, a few fruit trees, and then the jungle enclosing all. You would also have noticed that the houses each had their own individuality—some were larger, some smaller, some only roughly finished, others neatly made and even decorated. Yet there was a sameness about them all. All were roofed with attaps, all were raised from the ground on wooden piles, and all had verandas across their front. The intervening ground was largely worn bare, and looked clean and smooth with its pinkish-grey sandy earth. A well-worn pathway led, from where you were standing in the road, through the coconuts to this clearing, and you could just see another such path leading off to the right, which, as you would have surmised, led to the stream running under the culvert you had just passed over.

It was in these surroundings that I was born, this being the kampong of Batu Anam, in Selangor. My father was a person of no importance whatsoever beyond his own doorstep, but my mother was a person of some interest to the little community. Her grandfather had been a Sakai—one of those wild, aboriginal men of the jungles—who was reputed to be also a tiger, and she was supposed to be the possessor of strange powers inherited from this progenitor. This may, indeed, have been the case, since she was certainly a great luck-bringer, and used to compound strange messes of herbs and roots, with which she met the demands of her neighbours. She made potions for either internal complaints or wounds, not to mention aphrodisiacs, or even (so it was whispered), from time to time, those for more sinister purposes. She was in many ways a strange woman, and one of my earliest recollections

1

is of seeing her running stark naked into the jungle. I learnt later on that she would do this periodically, spending several days thus alone with Nature, though what she did on these occasions remained forever a mystery.

Looking back on it now, it seems to me that she had some deep-seated call to the wild, which undoubtedly was inherited from her jungle forbears, and which on these occasions proved irresistible.

Apart from this recollection of my mother, my only other recollection from these years is that of a dearly loved sardine tin—retrieved from I don't know where, but treasured beyond rubies by the little pale yellow, pot-bellied individual I then was. I say that this tin was a sardine tin, as an afterthought from my recollection of it; at the time it was merely a wonderful tin, which in some heaven-sent manner had the impression of a fish embossed on it, which in fact, I think, most endeared to me. Be that as it may, I nevertheless remember long happy days spent in company with my tin, and even now can recall something of my joy when one of my seniors tied a string to it, so that I could pull it about after me like a little cart.

I was still too young to remember very much when my father left the kampong to take up employment as servant to a Tuan on a European estate.

Here, indeed, my life may truly be said to begin. We lived in the boys' quarters behind the bungalow. There were my father and mother, my sister and myself crowded into the two small rooms which adjoined the kitchen. We children had, however, the area between our quarters and the back of the bungalow as a delightful playground; and even, greatly daring, could from time to time mount to the back veranda, where, if we were quiet and father in a good temper, we were allowed to play. I don't know what happened to my old friend the tin, but this new life was so rich in tins that doubtless it was early ousted from its erstwhile favourite position by the plethora of rivals. Tins there were, indeed, a 'drug on the market'!

Of my young life I do not intend to give any detailed account, as it was merely that of any ordinary Malay boy. I shall, however, mention one or two circumstances which I think may have had an influence in shaping or assisting in my future career. For instance, there is no doubt that the Chinese tin mine, which was only some quarter of a mile away, and near which there were many little Chinese children of about my own age, led to my learning Hokkien, without realizing that I was doing so, and to appreciate the difference between it and the Hailam spoken by the boys of the other Tuans on the estate.

Both these dialects I thus learnt conversationally at a time when I was also learning to speak my own tongue. In fact, I daresay I knew many Chinese words before I knew their Malay equivalents, and this knowledge has been of the greatest service to me throughout my work. On the estate, Tamil was in common use round me as Malay, in fact commoner use; so that it was another language which I came to know without learning.

You find me, therefore, at the age of eight or nine, already polyglot without any effort on my part; but at about this age my father insisted that I must learn some English, if I was to follow in his footsteps as a boy. I was just over ten when I had my first experience as a detective, and it was owing to my knowledge of Chinese that this came about.

My uncle, a man whom I had seen perhaps twice in my life, was employed in Kuala Lumpur, in the Government office of the Chandu Monopoly. He applied to my father for permission to employ me, as being an inconspicuous individual, to aid him in trying to discover the source of supply of the illicit opium, which was at that time flooding the country. From what he said, it appeared that the normal demand for opium, through the regular means of distribution, had practically collapsed over nearly the whole State of Selangor, to such an extent that the Monopoly had made no sales at all for the last fortnight.

Police headquarters had been engaged for a month in trying to get on the track of the smugglers, so far without any success at all. My uncle did not occupy any commanding position in his office, being merely a clerk, and he hoped that, should he succeed through me in laying bare this mystery, it would lead to his rapid advancement. Needless to say the matter did not rest with me, though, had it done so, the result would have been the same, for I was naturally overjoyed at the prospect of living in the large city of Kuala Lumpur, a place which I had visited but once or twice with my father on his weekly shopping expeditions to the market. Luckily, however, my father raised no objections—largely, I think, because of some mysterious financial transactions between him and his brother, of which I was not informed!

It was with the greatest delight, therefore, that I set out with my Uncle Ali to see life in the city. My uncle had warned me before starting that I must on no account talk to the rickshaw-puller in Chinese, nor must I speak to him, while in that vehicle, of the business in hand, since everybody, and all Chinese in particular, were to be considered as possible culprits. We were therefore careful to talk about nothing but the sights on the wayside, or the health of various members of the family, as we jogged along.

Before reaching the town we stopped at a wayside Khedai for refreshment, which was, of course, a great treat to me. It was here that my uncle, leading me aside, explained that I was not to live with him whilst engaged on this work, since he, being employed in the Monopoly, would probably be a suspected person, and all his household kept under observation by the criminals. He had therefore arranged that I was to stay with a distant relation of his wife's, who was a tailor in Java Street. This man was called Mat, and was to be waiting on the hill leading to the hospital, where I was to be unobtrusively handed over to his care.

All this mystery appealed very strongly to my youthful mind, and it was with the greatest sense of adventure that I made the final stage of our journey, talking volubly to my uncle about matters of juvenile interest, and eyeing the back of the patient puller, while, with grins of derision—thinking how marvellously I was hoodwinking him as to our real intentions. The poor man was no doubt as ignorant of one side of the question as I endeavoured to keep him of the other, but, to my eyes, he was the leader of a desperate smugglers' band, whose evil machinations I was about to thwart and whose constant suspicions I must evade. I thoroughly enjoyed those four miles!

We drove straight to the market, where the rickshaw was paid off. My uncle and I then mingled with the crowd, he going ahead and I following as though not connected with him, as he made his way deviously from one side of the square to the other. I then followed him over the river and up the hill towards the hospital, taking care on the way to be sometimes a few paces ahead, and sometimes a good way behind. His instructions had been to follow him 'as a dog follows his master', and these I endeavoured to carry out by running, as a dog will do, from side to side of the road, forwards and backwards, in a careless inconsequential manner. I soon saw my uncle stop and converse with a very old man who had been sitting at the roadside; this obviously was Mat, and my duty now was to follow him, which I proceeded to do in the same manner as I had followed my uncle, waiting the signal that he was to give before I approached him.

This signal was not given until we had reached the European shop of Messrs. John Little & Co., before whose windows Mat stopped, and into which we both gazed; I with spellbound interest. Never before had I seen so many wonderful things. When we greeted each other, Mat explained to me that for the future I was to be his grandson, who had just been left an orphan through the death of my father, Achmet, at Kajang. As we walked along to Java Street he gave me full particulars of my past life, and catechised me regarding it, until I was word perfect.

4

We then entered his house, which was situated behind, and over, the tailor's shop in which most of his family seemed to work. Here Mat explained to me my duties, which were very simple. I was to wander about the town at my leisure, keeping my mouth shut and my ears open, overhearing as many conversations as possible between Chinamen, and in this way I was to endeavour to find out where opium was now being bought. This was to be the first stage of the enquiry.

The next morning Mat provided me with a little money, and it was very little, and turned me out for the day. Even if I remembered where I went or what I heard that first day it would be of no interest to recount it here. It is sufficient to say that I spent about a week in learning the town of Kuala Lumpur, with special reference to the places where the Chinese 'most do congregate'.

I was, of course, a regular country bumpkin, and had to find my feet before I could become even a passable street urchin. I learnt, at the expense of my ears, to what places small Malay boys may not penetrate. Many is the time I was led forth, screaming lustily, practically suspended from one or other of these convenient handles, by a Chinaman, saying in very bad Malay: "*Lou mau chuli la? Pergi la, lekas*" (You wish to steal, eh? Hurry off, quick) or something of the kind. But I very soon learnt what may, and may not, be done in the way of wandering into buildings in the town.

I remember how delighted I was as I joined the crowd surging round a Chinese funeral. This was a spectacle entirely new to me, and one which met with my thorough approval. I was glad that in following it closely I was at the same time carrying out my duties in the best possible surroundings. The sight of the huge coffin, supported by its network of crossbars, borne along, undulating as it were on the crest of a wave, by the sweating coolies in their archaic funeral costumes; the tinsel, the banners, the queerly dressed officials and mourners, not to mention the crackers, the shouting and general air of excitement, all formed a scene of intense gaiety to my inexperienced eye. In fact I had been following it for some little time before I learnt it was a funeral, and not some joyous ceremony that was in progress.

I followed this funeral until it broke up at the cemetery, and mingled with the crowd of professional mourners as they returned from their labours. A small group separated from the rest at the corner of Petaling Street, and went along Kampong Attap Road. This group I kept with as they gathered round an itinerant vendor of agar agar—that jelly so sought after by the Chinese coolie. Whilst they were thus refreshing themselves I was busily engaged in begging a free helping, which I knew I had no earthly chance of getting. I overheard one of the groups

5

telling his companion that, with today's earnings, he now had two dollars fifty cents, which he proposed spending on opium from Li Hopp.

This was the first time that I had heard anybody say they were going to buy opium, and, though the news seemed to me to be of little value, nevertheless I hurried off to tell Mat what I had overheard. To my surprise, he was extremely interested in my story and questioned me closely as to the actual wording of what had been said. He then pointed out to me that, as it was a pot of chandu that this coolie had said he would buy, and that, since he had only two dollars fifty cents, he could not be expecting to pay the recognized price. He explained to me that the small quantities of chandu were sold in packets, the largest of which was of six hoons, but that the smallest pot sold contained three chees, the official price of which was three dollars; so that this man must be expecting to buy cheap opium, and we were therefore at last on the track of the smugglers.

The thing now to do was to discover the whereabouts of Li Hopp.

Mat was very pleased with my result so far, and advised me that the most likely way of hearing some account of Li Hopp was to frequent the neighbourhood of the rickshaw ranks. He thought that, rickshaw-pullers being great consumers of opium, when they could afford it, they would make a very fruitful ground to be gone over in the search; so for the next few days I was to be seen, playing about in the dust, near groups of rickshaws waiting to be hired.

In due course I came across my second clue, though not quite in the way that my uncle had expected. It was close on sundown, and I was about to leave the neighbourhood of three rickshaws, the pullers of which had been receiving my attention for the last half hour or so, when a very portly Chinaman seated himself in the one nearest to me. As he started off the only direction which he gave to the puller was "Li Hopp". Needless to say I pricked up my ears at this, and picked up my heels also.

As I did not want the remaining two coolies to be at all suspicious, I could not immediately run after the departing rickshaw, but, as this luckily turned a neighbouring corner, it was not far ahead by the time I was hidden from their sight, when, of course, it was an easy matter for me to catch up on it and keep it in sight within easy distance.

After having kept up the chase all through the town, I at last had the satisfaction of seeing the fat fare alight at a house in Gombak Lane. I approached this house some little time after, and to my surprise discovered that it was inhabited by Klings. This did not seem to suit my book at all, so I hurried home to report to Mat. The old man was very doubtful as to whether I had heard correctly or not. He said he would have the matter looked into, so he took me out with him in order that I could point out the house to which the rickshaw had gone. After having done so, he sent me home to bed.

Next morning Mat explained to me how I had been deceived. The house in Gombak Lane had a passage running along its side which led out into Batu Road, and it was obviously through this passage that the Chinaman had gone, and not into the house at all. It was a lodging house, the inhabitants of which were mostly Kranis in Government offices, some of them employed actually in the Chandu Monopoly office itself.

He was very angry with me for my carelessness in not seeing where the Chinaman had gone to, so I determined, to myself, to solve the mystery of Li Hopp, if I had to die in the attempt. I discovered that, by going up the hill on the other side of the river, I could from one place overlook the whole length of the passage in Gombak Lane, so I decided to sit there and keep the passage continually under observation, to see, if possible, where any other Chinamen using it went to. I spent two days at this occupation, and very miserable days they were; but at last, in the evening, I was rewarded by the sight of the same fat Chinaman alighting, as before, opposite the house and hastening through the passage-way; halfway along it he disappeared through a door in the wall on the left. This was good enough for me, and I returned home determined to say nothing about it, but continue my investigations myself.

Next morning I was out bright and early. I found that the door through which the Chinaman had vanished was the back door of a shop in Batu Road, kept by a Chinaman called Hopp Li Fun, a rotan furniture establishment. I thought that perhaps, Li Hopp being Hopp Li backwards, it was a secret way of indicating this back door, so I determined to try to get work in this shop, and overhear something useful if I could.

Chinese are not particularly fond of employing Malays, but, by dint of pitching a 'hard luck' story about my dear dead parents at Kajang, and asking for little more than my food, I managed to get employed here, on the job of stripping rotan. This was, of course, no new occupation for me, since I had often helped my mother at it when she was basket-making; so I felt quite confident of giving satisfaction, and hoped that I might soon learn something that would put me on the right track.

In my new situation I had to be very careful not to let my employer, and all fellow-workmen, know that I had any knowledge of Chinese, and I took no notice of remarks addressed to me, unless they were in Malay. I was tested several times by having sudden questions asked of me, which I understood perfectly well, but managed to show no sign of intelligence. After some time of this, conversation about me became quite unrestrained.

I had been working here for over a week before I heard anything in connection with my business, but when, at long last, it did come, I heard plenty!

First of all I was surprised to see the fat man, whom I had followed in the rickshaw, enter the shop from the back premises. He called to my employer, and they went together into a small room partitioned off at the back. It was against this partition that I was leaning as I worked, and I could therefore overhear all that was said. The fat man told Li Fun that he had brought him ten tahils, and that this would be the last supply, as the stock would be exhausted when this distribution was completed. They drank brandy together, and made a lot of fun, in conversation, of which I could not fathom the drift.

They were joking about the revered ancestor of Bak Heung, which, it appeared, was the name of the fat man. Now I knew enough already, about Chinamen, to realize that they are not given to making jokes about their deceased ancestors; there were, also, mysterious references to a 'coffin of plenty', which made me wonder whether I was translating what I heard correctly or not. In any case, I felt that I now knew enough to tell Mat what I had been doing, so I left my work that night with the intention of not returning.

When I told Mat where I had been, and what I had heard, no praises were too great for him to heap upon me, and he hurried off immediately to tell my Uncle Ali of my discoveries, giving me strict injunctions on no account to leave the house during his absence.

My uncle felt that the news was important enough to be reported to the authorities, and, on the matter being sifted, the story of the opium smuggling turned out to be as follows.

Bak Heung had applied to the Government for permission to land a coffin containing the remains of his grandmother, which he wished to have interred in the family vault he had lately built in the Chinese cemetery. This permission was readily granted, and, of course, the coffin passed the Customs authorities without being opened.

This was, however, unfortunate from the Government point of view, because the coffin had been completely packed with chandu, on the sale of which Bak Heung had made a vast profit.

There was no direct proof of these facts, since the grandmother (or an old woman who could quite well pass as such), who had really died in Taiping, was now peacefully reposing in the coffin which had been taken to the cemetery, and the imported duplicate had been destroyed.

So no proceedings could be taken against Bak Heung, and the only man who really suffered was my late employer, Hopp Li Fun, whose premises were raided. There the ten tahils of chandu were discovered, and confiscated, whilst he was heavily fined.

Bak Heung is now a highly respected member of the Chinese community, the large sum which he made out of his illicit deal in opium having formed the starting-point of a fortune, which he subsequently made by all manner of legitimate enterprises.

My success on this occasion was the deciding factor in my life. I am not sure whether my Uncle Ali got the promotion which he had hoped for or not, but in any case his story so interested one of the Controllers of the Monopoly that he was ordered to bring me along for inspection.

In due course, therefore, I had to accompany him to an office where I was introduced to Mr. Ogilvy.

This gentleman spoke to me in Chinese, but unfortunately I was quite unable to understand him. He seemed very surprised at my failure, and, speaking in Malay, said that he had been told that I spoke Chinese. I replied in English that I spoke Hokkien and Hailam. He seemed very impressed by this, and said that I must learn Cantonese as well, which was the dialect he had used, and is the dialect most frequently met with in offices. After further conversation, he asked me whether I would be willing to spend some years studying, with a view to Government employment; which, of course, I was only too ready to do.

Having given me a dollar and told me I was a bright boy, he sent me off, feeling as proud as a peacock, saying that he would see what he could arrange. My uncle was tremendously pleased with this interview, and, loading me with presents for my father and mother, sent me off back to the estate; where I spent long evenings recounting my marvellous adventures to my family.

Nothing happened for what seemed quite a long time, and my pride and sense of importance had quite evaporated—indeed it had changed almost to despair—when one day a visitor arrived at the bungalow and my father was ordered to produce me.

I followed him through to the front veranda where the Tuan and another white man were sitting drinking whisky. It appeared that the stranger was from the police department and had come to see what could be arranged about my future, in which it appeared that Mr. Ogilvy had been taking a great personal interest. A long conversation took place between my father and this Colonel Munroe, who said that he had come out to the bungalow, instead of calling me in to see him, since if I was to be of the greatest use to the Police, it was essential that they should appear to know nothing about me. He explained that Police headquarters were under constant observation, and it was never too soon to start taking precautions of this kind, as criminals' memories were long.

It was finally arranged that I should be sent over to Java, where I would receive a thorough education on European lines, and where I would, of course, learn to speak Javanese and Dutch whilst doing so. By doing this I could return to Kuala Lumpur, fully trained to help the Secret Police, without anybody in British Malaya knowing that I was anything more than an ordinary Malay boy, which would of course add tremendously to my value to them.

I did not feel at all happy at the prospect of being thus exiled, but the excitement of the travelling, the sense of adventure, and the pride in feeling myself once more a person of importance, more than outweighed my feelings of fear and depression. Nevertheless, it was a very heart-broken little boy who clung to his mother when the final good-bye had to be said.

As fate had it, that good-bye was, in actual fact, a final one; since I never saw my mother again. She, alas, died of cerebral malaria during my second year at Sourabaya.

I suppose everyone's mother means more to them than any other woman, and I can certainly affirm that this has been so in my case, though at the time, owing to my long absence from home, I did not feel her loss so keenly as might have been the case. Her withdrawal has left a gap in the pattern of my life, which I have been wholly unable to repair.

The Sakai language, and the many items of jungle lore which I had learnt from her have, during my life, proved of great, and in some cases crucial, importance.

I wish here to offer my tribute to the memory of one who, though perhaps uncultured in the European sense of the word, was, nevertheless, in every way a very gentle woman, and I look forward to seeing her again in that heaven in which my new religion has taught me to believe.

Chapter 2

MY JOURNEY TO JAVA COMMENCED at Klang, whence, in the early morning, we were rowed out to join a Dutch steamer lying in the Roads. I had been given a letter to deliver to the captain of this vessel and, as a result of this, was permitted to employ myself as an assistant to his boy.

The advantages of this position were, that instead of having to find a place on the crowded main deck, I could spread my mat in the pantry, not to mention the superior food which we, of course, shared from the officers' table.

If I had known anything about steamers, this one would have struck me as being of strange appearance, since the bridge deck was practically a cage, being entirely surrounded by heavy wooden bars about four inches in circumference. As it was, I merely took this to be the ordinary thing and it was not very long before I was to see the advantages of this arrangement.

The crowd of passengers inhabiting the main deck was largely composed of Achinese, and, in the early hours of the morning, after our first night at sea, these people made a determined effort to capture the vessel.

I was awakened by the sound of loud shouting, and, before I could rise to my feet, to this was added the explosion of firearms. The boy whose quarters I was sharing immediately ran into the saloon, where I followed him. Here I found the chief engineer busily handing out rifles and revolvers, apparently to anyone who asked for them. I did not realize at the time that this distribution was being made to the inhabitants of the cage only—these being the 'after-guard'.

As I approached the locker from which he was producing these weapons, he smiled at me grimly and shook his head, so I went on deck merely as a spectator. It was, indeed, a terrible spectacle into which I walked. The little deck was but dimly illuminated by one or two smoky oil lamps, with here and there an added gleam from an open porthole, which was sufficient, however, to let me see that the slime in which my naked feet were sliding was human blood, flowing from the stiffening corpse of an Achinese, over which the European officers and their assistants stumbled as they moved about, protecting the bars of their cage against the howling, murderous mob.

Not only were the bars to be protected, but none of the coolies must be permitted to reach the safety of the boat deck above, from which point they would have had the ship's company at their mercy. From out of the dark beyond the bars, the glint of a knife would be seen, and the hate-tortured face of its owner would be suddenly illuminated as he sprang to climb or strike. Crack! would go a revolver or a rifle, and, with a final scream, the face would vanish into the reeking murk from which it had emerged.

This scene was being enacted in half a dozen different places simultaneously, and, accompanied by the eldritch shrieks of the attackers, with the guttural curses of the defenders as a pulsating diapason, formed a scene of terror indescribable. After about half an hour things quietened down again, and, except that everyone on the bridge continued to carry their firearms, things seemed perfectly normal. The dead man on the bridge, who, I learnt, had led the attack and mounted the bridge before the gate could be shut, was thrown overboard, as were two or three others from the main deck.

When we arrived at Sourabaya signals were made from the ship, which resulted in a body of troops taking charge of the unruly passengers, and marching them off for trial.

* * *

Of my life in Sourabaya there is little that I need say. I was a student at the Roman Catholic school, and lived with the servants of one of the Fathers. It was a very hard life for me to begin with, as not many people spoke Malay, and I had great difficulty in making myself understood, but this soon righted itself as I became rapidly fluent in Javanese; after which time my days passed like those of any other school boy.

One day, some twelve months later, I was surprised to be called into the Father's bungalow, and found Mr. Ogilvy there. He said that he was pleased to hear such a good report of my behaviour and progress from Father Houten, and that he was going to take me away for a holiday with him.

The holiday which he proposed making was to take the form of an expedition to Borneo, where he intended to capture an orang-utan alive, if possible. For several days he was engaged in Sourabaya, in fitting out a suitable expedition for this purpose, during which time I continued at the school.

When Mr. Ogilvy had completed his arrangements we left by steamer for Pontianak, from which port we proceeded inland by boat, up the river. This was my first experience of travelling in small boats, and I was, naturally, extremely excited by my strange surroundings.

My position was that of assistant to Mr. Ogilvy's boy, who was a temporary servant he had engaged in Sourabaya, so we both had equally to learn our Tuan's peculiarities and methods as we went along.

After three days' travelling by river we came to Ngabang. Here we left the boats and proceeded through the jungle to the kampong of Bulit Api.

Omar Dang, the headman of this village, agreed to supply not only guides, but sufficient men to take part in the hunt.

Mr. Ogilvy's idea was that an orang-utan, or any other animal, could be captured in a net, if there were sufficient folds of the net to thoroughly entangle the animal's limbs in the meshes. With this object in view we had brought with us several large rolls of fishing net.

The Dyak guides led us through the jungle to the foot of a tall tree, high up in the branches of which they pointed out the large nest of an orang-utan. Of the animal itself there was nothing to be seen, and Mr. Ogilvy expressed doubt as to whether this was indeed the animal's home. It was most interesting to see the way in which the guides proved this. One of them, taking his parang in both hands, scratched the trunk of the tree several times with its point, making long grooved marks as he did so.

He had not been doing this very long, when his companion pointed upwards, where, sure enough, over the edge of the nest protruded the large, red-bewhiskered, face of an orang-utan; they explained to us that the noise produced by these scratches resembled that of a panther sharpening its claws, and, consequently, the orang-utan, thinking it had a panther practically on its doorstep, wished to keep an eye skinned as to what it was doing. Whether this was the reason or not, the effect certainly was produced.

When these hunters heard of the fishing nets, and the way they were to be employed, nothing could exceed their hilarity; they declared that these animals would think no more of a fishing net, and feel no more inconvenience therefrom, than we would of a spider's web; and, furthermore, they declined to take part in an endeavour at capturing them by these ridiculous means. They were, they declared, quite prepared to kill an orang-utan; but as to capturing one alive—they considered such a feat impossible.

My master explained to them that, with the large quantity of nets which he proposed to employ, there was every chance of curbing even the immense strength of these large monkeys; at last, after a long argument, he persuaded them to give his method a trial.

In order to do this, men were sent up neighbouring trees, surrounding that on which the animals lived, to spread the nets amongst the branches. This was no easy job, as, time and time again, the heavy roll of netting would fall to the ground, causing endless confusion; and, in the end, the encirclement by netting was a very scratch affair. However, in most places there were four or five thicknesses of net hanging above the topmost of the thicker branches.

This had not been done without considerable argument in opposition from the nest, when the first men appeared in the neighbouring trees. We then discovered that it was a mother ape which was there with a young one, and she sat up, voicing her grievance at this disturbance in no uncertain way.

Before very long, her husband was attracted home by the noise, and one of our men just escaped with his life, as the enraged parent crashed into the tree he was occupying, by sliding down a liana. Luckily, however, the father was more intent on defending his home while our operations continued, and, except for the occasional threatening rushes which kept our men on the sharp look-out, he stayed closely by the nest.

From the way these animals stamped up and down on their nest, shrieking out defiance, one would have expected to see the ramshackle collection of branches knocked to pieces; however, I suppose they knew where they could stamp safely, because the nest held together in spite of the rough treatment. When all the net had been used up, and the best use made of it that was possible in the awkward circumstances, Mr. Ogilvy's next scheme had to be put into practice; this was to frighten the animals into the nets.

For this purpose he had brought some rockets with which we were to bombard the nest from underneath, thus, if possible, setting it on fire, and scaring the inhabitants away from their home tree. Watching these proceedings was a great joy to me, as, apart from the crackers which the Chinese use so much, I had had no acquaintance with fireworks. To my great enjoyment several 'boss' shots were made before a lucky rocket entangled itself in the lower branches of the nest, where it fizzed away successfully, smoking the monkeys out.

Unfortunately for Mr. Ogilvy, they retreated in a most orderly manner, and not in the wild stampede he had hoped for; the consequence of which was that they walked quietly through the nets, for all the world as though these had no material existence; in fact there was no appreciable hesitation in the steady swing of their progress as they passed from our sight!

Thus ended my first experience of big game hunting. Mr. Ogilvy's leave did not permit of him pursuing these, or other, orang-utans on this occasion: and he was, I think, very disappointed at the tame ending to his ingenious hunting methods—but of course he did not discuss his feelings on the matter with me. From my point of view the holiday had been more than satisfying. I had enjoyed every minute of it, and the thanks which I expressed to Mr. Ogilvy, when we parted at Sourabaya once more, were entirely genuine and heartfelt. Then it was 'back to school' for another long spell for me!

If I do not mention all the various trips on which I was taken during school holidays, either by the kind Fathers, or by the captains of coasting vessels in whom they had confidence, it is because I do not propose to write a guide-book to Java and its surroundings.

After my mother had died, I was visited by Colonel Munroe, who put me through a very close examination; he was delighted when he learnt that I had added not only Cantonese, but Kheh, to my Chinese dialects. The time I spent with Tuan Munroe on this occasion made a great impression on me, not so much on account of the mud springs which he took me to see at Papang Dyang, but because he opened up a new view of life and its seriousness to me; and he encouraged me to stick to my studies, by pointing out how valuable I could make myself to my country, which was a view I had not considered before.

He explained that a great detective could do more for his country than a great soldier, because a soldier could only bring peace to his country during a period when there was a war; whereas a detective was constantly employed, throughout his life, or should be, in ensuring the peace of his country, by fighting the enemies of that law and order which are the foundations of a peaceful state.

I may say that, after a fairly long experience of life, I have found nothing to make me doubt the truth of this aspect of a detective's duties. Even during the Great War, though my employment kept me from the glory of the field of battle, I felt, nevertheless, that the work I was doing was of greater importance than would have been the case had I been in the ranks, or even a junior officer—but this is anticipation.

* * *

A noteworthy trip which I went, was one with Father Houten, to the Valley of Death on the Dieng Plateau. Of all the eerie sights I have seen, none has impressed me more than this uncanny spectacle. Possibly this was so because I was so young and inexperienced at the time, nevertheless the impression has remained. Before we approached the valley, Father Houten recited the poem to me which contains the lines:

The Angel of Death spread his wings on the blast,
And breathed in the face of the foe as he passed

I was therefore in a fit mood for the grim sights which met us as we inspected the Guevo Upas, as this rugged depression is called.

Death! Death! Death! All before us was death! Bones! Bones! and yet more bones!—glimmering palely in the bright sunshine, which, by the very contrast of its cheerful vitality, added to the ghastly horror of this natural charnel-house. Here lay a dead pig, there the panther who had been pursuing him. Here a deer, and, close by, a musang. Over yonder was a dead rhinoceros, and so on. It was, in very truth, the breath of death which lay before us! Father Houten explained that it was poisonous gases from a neighbouring volcano which collected in this valley, but under the glaring sunshine there was nothing to see but this widespread death.

You can picture me as having my student days broken by periodic holidays of this nature—visits to the tremendous temples of prehistoric builders, to volcanoes, and other places of interest, or sea trips to neighbouring islands.

* * *

Some six months after Colonel Munroe's visit, Father Houten called me in and told me that he had volunteered for a new mission, which was to be opened in Siam, at a place called Haad Yai. He was writing to Mr. Ogilvy, he said, suggesting that I should go with him as his servant, but, before writing, he wanted to know if I would like to go.

I was very fond of Father Houten, and would cheerfully have gone anywhere with him, so in due course I followed him to the founding of this new mission station. Here life was, in many ways, the same as it had been in my former life on the estate; lessons became less and less frequent, as Father Houten became more familiar with the language and his mission work expanded. It was whilst here that I heard of Mr. Ogilvy's death, from blackwater fever, and I was told that he had established a scholarship, worth twenty dollars a month, of which I was to be the first holder till I was sixteen years of age. I have more to thank this gentleman for than I can ever do in words, but I have tried throughout my life to make it as he hoped it would develop into when he first took me under his wing.

In my opinion, here is a shining example of what a patriotic bachelor should be. If a man has no children of his own who need to be brought up, what finer use can he make of his money than providing for the education of those less fortunately circumstanced? The more scholarships which are established, the better for the community.

We had been at the mission for over two years when it was wiped out. It would have been merely ruined, and not wiped out, I daresay, had it not been for the stupidity of the Siamese villagers, though I have no doubt they thought they were acting for the best.

For some weeks there had been rumours of a large herd of elephants which were reported to be moving northwards from Patani. Finally the news became definite that there actually was such a herd, since the brother of Headman Pringa said he had personally seen them, two days' journey away. He said they seemed to be moving towards the west, so we all hoped that they would pass to the north of us without paying a visit. However, this was not to be. On the fourth night after the news I was awakened by the noise made by the advance-guard of the herd.

I hurried in and awakened Father Houten, who said that if the elephants were allowed to do their will, no harm would come to us, since all they were after was the crops.

Luckily, however, I persuaded him that this would not be the case; and, together with the rest of the mission household, we ran out of the village by the path to the east, where we succeeded in reaching, after some difficulty, the branches of a big jati tree which stood there.

Whilst we were busy at this, things were far from quiet in the kampong. The villagers were trying to frighten the elephants away from the crops by the bangings of gongs, and, worse than that, the waving of lighted torches. This resulted in the herd becoming infuriated and charging blindly, in all directions, after the hated smell of man.

From our lofty perch we could not, of course, see anything of what was happening; except here and there small cameos of activity surrounding a torch-bearer. We could, however, hear the trumpetings and crashings of the elephants. It was not long until we got a better view of the scene, when one of the torch-bearers, flying for his life, tripped amidst the ruins of a demolished house which, of course, immediately burst into flames. This bonfire lit up a scene impossible to describe.

The elephants, and there seemed to be hundreds of them, driven completely mad by the smoke and flames, were charging about entirely regardless of what stood in their way. On several occasions we saw two running elephants meet head to flank, and together roll over in a squealing mass. The flames rapidly spread, until the whole kampong and the mission station was involved in the conflagration, the elephants being gradually driven off as the fire extended. For some time, however, odd elephants, seeming actually berserk, would come charging through the pillars of flame, screaming like demons in the pit of Tophet.

When dawn broke all was once more quiet, and what had been a thriving community was a smouldering ruin, surrounded by a trampled desert. No one had more than they stood up in, and already the returning villagers were exploring the ruins in the hopes of rescuing cooking pots and other fireproof possessions—though there were few of these undamaged. The loss of possessions meant more to Father Houten than to the rest of us, since, like all Europeans, he had more in the way of clothing and personal luggage than the rest of the inhabitants put together. On leaving the house he had, luckily, taken with him the bag containing his money, though money was of no use at the moment.

All the crops and stores of food had been burnt in the fire, eaten, or destroyed, and starvation stared us in the face. Everyone realized this, and, before nine o'clock in the morning, all had departed from the devastated village on a tramp to the nearest clearing where they had friends or relatives. Father Houten decided that he would have to report to headquarters and we therefore started off in a canoe down the river to Singora.

We had a very hungry day of it, as we dare not waste time waiting to spear fish, or hunt for fruit, but had to push on towards the certainty of food. At about five o'clock in the evening I was overjoyed to see a number of hornbills rising from the jungle, about a quarter of a mile down stream. I called Father's attention to this, and we landed at the nearest point; when, without much difficulty and using our noses as guides, we found, some hundred yards from the river, what I had expected—a durian tree in full fruit.

We made a feast of these luscious fruit on the spot, and were able to take a large number with us in the canoe—which, in fact, we seriously overloaded, realizing that the cargo would soon be consumed! This supply saw us safely to the sea coast, from where we made no delay in getting transport to Bangkok, and thence to Sourabaya once more, where I rejoined the classes until such time as Father Houten's position had been definitely settled.

In due course he was appointed to Tarulung, in Sumatra; but Colonel Munroe, who had taken charge of my destinies after Mr. Ogilvy's death, thought I could learn nothing useful by going with him to Sumatra; so I regretfully said good-bye to this good man, whom, as Fate decreed it, I was never to see again. He fell a victim to the Achinese—those wild men whose acquaintance I had so dramatically made when I first left home.

* * *

It was not long, however, that I was to be left at school; Colonel Munroe again paid a visit and, finding me a lusty lad of fifteen, decided that I should now be fully apprenticed to my work, and could well continue any further studies in my spare time.

He again impressed on me the urgent necessity for complete secrecy regarding my connection with the Police, in order to maintain which, not only was I to return a few days later than himself, but he had arranged that, for the future, I was to be engaged as a chokra (or junior boy) in the Officers' mess of the Artillery garrisoning Singapore. In this way my pay would be issued through the Army, and no clerk in the colonial, or the Selangor service would know even that I was on the pay-roll.

In about a fortnight I went to Singapore, and up to Fort Canning, where I had been told to report and hand in my chit.

My work as a chokra was of no more interest than that of any other boy; consisting, in the main, of running messages, washing dishes, polishing silver, and the like, but I found that a partial knowledge of Hindustani was thrust upon me by my association with the many Indian boys who had been brought over with their officers.

In due course I was called away to my first Police duties, which were simple in the extreme. In order to understand them, however, a slight description of the circumstances is necessary. In primitive Malaya, water was drawn from any running stream, or even stagnant ditch, which was convenient, or from wells dug in the courtyards of the more permanent houses. With the coming of the Europeans, the question of water supply was at once taken in hand, and pipes, hearing clean water from distant unpolluted catchment areas, were speedily laid throughout the towns, stand-pipes with taps being erected in the streets in the native quarters where household plumbing was not undertaken.

In spite of this benefit, many people preferred to use the customary wells in their yards and as these wells were, as often as not, supplied from surface-water drainage which often soaked through a neighbouring latrine, the order had gone out that all wells were to be closed. It was not very important that this enactment should be carried out by the private individual, but, in the case of eating-houses, it was the duty of the Government to see that water from these contaminated wells should not be used, to the detriment of the public health.

Many Chinese proprietors of restaurants had kept their wells open, and they would assure the Government inspectors that the water therefrom was only used for floor washing and similar purposes, but that all water used in cooking was brought from the Government stand-pipe. Although the inspectors realized that this was probably untrue, it was hard to prove it; so my first Police duty was to spend my time in closely watching these Chinese eating-houses, and keeping a daily count of the buckets of water which were carried into them from the street hydrants.

This was a very unheroic start to my career, but as I was to find out later on, the greater part of a detective's life is occupied in small unheroic occupations—only from time to time do incidents occur which relieve the usual monotony of seemingly unimportant detail.

Owing to the number of eating-houses to be checked off in this manner, and the length of time over which a count had to be kept, I was employed fully three months thus, tying knots in a piece of string to keep my daily account right.

Of course it would never have done for me to have gone up to the Police station to make my daily report and receive my instructions, so the method which Colonel Munroe employed of communicating with me will perhaps be of interest. In the first place I had been instructed to go to Kuala Lumpur, and, at sundown, to be at the entrance to the European church. Colonel Munroe would then walk past me at that time, and I was to hand him the letter containing these instructions, asking him if he could direct me to the address. He would take it from me, apparently to read the address, and, whilst pointing out the supposed direction, would return me, not my own letter but a further letter of instructions.

All this I carried out and, when I opened my letter, I found that it told me which eating-house I was to attend to on the morrow, and made a similar appointment for the day after tomorrow at a different part of the town. This meant that each of my sessions of watching would embrace a full thirty-six hours, and, as it was not always Colonel Munroe who met me on these occasions, there was no chance of my connection with the Police being suspected. I was to be, as I always have been, merely the 'information received' on which the Police acted!

In all my years in the Police Force, and in spite of my now being the senior detective sergeant, I have never taken an active part in an arrest—which is, I suppose, a rather unique record, regarded from the European point of view.

It is rather a coincidence that my first official duties were in connection with the water supply, since the occasion on which I came nearest to being discovered as a policeman was also a case connected with that supply—but at the other end of the limpid stream—as I shall recount hereafter.

Chapter 3

AS I HAVE KEPT NO diary and, owing to the nature of my employment, my doings appear in no available official records, I do not guarantee to continue telling the incidents of my life in strict chronological order—in fact it would be impossible for me to do so. Nor do I propose to make any further reference to my 'military' service at Singapore, though, from time to time between Police employments, I reported to do the duties there for which I was officially being paid.

It will be easier for me, and I feel pleasanter for my readers—for those of you who continue reading, at any rate—that I should pick out from my memory a selection of occasions where my duties have led into either strange surroundings or dangerous situations, and tell them in as nearly the correct sequence as possible.

The ordinary humdrum of getting information concerning petty thefts of all sorts, the mingling with the crowd, the loitering at khedais, the pretended sleep outside buildings; all this to pick up odd tags of conversation which may lead to the detection of someone who has stolen a hundredweight of rubber, or a bicycle, or a watch, or one of a hundred and one other things, whilst all part of the duties I have performed repeatedly, were, nevertheless, anything but interesting to me at the time, and would, I am sure, gain nothing in interest if I recounted them, in the full story of their deadly monotony, to you now.

The dead weight of the above paragraph is, in itself, proof of the anaemia of such a history—if proof was needed!

* * *

It was whilst living as a Sakai, up in the jungles of Pahang, that I witnessed the following scene, which has so far remained entirely unexplained to me. I have taken every opportunity I could of consulting doctors, and other scientists, but so far without any satisfactory explanation.

The duty I was on at the time does not enter into the story, and it is sufficient to say that it was a matter of smuggling on which I was engaged, and, in order to facilitate my investigations, I had succeeded in joining a band of Sakais as one of themselves. It was not, of course, very difficult for me to convince them that I was a Sakai who had grown soft through living in a Malay compound, but wished to rejoin my native people. I pitched them a story about having been picked up in the jungle by a party of Malays who had scared off the tiger which had just killed my mother, and how they had insisted on my going with them to their kampong, where I had been practically their prisoner for three years. On this footing I was willingly accepted, and was, incidentally, soon able to learn all about the smuggling.

One day we had a visit from another tribe of Sakais who were on the trek to new quarters. We made them as welcome as we could for two or three days, and the crazy houses almost collapsed under the extra loads of humanity thus nightly imposed on them. With these strangers was a Pawang of high repute, and one evening he was persuaded to give us an exhibition of his powers.

Across the middle of the clearing lay the trunk of a fallen tree, and on this Pawang Mahkit took his stand—first having warned us all to remain perfectly motionless, whatever we might see or hear. He commenced with an incantation, which certainly was in a language which I did not understand, and I know a good many; but, as this language was supposed to be that of the devil, it is one with which I hope I will never have to become fluently familiar!

Having offered up a sort of prayer, standing with his arms raised, and facing the four points of the compass in turn, he then crouched down on the trunk singing a crooning sort of lullaby. He had been doing this for perhaps five minutes when, to my surprise, I saw a large cobra coming out of the grass immediately behind one of my new friends. However, the cobra passed through between his legs, paying no attention to him whatsoever—though he, poor man, went grey with fear when he saw its evil head emerging between his toes. Looking back at Mahkit, I realized that the snake I had just seen was not the only one which had come out of the jungle. Several snakes were already climbing on to the tree trunk, and in a very few minutes the Pawang was literally covered with a writhing cloak of snakes, whilst he continued his murmurous chant.

If I tried to estimate the number of snakes there were, I would say at least fifty, though there looked hundreds at the time, and yet it may be that there were no more than twenty, for all were evidently in a great state of excitement and kept up a constant movement, twisting over his shoulders, through his hair, and all over him. He then changed his song to one on a higher note, till he reached a shrill piping almost like that of a bird, whereupon the snakes immediately turned from him and disappeared harmlessly back into the jungle from whence they had come.

It was a marvel such as I had heard of, but had never seen. The Sakais, on the other hand, whilst thinking it quite good magic, seemed to consider that Mahkit could not be so powerful as they had been led to believe, if this was the best he could do in the way of demonstration. Of course they did not say this to the Pawang himself, being far too afraid of his powers, but, amongst themselves, it was the impression which they held.

They had, however, been too hasty in their judgment, for later in the evening Mahkit announced that he would now show them some real magic. Two large fires were lighted, with a space of about ten feet between them and the fallen tree trunk some eight feet behind them—the space between the fires and the trunk thus forming a fairly well illuminated stage; twenty feet or so in front of which we all gathered, sitting in a rude semi-circle. Mahkit took up his post, stark naked, between the fires and again went through the formality of calling to the cardinal points, then he threw himself to the ground, wriggling about and hissing like a snake. He then arose upon his hands and knees, and tucking his feet between his flanks, ran about in this position with extraordinary agility, and looked for all the world like a four-footed animal.

Presently he bleated like a goat and capered about till it was hard to believe that it was not a goat one was looking at. Soon we heard the hungry snarl of a tiger from the darkness beyond the trunk, whereupon the Pawang, once more stretched out as a snake, wriggled to the trunk and disappeared over it. Almost immediately a large tiger raised itself, with its paws on the trunk, at the very spot where Mahkit had disappeared. In the bright flickering firelight its white front, heavy square white jowl, gleaming green eyes and flattened ears, were clearly visible, as it lifted its whiskered lips in another snarl. A thrill of fear passed through the crowd, but the fascination of the sight, and probably the subconscious feeling that it was magic, kept all seated; the tiger, showing his gleaming fangs, snarled menacingly upon us but did not venture further.

Again we heard the bleating of a goat—this time from the jungle edge behind the tiger, which thereupon vanished from our sight as it dropped behind the trunk. Without a second's interval, the Pawang appeared at the very spot where the tiger had sunk down. He was still in his snake attitude as he slid over the trunk and reached the sandy stage; but when once more between the fires, he rose to his feet and, after a final address to the powers of darkness, he declared the exhibition over.

I have heard many explanations of this scene, but none of them have convinced me. I suppose I shall die, still without understanding exactly what it was that I saw—but that I saw it there can be no doubt.

* * *

I was borrowed by the Penang Police to assist them in what appeared to be an extremely grave case. It appeared that a Malay named Sehidin had a very beautiful daughter whom he had brought up in the strictest seclusion. Never was the fair Malilah allowed out unless accompanied either by her mother or one of her aunts, and yet in spite of all precautions Malilah had disappeared; the jewel had been torn from its setting!

Neither Sehidin nor any of his numerous relations had been able to get on her track, until at last what appeared to be news of her came to hand from a very unexpected, and extremely dangerous quarter. A distant relative reported that, happening to visit the Chinese temple at Ayer Itam, he had overheard one of the priests instructing a workman regarding "the room of the new Malilah".

Sehidin immediately rushed to the Police with this, demanding that they immediately raid the temple and rescue his fair progeny from the evil clutches of the unbelievers.

Any such proceeding was, of course, quite out of the question, at any rate until much clearer evidence of the girl's detention at the temple was forthcoming. Even then it would be an extremely delicate business to handle, as the least mistake would, in all possibility, raise an international riot. In these circumstances the local Police had called me in to see what information I could gather as to the whereabouts of Malilah.

I made my first visit to the temple, as an ordinary visitor, on a day when it was crowded with Europeans from a passenger boat. Having made this preliminary reconnaissance, I decided that the best character for me to assume, if I was to succeed in carrying out my investigations unremarked, was that of a Siamese Buddhist, and I therefore frequented the temple in that guise during the following days. It was not very long until, to my surprise, I sure enough heard a reference to Malilah. I say to my surprise, because I had considered the whole story a 'mare's nest' from the start. It was absolutely inconceivable to me that the Chinese priests of any temple, least of all those of an important temple like this, should mix themselves up in a kidnapping case of any kind, and certainly not in the kidnapping of a Mohammedan girl. After all, if the priests wanted a girl, there were doubtless plenty of Chinese girls that they could kidnap, and who would be, I considered, much more attractive to them.

However, there it was! How it came that her name was being mentioned, if they knew nothing about her? It all seemed very mysterious, and I haunted the temple assiduously. I ran up quite a respectable expenses account with my purchases of crackers, joss sticks, and of kangkong for the temple tortoises.

I spent my days thus about the temple. Most of the intervening nights I spent uncomfortably crawling about the rocks in the neighbourhood, by which means, I think, I managed to look into every illuminated room of the priests' quarters, and I certainly overheard a vast amount of irrelevant conversation. At last it dawned on me that, though I had now heard the name Malilah mentioned some half-dozen times or more, it had never been in conversation between the priests themselves, but on each occasion the priest mentioning the name had been using the Malay language.

In fact the conversation of the priests amongst themselves, when it was not concerned with the purely mundane questions concerning the household affairs of the temple—such as cleaning, repairing, or provisioning—seemed to be confined to interminable discussions on the finer points of ethics, into the sense of which it was almost impossible to follow them. So far as I recollect, I never heard any woman's name mentioned in their own language at all.

I determined, therefore, that the next time I heard a priest use the name I would boldly ask him who was this Malilah that he named, and see what the effect of this query was on him.

I had to wait another two days before this opportunity presented itself, and, on putting the question to him, the surprising result was that the priest said "Come and see, brother." He led me off through a dark passage, which appeared to lead into the very bowels of the mountain itself, then turning a corner we found ourselves in a small room, facing a standing figure of the Buddha, dimly illuminated by several small lamps.

The tall, peaceful figure stood with beckoning hand upraised, an attitude which I had heretofore not seen. "Here is the Malilah," said the priest, and at once the mystery was revealed to me. This beckoning posture the priest had named the 'come here' presentation, and in talking pidgin-Malay they called it the 'Mari-lah', but, as is usual with the Chinese, they pronounced the 'r' as an 'l'. The priest explained to me that they had only recently had the good fortune of getting this rare 'Mali-lah' Buddha, and would soon have completed the public altar on which it would be set up.

This settled the question as regards the Chinese, but in the meantime, owing to this futile enquiry, all chance of tracking the real Malilah seemed to have been lost. Having done what I had been called upon to do, I was leaving further investigation to the Penang Police. However, they asked me to continue working with them, since, being entirely unknown, I stood a better chance of getting on the right track than the local men, who were all more or less widely known. I therefore spent a lazy, but nevertheless busy time in Penang, with ears wide open to pick up any chance remark which might lead me in the right direction.

I picked up an acquaintance with Sehidin himself, and in due course visited him at his bungalow, where I heard the story of his daughter's ravishment by the Chinese, and the scandalous inactivity of the Police in spite of the clearest evidence. Sehidin did not for one moment believe the story of the new Buddha. To him it was obvious that this figure had been purchased and set up merely as a cover to their nefarious doings. Needless to say, I was entirely sympathetic to him. In course of time I met most of his relations, and became suspicious of one of his sisters.

It seemed to me that this lady's protestations of dismay at the girl's fate did not ring true, and I therefore turned my attention to this old dame, Timah, who lived in the Dato Kramat Road. Through the aid of the local Police a watch was kept on her correspondence, and in due course a letter turned up from one Braham, at Alor Star, which seemed to mean much more than it said—it was so glaringly discreet—so I thought a visit to the writer might prove instructive.

Sure enough, on visiting Braham, I found him a strapping young man who had lately set up house with his wife Malilah in a small coconut grove, and learnt from him the full story of the 'rape of Malilah', which turned out to be prosaic in the extreme.

Having seen her on one of her outings with her aunt, Timah, he had straightaway fallen in love with her, and she, it appeared, with him. He had thereupon laid siege to the aged duenna and persuaded her romantic old heart into assisting in an elopement, which had been duly carried out in the good old-fashioned style. The actual wedding ceremony had been performed at Ipoh in order, if possible, to throw pursuit entirely off the scent. This closed the case so far as I was concerned, and I left the local Police to deal with the inevitable squabble which would follow.

Chapter 4

I WAS UP IN TAIPING looking into the question of a Wha-Wei, which is a Chinese lottery of the illegal kind which, it was rumoured, was being run by the gambling farmer himself, when an atrocious murder took place. There was no question as to the murderer's identity, as the following story will show.

Chow Tiang was a quiet, peaceable merchant in the market, who lived with his wife and small family of three in a well-built Chinese-style house, fronting the Kamunting Road in the Klian Pau district. He, unfortunately, was of an amorous disposition, and had succeeded in winning the affections of Lechumi, a charming Kling lady.

This was unfortunate, because Mee Kow had long considered Lechumi as his; the lady had, in fact, so assured him—and what more convincing assurance could man have?

Chow Tiang had been enjoying this lady's favours for some weeks before the news reached Mee Kow—through the intermediary of another lady, as this sort of news always does reach the interested ears, in time.

Now Mee Kow was a very different type of man to Chow Tiang. He was a tin miner, and had been a butcher in his native town, where he had also, doubtless, been a criminal of some note; in any case, his reputation on the mine was that of what a New Yorker would call a 'tough guy'. This being the case, he dealt with the situation after his own manner. He offered no physical injury to Chow Tiang himself, but gagged him and tied him firmly to a heavy blackwood and marble stool in his own house. He lashed the whole to a pillar, and proceeded to provide a little entertainment for his enemy, which took the form of dealing with his wife and children as he had dealt with pigs in his previous occupation.

He split them open neatly and eviscerated them before the eyes of the loving parent and husband, and hung the bodies up on meat-hooks from a beam, with the backbones neatly split through and a stake of wood keeping the sides apart—in exactly the same manner as a pig is dealt with and displayed for sale. In order to make the entertainment really complete, he heaped the entrails round the feet of his victim, and tenderly placing his wife's heart on his knees, departed; leaving the bound and gagged Chow Tiang with the sneering assurance that he would soon join his dear ones, as he would starve to death. This doubtless would have been the case had the affair taken place at Mee Kow's home in Northern China, but in making this prophecy he was forgetting the climate of Malaya.

It was only three days later that Mr. John Meek happened to be cycling past the house, and noticed the obnoxious smell borne from it on the evening breeze. Like all residents in the East, he was accustomed enough to a variety of stinks, but this stench was so appalling that he had enquiries made, which in a short time resulted in the discovery of Chow Tiang in the situation I have depicted—swarming with ants and tortured by the myriads of flies.

I was one of the first to enter the house, merely as an 'idle spectator', of course, and I well remember the sickening horror of the scene.

I suppose anyone but a Chinaman would have lost his reason after undergoing an experience of this kind, and probably also lost his life through suffocation by the poisonous gases from the putrescence by which he was surrounded. Chow Tiang, however, though in a very bad state, revived sufficiently in the hospital to tell something of the circumstances, and the name of the assassin. The Police immediately hurried to the *kongsi* where Mee Kow lived, only to find that he had hastily departed some ten minutes earlier.

It was dark when I was sent for officially, to be told that I must immediately transfer my duty to assisting the local Police in the tracking of this murderer. The story of his association with Lechumi having come to light, we learnt that it was through her agency he had so swiftly heard of Chow Tiang's discovery, but no amount of questioning could elicit from her what his plans were. She was, however, taken to the gaol and charged as an accessory after the fact; a charge which, I may say, subsequently failed owing to lack of evidence. My own opinion of the matter was that, as a matter of fact, she knew nothing of what had happened, though doubtless she had her suspicions.

It was nearly midnight before I discovered that the murderer had borrowed a bicycle from the barber whom he usually patronized to ride to Matang, which naturally made me enquire more particularly along the roads leaving the other side of the town; there, however, I could gather no news of the fugitive, and it was not until next morning that we discovered that he had actually left the town to the south. The Police at Kuala Kangsar were warned, and a party of them came north along the road, but heard nothing of him. As there was also no news from Matang, it appeared that he was making to the north by the Perak valley road.

When the Police reached Lenggong they found that this surmise was correct. Mee Kow had left the bicycle there and taken to the jungle. In face of this I was detailed to keep on his track, the idea being that he was obviously going to make for Bandar Bahru, and so through Kulim to Penang. The theory was that he would appear under another name on emerging from the jungle, and either hide himself in Penang or take fresh employment if opportunity offered on the way. I was to follow him and be ready to point him out to the Police in either case.

I speedily arrived and had no difficulty in getting on to his track, which, to my surprise, soon changed from a westerly to a northern direction, and bearing round still further to the right, by evening I was marching due east. This did not at all fit the Police theory, and I began to wonder if my quarry had lost his way. The most amazing thing to me was the speed with which this Chinaman managed to fight his way through the jungle, for the Malay jungle is a hard enough proposition to find your way through even when you are fairly experienced; but here this man, to whom such progress must have been a complete novelty, was making his way, at the least, two miles per hour.

Following on his track as I did, my difficulties were not so great as his, since I had the benefit of his cutting the way, so had I pressed forward I would have had no difficulty in overtaking him; but, of course, my instructions were merely to keep on his track and it was not part of my duty to attempt an arrest. He evidently felt himself entirely safe, for no sooner had night fallen then he built a fire for himself, so, as he showed no signs of making another night's march of it, I retreated a mile, and there made a hasty shelter, but did not risk the comfort of a fire in case Mee Kow should return on his tracks to discover if he was being followed.

Early next morning he started off and I again took up the chase, with the result that before mid-day we had reached the bank of the Perak River. Here I was unfortunate, as on my arrival at the river bank I was just in time to see a canoe disappear round the next corner up stream, which apparently bore my fugitive. He evidently had reached the bank just as this boat was passing, and had been given a lift.

In one way I was not sorry that this had happened, since, once on the river, it was unlikely that he would leave it, and following him would be a much more comfortable matter than tramping through jungle. I knew that if I made my way slowly along the river I would sooner or later reach a kampong or be overtaken by another boat, and that I could get definite information regarding my quarry from the crew of the boat which I had just seen disappear up-stream. What worried me, however, was the direction taken by Mee Kow. It was, of course, impossible to say yet with any certainty what his intentions were, but he did not seem to be following the suggested programme.

About five o'clock in the afternoon I was pleased to hear the sound of poling, and was overtaken by a boat on its way up-stream, which turned out to be that of a Chinese trader on one of his regular journeys to the upper reaches of the stream. Nothing could have suited me better, as even the Sakais were accustomed to trading with this man, and as we called in from place to place I could hear all the gossip of the river, and have no difficulty in keeping track of the murderer who was now some six hours ahead of me.

At our first stop I learnt that the boat which carried him came from Grik, and to that place I followed in a leisurely fashion on my travelling shop. I felt quite safe in doing this, for unless he returned by the stream, in which case I would, of course, immediately hear of it, he would have to take to the jungle again somewhere, and I felt quite confident of being able to keep on his track there and catch up with him without much difficulty.

I thought it possible that he might try to make from Grik to Baling, and so down the Sungei Ketil, but on arrival at Grik I was surprised to learn that he had again sailed further up the Sungei Perak with a boat returning to the kampong of Beting Kotor. This altered the whole aspect of the chase, as it now seemed to me certain that he was aiming to seek safety by making his way into Siam, in which case it would be useless my merely following him. I decided therefore to push forward with an idea of overtaking him, which, as he was now nearly four days ahead of me, meant a strenuous effort on my part. However, I hired a canoe with a crew of three, and with the four of us at the paddles we made good speed up-stream, continuing steadily day and night.

When we reached Beting Kotor I learnt that my suspicions were quite correct, as Mee Kow had been asking which was the best direction to take on the road to Siam, on which journey he had left twenty-four hours ago. I was still in grave doubt as to what my procedure should be, but felt that my duty was to overtake this man and, if possible, by some means or another bring him into the hands of justice.

I hoped that I would meet some Sakais who I could persuade to make him a prisoner, pending the arrival of the Police. In any case I decided to push forward with all haste, which I proceeded to do. The jungle here was not so dense as that of the lower ground, but the going was almost equally hard, owing to the hills and ravines which had to be traversed. Travelling at my best speed, on the second night I came within sight of Mee Kow's fire. The stream, on the bank of which he had made his camp for the night, ran down the floor of a valley on which owing to the contour of the ground, it caused a series of swamps, strung along its course like beads on a thread.

It was one of these swamps which separated Mee Kow's sleeping place from my position; the actual distance between us, as the crow flies, being very much less than the ground to be covered walking round the swamp. Realizing that we were now within a very few miles of the Siamese border, and having seen nothing of any Sakais, I decided that something had to be done immediately. I sat up long and debated with myself what should be done, then, having reached a conclusion, I skirted the swamp and approached his fire.

As I drew near him I proceeded with the greatest caution, but I need not have been so careful, as I found that Mee Kow had camped on the very edge of the stream, and was lying asleep on the ground between his fire and the banir of a large tree, one of which roots he was using as a pillow. Creeping stealthily up to him, I struck him one blow on the head with my parang. At the shock of this he made a convulsive movement of almost sitting up, then overbalanced and fell into the stream. I had no doubt the man was dead, and after kicking the crown of his head, which lay like a shard on the bank, into the stream after him, I put out his fire and returned to my own rough shelter for the night.

On thinking things over, I thought I had better report direct to Colonel Munroe, as I was not at all sure whether I had exceeded my duties or not. I returned as quickly as possible to Kuala Lumpur, and, having arranged to meet Colonel Munroe, told him what I had done. He told me that, though as a man I had done quite right, yet as a policeman I had done worse than wrong, though in all the circumstances he did not see what else I could have done.

As a result of this interview I reported to the Police at Taiping that Mee Kow had, in my sight, fallen into a stream and had not risen to the surface again, the presumption being that he had either been drowned or taken by a crocodile. They were glad to hear that this murderer had met his fate, though sorry that he had not been brought to justice.

Several months afterwards, Colonel Munroe handed me a free pardon, signed by the Sultan of Perak, for the murder of Mee Kow; in order, as he said, to regularize my position. It had been arranged to have this pardon signed before my name had been filled in, in order to preserve my anonymity.

Chapter 5

AN INTERESTING JOB, WHICH I was allowed to undertake as a private detective during one of my long leaves, was my search for the Pontoh Mujizat Kemewahan, or 'wonder armlet of abundance' as it might be translated. The difficulty was that nobody quite knew what this thing actually was, what it looked like, or of what it was made! In fact, its very existence was rather a doubtful point—so you can understand that setting out to search for it was an undertaking which required considerable optimism and ingenuity.

This article was reputed to have formed part of the regalia of Perak, and if it was in existence the Sultan was anxious to recover it. I had better explain that, at the time the British first took an interest in Perak, that country was distracted by internecine wars between rival claimants to the throne. The British supported the claims of Rajah Abdullah, but he, unfortunately, was not in possession of the regalia—which was held by Rajah Ismail in Upper Perak. Nothing could persuade Rajah Ismail to give them up and, after having been hunted more or less from end to end of the country, he carried them off with him to Penang, where he gave himself up to the British.

The regalia remained some time in Penang, and was then transferred to Singapore, whence, when the country became definitely peaceful and settled, they were delivered to the reigning Sultan. By this time so many years had passed that the inventory of the regalia was more a matter of tradition than of history, and it appeared that the Pontoh should have been with those handed over, but was not. The prosperity of the country was reputed to depend on the possession of this token by the reigning monarch, though as a matter of fact the country had been infinitely more prosperous since this wonder armlet had been lost than it had ever been in the days when it had formed part of the throne. The regalia had passed through so many hands in the vicissitudes of its journeyings that it was difficult to know where, if at all, this part of it had gone missing.

On its arrival at Singapore a very detailed list had been made out, but this unfortunately had not been the case in Penang, where the principal items only had been enumerated and the rest lumped together under a heading of 'other small articles'. It was therefore left in doubt as to whether this armlet had ever been handed over by Rajah Ismail or not.

There were many people still alive who claimed to have seen the regalia worn by Sultan Ali, Abdullah's predecessor, but the majority of these, if they spoke the truth, must have been mere babies at the time. There were, however, several very old men who, no doubt, could remember, but unfortunately the descriptions given by these old people were, almost without exception, entirely different in each instance, and no reliance could be placed on any of them, so the matter of the armlet had remained unsettled up to this time.

I thought my enquiries had better begin in Johore in which State Ismail had been allowed to end his days. I therefore went to Kukub to start the investigations, and there, after endless enquiry, the only semblance of a clue I could find was the recollection of an old woman who had known Rajah Ismail when she was a girl. She remembered him saying how that, at one time when he was being closely pursued by his enemies, he had saved his life by bartering the 'Luck of the State' with some Sakais over the Kelantan border. This seemed very vague but was the best result I could obtain, and as no more was to be learnt in the south, I determined to pursue my enquiries in Kelantan, where, if there was any truth in this story, I had hopes of confirming it, since Sakai memories are very long.

This meant once more living as a Sakai, and I did not look forward to the prospect, but duty is duty, so off I went.

The whole business started rather badly for me, as having discarded my clothing and penetrated the jungle as a Sakai, I had not proceeded far before I had the inestimable misfortune to disturb a hamadryad. These snakes are far and away the most dangerous snakes in the world, not only because their poison is fatal within three minutes, but because they are the only snakes which will actually pursue man. They have been known to follow a man relentlessly for miles; the nearest approach to their malignant pursuit, which I have heard of, is that of a stoat chasing a rabbit.

Having not yet thoroughly got into my stride again as a 'jungle wallah', I was careless enough to attract the attention of a twelve-foot fellow, who proved no exception to his kind and proceeded to chase me. Luckily for me I happened to be on a well-defined elephant track, and could therefore put my best foot forward to some purpose, though I realized that it was a hopeless endeavour, in any case, to outdistance my pursuer—even more hopeless in my present circumstances, unfit as I was from my softening life amidst the fleshpots of the towns.

I ran! Oh, yes! I ran all right! Even a paralytic would put up some sort of a sprint with twelve feet of browny-green death wriggling at his heels. As I ran I recalled my mother's advice to me, of what to do should I ever be placed in the circumstances in which I now found myself, and therefore swept my eyes eagerly over the jungle surrounding me.

With my legs almost falling beneath me, and my breath coming in hoarse gasps, which seemed to tear the very skin off my throat, at last I saw what I was seeking, and drawing my parang, rushed towards a rungus tree which was growing close to the left of the track. I had no time to treat this tree with the respect that should be given to it, but hastily slashing with my parang, quickly separated a strip of bark some five feet long and, dropping it across my path, continued to stagger forward. The snake, swiftly following, slid on to the wet bark of the tree, and looking over my shoulder I was delighted to see that my mother's advice proved true; for I saw the hamadryad writhing in agony on the ground, rolling over and tying himself in knots as he struck furiously at his own body.

It was only now that I could realize the condition I was in myself, owing to my hasty handling of this deadly poisonous tree. My left hand and part of my left thigh were the worst, but there were many other places where the sap had splashed me, and they looked as though they had been dropped into boiling water. The agony was fast becoming unbearable, and it was necessary, therefore, for me to find a root of mulgoh isap as soon as possible. It took me nearly half an hour before I found a good root of this, and by the time I had split it open and rubbed the juice over my sores, I was more dead than alive.

The milky juice from the root soon took the worst of the pain from my scalds, and when I had managed to crawl to a flourishing bush of paskok, I completed the antidote; I chewed plenty of the leaves of this low-growing shrub, which soon began to put new life into my veins. It was, I may say, many weeks before the marks of where the rungus sap had bitten in entirely disappeared from my body. My present appearance, however, although its acquisition had been heroically drastic, nevertheless made one of the best make-ups man could think of for my character as a Sakai—their skins being generally covered with blemishes.

All this had naturally taken a long time, and night was upon me before I had reached the Sakai encampment I was making for, which meant an uncomfortable night in the open for me. However, I reached them next morning, and my story of the trouble I had had with my tribe in Pahang, and my journey north, was accepted without question. It was lucky I reached them when I did, as within two days we were on the trek to establish a new clearing, which wandering life, of course, suited my book excellently. By judicious questioning I soon learnt that the people I was with had never even heard of Rajah Ismail, but I had hopes of finding memories of him amongst others whom we were sure to meet on our journey.

Sure enough, I found what appeared to be a clue to my search when we had been on the move about three weeks. I was talking to a wrinkled old Sakai, the leader of a tribe who were hospitably entertaining us for the night after our late arrival at their clearing. He told me of a certain Pawang Hitra, with a tribe who were generally to be found in the district round the headwaters of the Sungei Desat, some sixty or seventy miles away. This old fellow said that this Pawang had added greatly to his powers, some forty or fifty years ago, by becoming possessed of a talisman which he called 'Iscandar's Belt'.

This seemed a likely enough name to have been given to the object of my search, and the time of its arrival in the jungle also seemed to fit in. In any case it was the only suggestion of a hint I had received so far, and—with all news or clues so nebulous—anything which seemed even vaguely definite was worthy of attention, so I decided to investigate this matter further.

As we were moving west we would in due course be crossing the territory named, so there was no necessity for me to alter my arrangements, and about a week later we met a hunting party from the very encampment I wished to visit, with whom we joined forces and returned to their home, where we were heartily welcome.

I immediately found that Pawang Hitra was a comparatively young man, and it was only by dint of the most delicate enquiries that I learnt from him that it was his father who had acquired the belt of Iscandar, but by no means of persuasion could I obtain a sight of this treasured possession. The one bit of news which I did learn, was that it was from an 'Orang Farsi' that the talisman had been obtained. This did not seem to fit in with my theory at all, for at that time I did not know that Rajah Ismail was, as a matter of fact, not a pure-bred Malay. However, in spite of the evidence against the identity of these two 'luck bringers', I decided that the evidence in favour of them being the same was the greater, and that it was up to me to obtain a sight of the belt by hook or by crook, and decide from its appearance whether it was the Pontoh or not.

Expressing the greatest satisfaction in the company and the surroundings of our hosts, I announced my determination of not continuing with my party, but of remaining where I was, if permitted. As I was a strong, lusty young man and would add greatly to the hunting powers of the tribe, I was welcomed into their community; then I settled down immediately to the task of persuading Hitra to let me see, and to, possibly, depriving him of his most valued mascot.

I had, of course, much greater knowledge than any of my new friends, so I was soon able to impress them with my capabilities, and the Pawang, being a wise man, felt that it would be worth his while to cultivate my closer acquaintance. I, of course, was only too ready to fall in with this desire of his, and eventually tentatively suggested that he should make me his assistant. I had been able to teach him one or two simple bits of 'magic', with which he was greatly impressed, and for the knowledge of which he was very grateful. His astonishment at my demonstration of thimble rigging, with three half-coconuts as the thimbles and an areka nut as the pea, was immense. When he found he could never lift the shell which covered the nut, he felt that here indeed was a magic as powerful as his own! His sly enjoyment when I showed him how it was all done, convinced me that many, if not all of the powers displayed by these 'witch doctors' are trickery of some sort or the other—though I must confess I have seen them do things the trickery of which, if it existed. I have been unable to fathom.

Becoming thus friendly with him I was, in due course, permitted to see and even handle the famous belt. This proved to be, without doubt, the armlet for which I was in search. If it had been, as a matter of historical fact the belt of Iscandar, then Alexander must have had a waist of a slimness which no woman could rival! Even at its best the armlet cannot have been much to look at.

It was a narrow belt of plaited leather, and at one time each of the strips forming the plait had evidently been brightly coloured, but there were only faint traces of the colours left. Several strips showed the remains of gilt, but, when new, it had been nothing more than a gaudy trifle. Attached to the centre was a little pocket of leather, on which was left a mere suggestion of the stamped inscription in Arabic characters with which it had been at one time decorated; now not sufficiently clear to distinguish even one character distinctly. No doubt there was a text from the Koran contained in this sewn-up pocket.

The object which I held in my hands, having been for many years trailed about the jungle in a bundle together with all the paraphernalia of a wizard, looked and smelt more like a bundle of dead rats' tails than the proud possession of a king. I could hardly imagine that the Sultan of Perak would be grateful to have such a greasy, loathsome rag placed in his hands. However, that was not my business, and I set about getting possession of it in the following simple manner.

At the sight of it, I first went into raptures of delight at the marvel thus displayed to me, and then, working myself up on the subject of its intense holiness, I slowly came round to anger that it should be subjected to the treatment which it was receiving, and protested that such a rare relic should be protected from further injury. Its powers, I exclaimed, would not be the less if it was put in a sealed-up receptacle, and if that was the case there would be no fear of it becoming further disintegrated with age.

I quite carried Hitra with me in these transports, and persuaded him to seal up the armlet in a short length of bamboo, on the outside of which I undertook to brand some further powerful cabalistic signs. Needless to say, whilst I was engaged on this mystic ritual I had no difficulty in substituting another, exactly similar, length of bamboo which I had carefully prepared, in place of that containing the armlet. I felt that the strips of monkey skin, with which my bamboo was loaded, would be quite as efficacious to his magic as the armlet had ever been, and that robbing him of it in this manner deprived him of nothing.

Had I merely taken the armlet and disappeared into the jungle with it, I have no doubt that misfortune would have overtaken my new friends, merely because they would have expected it to do so; as things were, they would go on being as fortunate as ever, firm in the conviction that they carried their fortune with them in the small bamboo box.

My having an attack of fever, the intensity of which I exaggerated by simulation, gave me an opportune excuse for leaving my new home, and I lost no time in returning to Kuala Kangsar, where, as I had expected, the recovered Pontoh Mujizat Kemewahan received a very cold reception! Whether it is at present resting in the Royal Treasury or not, I do not know.

Chapter 6

OF COURSE I HAD LONG made it my business to become acquainted with all that there was of a criminal fraternity in Malaya, but conditions with us are very different from those existing in the more advanced civilizations of the West. Crime here tends to be more childlike and extreme; the majority of the cases with which we had to deal with tended to group themselves under three headings, either petty pilfering or murder being, as one might say, the natural two crimes of the country, to which was added a class which could be conveniently grouped under the heading of revenue evasions and the like. Under this last class I group the varied intricate financial transactions of the Chetti and the Sikh.

It was a rare thing for a Malay or a Chinaman to go in for simple robbery, and robbery was rarely the incentive for murder, in fact, it was rather the other way round; his enemy being dead, the murderer did not see why he should not take possession of his effects—but quite as an afterthought.

There was practically no floating criminal class, such as is found in the cities of Europe, or the United States, though in course of time small populations of this kind gathered in the larger towns. There were, however, a fair sprinkling of traders who were not averse to dealing in stolen goods, and it was to these gentry that I first gave my attention.

By arrangement with Colonel Munroe, and with his successor, Major Ritchie, I was from time to time supplied with a parcel of goods which I would dispose of to one or other of these receivers, who were nearly all, whether Chinamen, Parsees, or Tulacans, 'curio dealers'.

The Police would make a great fuss of enquiring for these goods, and it would be noised abroad that they had been stolen from 'so and so'. In this way I established confidential relations with most of these folk, which of course greatly aided me in my various enquiries. Needless to say I was known to them under a variety of different characters—to one I was a Javanese coolie, to another a Burmese clerk, to a third a Malay boy, and so on.

As the number of white men increased in the country, the value of the articles pilfered naturally increased, since both the opportunities for theft and the value of the available harvest were greatly enhanced by the property which these gentlemen brought with them. Cases in which white men were concerned became more numerous, though needless to say, almost without exception, they were the prosecutors which brings me to an extraordinary case on which I was engaged.

For some time past planters, mine managers, merchants and their clerks, and the white population generally, had been suffering from an unprecedented plague of theft. Reports were the same throughout the whole country from Singapore to Kuala Lumpur, and in no case could anything definite be discovered as to the perpetrators, the robberies being so wholesale that it looked like the work of an organized gang.

When this was realized, the matter was put into my hands for special investigation. I gathered the Police reports from all of the many robberies, and on analyzing them the following fact stood out. In every case the thieves had known exactly where to go for their plunder. Nowhere had there been signs of the general ransacking of premises which usually accompanies a casual housebreaking. This fact seemed to point to the indoor servants having been concerned, since they would, of course, know exactly where to lay their hands on their master's most valuable property. Against this, however, was the startling number of thefts. Why should so many boys all take it into their heads to rob their masters within the short space of time covered by these cases?

This brought me to the question of time, and, on making out a chronological list, it seemed to me that all the robberies might well be the work of one man, travelling slowly northwards through the country. After my most diligent enquiries amongst the fences I could obtain no news of any of the stolen property, so I determined to follow in the footsteps of my supposed travelling thief, and see how far any new fact I might gather, by enquiries on the spot, would support my theory and help me to identify him. In Singapore itself there had been a regular epidemic of thefts dating over some three weeks, and I decided it would be better to start my enquiries on the mainland, where the population was not so dense and news of any strangers in the district would probably be more easily come by.

When I had interviewed all the Tuans who had been robbed, which I did in the guise of the agent for a Chinese Mutual Security Insurance Company (in which I was quite sure that no white man would care to take out a policy; indeed it would have been impossible for him to do so, as such a company did not exist—though I had some very convincing-looking literature on the subject!), and had thoroughly discussed the robbery question with their various servants whilst waiting for the interviews—always a long period, since it was invariably my misfortune to call at a time when the master was not likely to be at home—I amassed an amount of information from which I was interested to note that all these houses had been visited, some weeks before the robbery had taken place, either by an Italian named Marchesi, or by an itinerant French conjuror who called himself the Great Sardou.

The Italian appeared to be a capitalist who thought of investing money in an agricultural, or mining venture, and in this character had spent a day or two at many bungalows, as a welcomed guest, whilst inspecting the properties. The Frenchman, on the other hand, had given conjuring entertainments, and had in turn been entertained for the night in many cases. It seemed to me, therefore, that these two were in some way connected with the robberies, and I had enquiries instituted at once as to their whereabouts. There was no difficulty in getting on to their tracks, as both appeared to have followed the same itinerary to some extent.

The first news which could be obtained in either case was of their appearance in Penang, but they did not seem to have landed there at the same date, in fact the Italian had been a well-known figure, staying at the Eastern and Oriental Hotel, at least a month before there was any news of the Frenchman's first performance in Chulia Street. At the other end of their trip through the country, the order of their departure had been the same, for the Italian, after staying there a few days, had left Raffles Hotel, Singapore, on his way to Colombo, again some weeks before the Frenchman was reported to have left the same port for Saigon.

This news seemed to knock the bottom out of my supposition, and in the meantime several fresh robberies had taken place in the town and district of Ipoh. I therefore decided to travel over the ground again, this time paying no attention to the houses robbed, but gathering what news I could on the roadside. I started my trip on foot from Johore Bahru, and it was not long before I made a discovery which brought me post-haste back to Kuala Lumpur, where my report immediately brought the Police into action.

The facts, as they emerged at the subsequent trial, were as follows:

A well-known international thief, finding that things were getting a bit too warm for him in Europe, thought that a visit to Malaya might serve a double purpose. It would both form a sunny holiday for him, whilst the memory of his recent activities faded from the minds of the European Police; and, at the same time, such a visit might, by judicious speculation, be rendered profitable. He had toured the country, first in the guise of an Italian capitalist, in which capacity he visited only the managers or owners of properties, and marked down the most likely places to be robbed.

When he left Singapore he had not gone to Colombo as was supposed, but had landed again at Penang, and from there had gone over the same ground once more, this time as the Great Sardou, giving his famous conjuring entertainment, and visiting the bungalows of the smaller fry, thus adding enormously to the number of his prospective victims. In this latter guise he had simply not left Singapore when he had booked his passage to Saigon, but had dressed himself as an Arab. This was a character which he could well support, as he spoke Arabic fluently, owing to his frequent winter visits to Cairo—following the wealthy in pursuit of his 'business'.

As an Arab, and accompanied by a Malay woman he had picked up in Singapore, he had been, and still was travelling slowly back over his tracks in a bullock cart, and from this inconspicuous headquarters was making his hauls. Day or night, the cart could stand at the side of the road without remark, when the couple wished to sleep or eat—and when he was netting his catches.

It was a well thought out scheme, as there is nothing in Malaya more unremarkable, or unremarked, than a bullock cart. The drawback to it was the time factor. Had he used a motor car he would have finished his clean-up quicker, but would have been so conspicuous that the Police would have caught him correspondingly quicker also. The only thing which would have balanced these two factors, and ensured his safety, would have been for him to have been content with a small haul and ceased operations sooner. Greed undoubtedly was his downfall.

In the cart was found the whole of the stolen property, so that the case ended satisfactorily all round.

* * *

It was not often that I was thus employed on a case where a white man was the criminal, though I was called in, and actually engaged for about two hours, on the case which has become so widely known through the play and cinema film called 'The Letter'. The facts as given in this play are not quite the true facts of the case. The letter in question was found in the murdered man's bungalow quite openly, and there was no question of blackmail concerning it, as given in the play, at all. Furthermore, the lady who committed the murder was condemned to death, and afterwards pardoned by the Sultan. The film picture is, of course, merely a farcical travesty of either the play or the truth.

When Doctor Knight first reported his discovery of the body lying in the compound to Police headquarters, it was thought that my services might be needed, and I was detailed for the case; but very short investigation showed that it was to be all plane sailing, and I was taken off again to other work.

Chapter 7

WHEN THE CHINESE EMANCIPATED THEMSELVES, by revolution, from the rule of the Manchus, it was a busy time for us in the States Police, since the various Chinese Tongs were in the process of making up their minds as to which side they were to take in the question. This led to very considerable unrest amongst the Chinese population, to say the least of it.

So long as the troubles were confined to the Chinese amongst themselves this was not so bad, as it was all part of the game to them. Unfortunately, however, many unruly elements amongst them thought this was a grand opportunity for some general lawlessness. The roads were being picketed by the parties in favour of the new republic, who were compelling all passing Chinamen to sacrifice their pigtails, unless they had already done so, as a sign of partisanship with the new movement.

Advantage was taken of this situation by the criminal minority, and for a time the roads were rendered unsafe by their marauding bands, who held up not only passing Chinese but everybody else; and several murders by these highwaymen took place as a result of resistance to their demands.

I had a very narrow escape from falling into a regular ambush laid by some of these men. I had been busy investigating a murder by one such band in the neighbourhood of Klang Gates, and, on my return to Kuala Lumpur, was immediately ordered out to look into a similar affair which had just been reported from Ulu Langat. I at once started off on a motor bicycle, and about half-way between Pudoh and Cheras, as I came round a corner, I found that an attempt to block the road had been made by laying a row of rocks across it.

I immediately realized that, if I were to stop, I would be at once surrounded by Chinese and entirely at their mercy, and that it was preferable to 'take a chance' at the obstacle than to submit to intimidation without any chance at all. The stones were of varying sizes, the smallest being about the size of a man's head, so, choosing a place between two stones which looked the most likely, I opened the throttle and charged at full speed at it. The bicycle bumped over somehow, and it was with some little surprise that I found myself speeding along the road, apparently without damage to the machine.

I made directly for Cheras Police station, since it was the nearest, and there reported the ambush, when it was arranged by telephone that parties of Police should proceed from both ends of the road simultaneously in an endeavour to capture this gang. This was done and they were partly successful, since four or five men were taken out of a party estimated at fifteen.

When I examined my bicycle, I was even more amazed at my luck in getting through, for the metal rim of the front wheel had been folded back, where it struck the rock, exposing the rubber bead for a distance of at least three inches, and it was a mechanical miracle that the inner tube had not blown out and burst.

The success of the Chinese rebellion, involving as it did the doing away with pigtails, aided me very considerably in my work. With all Chinamen wearing their hair dressed the same as other people it was now possible for me to pass unremarked when dressed as a Chinaman, a disguise which their peculiar form of hair-dressing had rendered it too risky for me to assume heretofore, though, owing to the unusually light colour of my skin it was one which I was particularly well suited to enact. I have since spent so much time disguised as a Chinaman that I feel almost as at home in that capacity as I do in my natural state.

* * *

The custom of white bachelors taking Malay girls to live with them was one which was very apt to lead to murder when such a man wished to replace this housekeeper by a legitimate wife. These girls sometimes become deeply attached to their white master, and, looking upon the white woman as a usurping enemy, set out to murder her by whatever means they found possible and practicable. Though these murders were comparatively obvious, it was not always easy to bring the charge home to the right party, and I was sent out on several occasions to make local enquiries with a view to establishing the guilt where possible.

There was a sameness about all these cases in that the outstanding facts were the same, though of course the individual surroundings, the moves made, and the methods of murder were varied. I do not therefore propose to give more than one instance of this type of case, which is quite representative of them all.

The estate of Pukul Satu had been opened up from the original jungle on the hillside of Bukit Tidah by a Mr. Nemo who, at the time, was assistant to Mr. A.N. Other on the flourishing estate of Bukan Stingah, alongside of which the property was situated. Almost immediately after he first came out to Malaya, this Mr. Nemo had taken Sarefa, then a pretty girl of sixteen, to live with him. Sarefa had looked after Tuan Nemo as a mother looks after her child. She had interpreted for him, washed for him, mended for him, occasionally cooked for him, and had nursed him tenderly through numerous bouts of fever. She had borne him several children, though only one lived, and that one was being brought up in the Catholic Convent.

When the Pukul Satu clearing became sufficiently important, Tuan Nemo, when at home in England on leave, had succeeded in selling his estate to a company. Things were now looking up with him, and he doubtless felt it was time to settle down, so in addition to floating his company he became engaged to Rosie, the beautiful daughter of a wealthy Scottish landowner—Isaac Cohen (or whatever his name was).

Thinking of Sarefa, Nemo decided that he must return alone. "In order to prepare a bungalow", as he said, and get things ready for married bliss. When this was all prepared, Rosie would follow him; they would get married in Colombo, and 'honeymoon it' across the Indian Ocean.

On his return, Nemo had many scenes with Sarefa during the building of the new bungalow—which were heartbreaking to her and incomprehensible to him. He explained to her, *ad nauseam*, how it had been from the start a purely business arrangement—"as well she knew". "Had he not paid her thirty dollars a month regularly? It was like any other business arrangement, liable to curtailment at any moment"— and this was the moment.

Sarefa could not see all this, and, on her side, she argued. "How had she failed in her duty as a wife? In what way had she not been a wife? Had he not told her countless times how he loved her? Did he not remember how wonderful they had both thought their first baby was?" This was the one now at the Convent. "Did he not use to crawl along the floor of the veranda playing bears with this little one?" She insisted that she loved him deeply and would not give him up for any insipid white woman.

Nemo, however, had been firm, and packed her off with a present of a thousand dollars to solace her wounded heart. Packing her off, however, did not mean so much as it sounds—since it only meant her returning to her own people, who lived just beyond Bukan Stingah estate at the cross-roads; in other words, practically on his doorstep.

The actual parting was a very hectic scene. Words ran high on both sides, the woman as usual being the more verbose and biting, so Nemo was very touched when she returned in a few days' time, full of a spirit of sweet reasonableness and apologizing for the scenes she had made.

He told her that he had been quite sure she would understand after she had thought the matter over, and was glad that this had been the case. He said that, after they had been such friends, it would have been a pity to have parted thus in anger, and he was delighted that his faith in her common sense had been justified. In fact, he said a lot of nice things to her about herself; told her that she would like the new Mem Sahib when she saw her, and rather enlarged on Rosie's many perfections. To all of this Sarefa dutifully agreed, so he kissed her quite after the old style when they parted, and went off with a light heart to his marriage in Ceylon.

After Rosie had been established some six months as mistress of the new bungalow, she was taken violently ill with agonising pains in her stomach, wherefrom, after a few days' torture, she died, in spite of the best medical attention available.

In the circumstances, older people shook their heads, and suspected poison; Nemo laughed such a suggestion to scorn—who was there who would wish to poison his beautiful Rosie? When the name Sarefa was suggested as a possibility he was even more emphatic; he was sure she would never dream of doing such a thing. He knew her well, and she was far too kind and gentle in her nature even to hurt anyone, much less kill them, and, in any case, Sarefa had gone on a visit to distant relations more than a month before Rosie had been taken ill.

Such were the circumstances given to me when I was despatched along the road to investigate the matter.

Realizing that a new face in such a small community would need to be definitely accounted for, I started from Ulu Kerbau, which town is situated some sixteen miles further along the road beyond Pukul Satu. I was an impresario searching for talent to appear in a series of Malay plays, which I was going to produce in the near future.

In this capacity I gradually approached the little kampong by Bukan Stingah, and, of course, news of my doings had preceded me, so my visit was expected. Needless to say I had arranged my programme so that I arrived in the evening, and must spend the night there. My manner of approach was peculiarly suited to my enquiries. Almost the first person mentioned as a possible success on the stage was Sarefa, which brought the conversation in the direction I desired without any effort on my part. There was a young man called Lasam who, I noticed, did not seem overjoyed at the prospect of my engaging Sarefa when she returned; so, a little later on, I expressed the opinion that he was just the sort of fellow who would suit me, and discussed theatrical work at some length with him, pretending to be highly satisfied with his qualifications. When I returned to the subject of Sarefa, I noticed that he was now quite keen on the idea of her being also engaged in my company.

I do not propose to weary you with further details of my conversations. It is sufficient for me to say that, having thus established confidence with Lasam, I eventually succeeded in eliciting the following facts— partly from him and partly from others.

Lasam had long been 'casting sheep's eyes' at Sarefa, and, when she had been thus cruelly turned away by Nemo, he had at once proposed marriage to her. She had blown hot and cold, until finally she had told him that, much as she would like to marry him, she would never do so as long as the Mem Sahib lived. Lasam had been in the habit, from time to time, of supplying fish to the Chinese cook at Nemo's bungalow, and he had determined to make use of this custom in winning Sarefa for his wife.

Choosing a morning when he had seen Nemo going into town alone, he had appeared at the cook-house with a small catch of three prawns from the neighbouring swamp. The reason why this catch was so small he did not explain. He could hardly have been expected to do so, as the reason was that, by this means, he was sure that no one but the Mem Sahib would partake of these fish, three being a meagre helping, even for one.

Into the flesh of these prawns he had cleverly introduced thin slivers of bamboo, neatly pointed and barbed at either end, and rolled up, after the fashion of a watch spring, into a very small compass. He knew that *makan udang* was a favourite dish with the Mem Sahib, and trusted that, the flesh of these crustaceans being of a tough nature, his morsels would be eaten by Rosie without his scientific additions being detected.

These threads of bamboo, straightening out as the food was digested, would lacerate the bowels from end to end during their journey, and, in passing, would leave nothing for a post-mortem to discover, which might not have been caused by any of a hundred and one errors in diet.

This, then, was the cause of Rosie's demise, but since everyone concerned would deny all knowledge of the circumstances except perhaps the perfectly innocent cook, and since what had been said to me was one thing, while what would be said in the Magistrate's court was quite a different matter, nothing could be done to the perpetrator.

Cases of this sort were, whilst never frequent, still not uncommon some years ago—but nowadays one hardly ever hears of them.

Chapter 8

I HAVE BEEN FORTUNATE, in that I have been in the immediate neighbourhood of several cases of amok, and escaped from all without injury. The most fatal of these cases which I witnessed was one near Malacca. Here a man named Abu was sitting one morning on his veranda gossiping with his wife Maimunah, and her brother Mat Aris, whilst he was sharpening his parang. He then stood up and quietly tested its edge by decapitating his youngest child, who was playing at the door of the house behind them. He next struck down his wife— while Mat Aris reached safety by jumping from the end of the veranda.

Abu then went into his house and murdered both his other two children and his mother-in-law, before quietly walking down from the veranda with his streaming parang in his hand. Mat Aris had at once called Abu's father, who, he thought, might have some influence over him. This foolish old man walked up to his son as he descended the steps, calling to him to put away his parang and stop this nonsense. I was a witness of the scene when the son, telling his father that "it was not his fault", and that, "these things happened", struck the old man to the ground with a blow which split his head almost in halves.

At this time most of the men folk of the kampong were out in the plantations, and the Penghulu, to whom I was talking, realizing that there was nothing else to be done if this wholesale murder was to be stopped, snatched up a sporting gun which he had and rushed towards Abu, who was, by this time, pursuing a wildly shrieking woman. The Penghulu, being an oldish man, unfortunately did not overtake him before he had added Marian to the list of his victims. But, as he stood over her, the gun was fired at close quarters, killing him instantly.

In other cases which I have seen it has been rare for there to be more than three victims of these possessed people. The cause of this form of murderous obsession has long been sought for, but so far without definite success. In the case which I have just mentioned, the man Abu seemed to have been living a perfectly happy life, both with his family and neighbours; the only possible cause of annoyance which he may have had being a matter of nine months old, regarding the death of a buffalo of which he was part possessor, and about which there had been a dispute. The matter had been taken to court and settled in his opponent's favour, which Abu considered a most unjust settlement.

Possibly it was brooding over his supposed wrongs in this case which led to his sudden breakdown, though this seems almost beyond belief. In any case there was nothing else that could be put forward, with any more justification, as a possible reason; so, unless these things happen without reason at all, it certainly would appear that the reasons which cause them are utterly insignificant when compared with the result produced.

* * *

Whilst I was engaged on quite a different enquiry, I ran across a thread which I was subsequently instructed to follow up, to see whether it, in fact, led in the direction which it seemed to indicate. From a chance remark I had overheard, it seemed as though a Mr. Jackson, who was an assistant on Chelaka estate, had been guilty of murder.

Getting into touch with the boys at his bungalow, 'I could find no confirmation of this rumour, but learnt that, some months ago, he had taken a very pretty little Malay girl as housekeeper, who answered very well to the description of the victim. The original negotiations regarding the acquisition of this girl Mr. Jackson had carried out with an elderly man, whose name the boys thought was Mat Sah. This girl had only stayed about a fortnight when she had mysteriously disappeared one night, but the boys ridiculed the suggestion that Tuan Jackson had had anything to do with her disappearance; they were quite sure that it had surprised him as much as themselves; he had, in fact, instituted searching enquiries in an endeavour to discover when she had left, why she had left, and where she had gone.

The boys could give no answer to any of these questions, and had never seen her since the day of her disappearance. They had, however, seen Mat Sah since, as he had called at the bungalow to see Mr. Jackson two or three times, the last time being about a month ago.

On making the most careful enquiries all round the district, I could find no one else who knew Mat Sah or anything about him, in fact he seemed to be a regular man of mystery. Since it seemed to be on the strength of this disappearance that the remarks I had overheard had been made, I determined to get on the track of this old man and investigate the matter further.

49

In about a week he turned up once more at Chelaka and visited Mr. Jackson, which was very convenient for me; as I simply had to follow him to find out where he lived and all about him. Following him turned out to be not quite such an easy job as I had anticipated; from his actions he appeared to be expecting pursuit and took every precaution against it. For instance, during the day he twice took to paths through the jungle, in the first instance turning about and returning rapidly along the same path after he had penetrated it for about half a mile.

In this case, had I not had the training which I have had with Sakais I would certainly have been discovered. Thanks to my ears being thoroughly used to the multitudinous noises of the jungle, this was not the case, and I found no difficulty in following the sound of his sandal-shod feet, so had plenty of warning when he turned, to enable me to step off the path. It was of course only necessary for me to go a very short distance to one side to render myself invisible.

In the other case, having entered the jungle, he commenced running the moment he was out of sight and doubled back along a branch path to the right, which brought him out again within a hundred yards of the point where he had entered. In this case, however, as I knew the path he was taking, the moment he commenced running I suspected what his ruse was, so sat down just within the jungle edge and waited for him to emerge, as he did in due course, very much out of breath. Finding that he was taking these precautions, I was convinced that he was up to some nefarious operation or other, so I stuck to him like a leech. I followed him in this manner for nearly a week, and found that he was calling on a widespread clientele of junior assistants. By sticking to him, he finally led me to his home among the paddy fields in a neighbouring state.

Returning to the various bungalows at which he had called, and making close enquiries amongst the servants, I discovered that the story in each case was practically identical with that of Mr. Jackson. All these assistants were very young men, and none of them had been in the country longer than eighteen months when they had first seen Mat.

It seemed to me a clear case of blackmail, and so I reported it to Major Ritchie. The matter, of course, then passed out of my hands, but it ended as follows:

Each of these young men was being accused by Mat Sah of having murdered and done away with his charming grand-daughter Puteh. Being very young and inexperienced, and being too diffident to have their amours dragged into the light of the police court, with the probability of newspaper paragraphs which might reach the eyes of their people at home, all these victims were submitting to the extortion demanded.

The old man had done very well out of the business, since in every case it had been necessary for the Tuan to pay fifty dollars "to free her from debt" before the lady arrived, and each of them had paid her an advance of thirty to fifty dollars, "to buy clothes with", before she disappeared. On top of these payments came Mat Sah's blackmailing demands, and the old rascal had been very skilful in scaling these. Knowing that these young men would be feeling the pinch of the initial outlay, he had started with a simple ten dollars with each, "to keep the girl's mother quiet". He had raised the sum on each of his subsequent visits, until the oldest standing claims were paying as much as forty dollars at the time of my enquiry.

Naturally enough, Major Ritchie found it almost impossible to persuade anyone to prosecute, in fact they were all extremely upset to find that the Police knew anything about the transactions at all! It looked as though the miscreant would escape, with nothing worse than a visit from the Police and a warning regarding his future behaviour; and such, undoubtedly, would have been the case had he not conveniently hanged himself, by playing his game once too often, and this time by choosing the wrong man for it.

The man he had chosen was certainly young enough, and innocent enough, but, unfortunately for Mat, he was a Scotsman, and after the girl's disappearance he was hard hit by the loss of his good money. Mat's subsequent appearance, and his talk of the Police court, came as a bright light to this boy. He had never thought of the Police court as a possible remedy, and no sooner had Mat mentioned this institution— which had usually produced such desirable results—than it was greeted with a veritable hoot of joy, and Mat found himself being hurried thither by the stalwart Caledonian, who did not care a tinker's curse what was said about his morals so long as there was the least chance of saving his bawbees!

The case did not provide any general sensation, for the widespread operations on which Mat had been engaged were not mentioned in open court, and only the Magistrate was given full details. Mat and his alleged grand-daughter were duly given a chance of contemplating their misdoings for a considerable time at the Government expense, and the defrauded Scotsman even managed to recover the thirty dollars advance which he had given to his charmer by instituting a case against her for "absconding with an advance of wages"! If it were not for these public-spirited characters, Police work would often be rendered very unproductive.

* * *

Like everybody else who has moved about the country at all, I have rather more than a nodding acquaintance with our ubiquitous friend the crocodile, though I am glad to say I have so far managed to keep that acquaintanceship a distant one. It has, however, been my misfortune, from time to time, to be an eye-witness of some distressing scenes caused by them. I once met a man who had been taken by a crocodile whilst bathing, and carried to its lair, from which he managed to escape; which is an experience very few can have had, and should, therefore, bear repeating.

Towards the evening a large number of people had been bathing in the river, and this man arrived just as they were coming out of the water, seeing which he entered the water himself without the least suspicion that it was not perfectly safe. He was standing up to his waist, and had ducked himself twice, when he was caught about the middle by a crocodile and immediately dragged into deep water.

It was lucky for him that he had been ducking himself, for he had taken a good breath of air before going under, and, as the crocodile was not hurting him much, he kept his head—and his breath—thinking that he might yet have a chance. The crocodile was holding him about the hips, firmly but not cruelly, "like a cat carrying her kittens" was the way he expressed it. Soon he was surprised to find himself thrust above the water, and he seized this opportunity of getting another breath of air. He was above only for an instant, whilst the crocodile shifted its grip, from directly across the thighs at the back, to one which put him sideways in the reptile's mouth. Again he was plunged under the water, and soon found himself being pushed under the arching roots of a mangrove.

The crocodile did not bite him, but, having placed him in position, pushed him firmly in with its nose. Waiting for a second after this had been done before moving, he then seized the roots immediately on his right and, fighting his way through their tangle, managed to get his head above the surface of the water just before he was suffocated. He found himself in a very precarious position, since he was still more or less wedged amongst the roots, and he knew that the tide was rising.

Eventually, after a violent struggle, during which he had to submerge himself again twice, he managed to free himself and haul himself up the mangrove. By this time it was quite dark, but was light enough for him to see that he was on the other bank of the river. He did not dare risk swimming across, and had to spend the night so, clinging precariously to this tree, very much more dead than alive, until he was rescued by a boat in the morning.

I have never seen a fisherman knocked out of his boat by a crocodile, though I am well assured that this is by no means an exceptional occurrence. I was present on one occasion, however, when a child was taken from the river bank, where she was playing, whilst the mother was engaged washing clothes only some three yards distant. It was all over in an instant. The innocent child, playing peacefully; a splash; a shrill cry; the empty bank; and only a swirl in the waters to show that anything had happened. In this case certainly, the crocodile did not lift his victim again above the water, as they are reputed always to do.

The legend is, that a crocodile always thus lifts his prey to show that it is not he who is causing the death, but the water. From the experience of the man who escaped, above related, it would appear that this is only done when the reptile finds that he has made an inconvenient grip at the first snap.

At one time, when I was searching the fishing villages of the coast for smugglers, I lived for weeks in the society of almost more crocodiles than men. These villages, built for the most part over mud flats which are covered by every tide, have crocodiles about them at all times; and the Orang Laut, in spite of their familiarity with these reptiles, have not yet reached the stage of treating them with contempt—any who may have done so having probably been eliminated.

There is no doubt that the crocodile is the most formidable menace with which mankind has to contend in the coastal regions, and even far inland.

Chapter 9

A LARGE NUMBER OF THE cases with which I had to deal were caused by the habit, which seems to be almost universal amongst the Sikhs who come to Malaya, of lending money at interest. It would sometimes take me even as long as a week of careful enquiries, to straighten out the story of the complicated financial transactions of some Sikh cart driver, who had been severely assaulted whilst travelling peacefully along his customary road. It inevitably turned out that the assault had been committed by some exasperated client who, having originally borrowed fifty cents, now found himself owing a capital sum of six dollars, and was met with a demand for interest of fifty cents a week, which of course he found himself utterly unable to continue paying.

Cases of this sort were constantly cropping up and they, of course, were very important to the people concerned, but I feel sure the sordid details would prove very poor reading even though, as sometimes happened, it was the more serious eventuality of murder which, had followed on these extortions—which was by no means an exceptional occurrence.

Another class of case which occupied a good deal of my time, but can be of no general interest, was that brought about by the influx of Tamil coolies to the rubber estates. Each of these coolies costs an estate a considerable sum of money to recruit and bring over from India; so it is important that they should continue working on the estate which has paid these sums.

From time to time, however, coolies were tempted away from their estates to work elsewhere; their new employers thus acquiring labour cheaply. I was frequently employed to discover the present whereabouts of coolies who had absconded in this manner, sometimes a matter of no little difficulty, but always an affair of no general interest whatsoever.

The finding of a dead Chinaman by the roadside was frequently reported, and I was from time to time employed on the fruitless task of discovering his identity and the circumstances of his death. I say the fruitless task, because in such circumstances it was quite impossible to find anyone who would admit to the slightest knowledge of the man. He might be found on the road within two miles of Chinese coolie lines, perhaps with no other Chinese within miles, the obvious inference being that he had been a coolie living in these lines. Yet the Mandor would deny all knowledge of him, and the coolies express equal ignorance.

The facts of the matter probably being that, the man having died with a certain amount of wages due to him, the Mandor had had his body removed to the place where it was found in order that there might be no inconvenient enquiries and he might quietly pocket the balance of wages due. Here again the incidents of such an enquiry do not deserve repetition, even if I could recall the actual facts of any such individual case, which I very much doubt.

Talking about Chinese brings me to a case with which I had to deal, in which an assistant on a rubber estate was found by his servant in the morning lying dead in his bed, with a wound in his neck which had practically decapitated him. On investigation it appeared that this savage attack had been made by a Chinese carpenter who had been employed in the building of some new coolie lines on the estate.

I appeared on the scene as a Krani seeking employment. From what I gathered I pieced together a story which was as follows. In the course of his employment this carpenter, a man named Wee Chit, had to lay out his roof beams on the ground before erecting them. He chose for this purpose a footpath much frequented by Mr. Tulloch who, finding him commencing this obstruction, told him, as he passed, to do the work elsewhere. On returning along the path later on, Mr. Tulloch found that Wee Chit had taken no notice of his instructions, and was gaily going ahead laying his timbers across the pathway. So he slapped his face for his impudence and disobedience.

From this slight cause had tragedy developed. I heard that Wee Chit had been very incensed and, refusing to continue working for such a master, he had packed up his tools, collected his wages from the contractor and left the estate that evening. But, from the careful cut made in the mosquito net, the nature of the wound and the marks on the pillow, it was obvious that the attack had been made with a carpenter's axe, and after very delicate and careful investigation I managed to prove that he had not, as a matter of actual fact, left the estate until about five o'clock the next morning.

On leaving the estate Wee Chit had expressed the intention of going to Kajang, but from what I could learn he did not seem to have appeared anywhere in that district. This necessitated endless enquiries on my part, and it was some time before I ran him to earth in Tampin, where he provided considerable excitement when the Police made his arrest.

Chinamen are generally supposed to be placid individuals, but this man put up a scene which was only to be exceeded by that of an amok.

The two Sikh Police who originally entered the shop where he was employed barely escaped with their lives, and of the dozen or so who were then called out, he succeeded in injuring five before he was finally overpowered. He was in due course condemned to death and executed, which made a satisfactory case of it from my point of view.

* * *

The gold mines at Raub did not provide so many cases as one might have expected. On one occasion they had a serious robbery, which practically amounted to an armed raid. The raiding party were Chinese, and after having killed three of the guards, they had actually broken open the strong-room before help arrived and they were overpowered, four of their number being killed outright in the process. The remaining seven had been collected into a store-room, which was turned into a temporary prison, when, to the surprise of everyone, it was discovered that fifteen hundred ounces of gold were missing.

The prisoners and the dead were carefully searched, but no trace of the gold could be found, and matters were at a deadlock. It was in these circumstances that I was despatched to discover where the gold was, and recover it if possible. After exhaustive and delicate enquiries amongst the Chinese I could not learn of anyone else who had been a party to the raid, except the eleven who had already been accounted for. The more I enquired into it, the more mysterious became the disappearance of the gold.

In this *impasse* it struck me that a useful line of enquiry would be to discover how these Chinamen had intended to dispose of the gold when they had plundered it. It seemed unlikely that their intention had been merely to divide it and risk having it found on them.

By arrangement I was arrested for creating a disturbance in Petaling Street, and thrown into Kuala Lumpur gaol beside these criminals, who were there waiting their trial. Whilst there, of course, I was supposed to be completely ignorant of Chinese, and in consequence was able to overhear all of their conversation, some of which put me on the right track.

Needless to say, when I appeared before the Magistrate the next morning, I was dismissed with a caution. I at once proceeded to follow up the clue which I had thus obtained—which took me to Bentong, and thence into the jungle in search of a Sakai named Tahir. This man, from what I had heard, had been going to guide these Chinamen through the jungle to a spot on the Sungei Pahang near its junction with the

Sungei Lompat, where they had arranged to meet a Chinese trader, in his boat, who would take the gold from them. It seemed to me extremely likely that this man, Tahir, had been near at hand when the raid had taken place and, seizing his opportunity, had succeeded, in the general excitement, in entering the strong-room unobserved and carrying off the gold.

From what I had heard it did not sound as though Tahir knew the Chinese trader, and I thought it probable, therefore, that he would have the gold with him and would now be wondering what on earth to do with it.

It was rather like looking for a needle in a haystack, as I did not know whether he was the leader of a Sakai band or merely one of the members. In the latter case, unless I could strike the right band I would have the greatest difficulty in discovering his whereabouts. However, I knew of a Sakai encampment not far from Bentong, so made for them as a jumping-off place at any rate. Having joined this band, I found that they had no knowledge of anyone called Tahir, who was evidently a person of no importance, thus adding greatly to my difficulties.

Being thus unable to fix any definite spot for which to make in my search, I thought it best to start at the one definite place I had heard mentioned, and work back westwards from there in the hope of finding my man on the way. In pursuance of this plan I persuaded two of the Sakais to accompany me to the Sungei Pahang, calling in at three other clearings, of which they knew, on the way.

We reached the banks of the river many miles below the place appointed, but at one of the few places where the bank was not completely overgrown with vegetation, making the river almost unapproachable, as it is for most of its length, there having been a clearing here. It was an ideal camping ground for the night, as close to the river's edge there was a sandbank left by the flood-waters, which made a splendid site on which we erected our simple shelter and from which we gathered our firewood without any necessity to search for it.

Early next morning, when my companions were in the jungle hunting something for our breakfasts whilst I 'tended camp' and was boiling the water, a Chinese trader came down the river in his boat.

When he saw a Sakai on the river bank, he came across and commenced bartering with me. I wondered whether this was the man to whom the gold was to have been taken, but could think of no way in which to find this out; so, to give myself time, played my part of a trading Sakai, assuring him of the large quantity of gambier I had collected together only a little way off. He displayed his trading goods, and the discussion was going fairly well when one of my companions appeared on the scene with a plandok which he had shot with his sumpitan. I felt very relieved to have him take up the argument, since I was not at all sure of myself in a trade of this sort, in which I had never taken part before; I was afraid of saying something which would make the Chinaman 'smell a rat'.

Before long the other Sakai arrived—he had had no luck in his hunting—and the argument became fast and furious. Mirrors, bits of cloth, showy knives, cooking utensils, and all the shoddy paraphernalia of the Chinaman's stock were produced, and the value of them in gambier and monkey skins fiercely contested on both sides. Whilst this was going on I heard the Chinaman mutter to himself, as he was opening a new bundle, that "it was taking more trouble to get gambier out of these three savages than he had had in getting gold from a solitary one the day before".

I at once realized that Tahir must have known more about the arrangements than I had suspected, and had transported the gold to the appointment; no mean feat, since it weighed one hundred pounds or more—which itself accounted for the length of time it had taken.

Drawing my companions to one side, I hastily explained to them something of the story. I had heard, I said, something about the theft of this gold, and that the Police would pay a large reward for the capture of the thief. This Chinaman undoubtedly was the thief, and if we captured him, they could hold him a prisoner in the jungle whilst I reported the matter to the Police, who would then come and take him, paying us the reward at the same time. They at once agreed that the capture of the Chinaman would be an excellent thing, doubtless feeling that the trader's stock would be an unconsidered trifle which would fall as a perquisite into their hands.

Unfortunately one of them, Suliap, having more courage than discretion, immediately sprang into the man's boat to seize him. The Chinaman, immediately scenting danger, without an instant's hesitation drew a large knife and stabbed him to the heart. It was all over in a second, and the Chinaman was poling his boat from the bank almost before I had realized what had happened—not so my companion. Before the boat had gone five yards he had landed three darts from his blow-pipe into the broad of the Chinaman's back, and another got him in the neck just as he turned with a revolver in his hand.

I felt that we had missed our capture for the present and, at the first crack of the revolver, hastily dragged Kenapi into the shelter of the jungle, where I expressed my sorrow at the murderer's escape. Kenapi laughed and said that he had not escaped, but, on the contrary, was a dead man. He had prepared his darts freshly that morning before going hunting and, with the five darts which he had in his body the Chinaman would not live more than half an hour, if so long. The poisoned points, having been nicked all round, would break off and remain in the wounds when he pulled the darts out.

This was good news to me, since it meant that I would recover the gold, but I was afraid that it would be looked upon as murder by my superiors. I determined, therefore, that the Police would arrest Kenapi for murder when they came to collect the gold. In the meantime, however, it was as well to say nothing of this, and I merely joined in his jubilation. We could see that by this time the Chinaman was feeling the effects of the poison, as his poling down-stream became very erratic. So, leaving him to die quietly, we set off along a jungle path which would bring us out on to the river bank again some mile or so further down-stream. When we had reached this point we had not long to wait before we saw the boat drifting towards us; the set of the current carried it to the bank some distance above us, where it became firmly wedged in the river-side growths.

There was no sign of the Chinaman at all, so we made our way through the jungle till we could look down, from the overhanging branches, into the boat, and there we saw him lying dead. He was horribly contorted and had evidently died in the greatest agony, but the main thing was that he was dead. He was quite alone and had, presumably, thrown Suliap's body overboard, so, climbing into the boat, we treated his body in the same way.

Kenapi and I made the boat secure, concealing it amongst the greenery of the river bank. Then, dividing the gold between us, we started our long journey back. Having such valuable luggage, we refused the friendly hospitality offered us at the clearings we had visited on our outward journey, and we reached his people by forced marches. There I left him, and that was the last I ever saw of the man.

I returned home at once to Kuala Lumpur and reported the whole incident to Colonel Munroe, who decided that it was unnecessary to take any proceedings against Kenapi as, considering the fact that the Chinaman had just murdered his brother and was, moreover, attacking us with his revolver, the Chinaman's death, caused by Kenapi's action, had been in self-defence, and was therefore justifiable homicide. I was relieved to hear this as I had been afraid that I was in for another wigging for having exceeded my duties, although, as a matter of fact, what had happened was a matter over which I had had no control. The whole incident therefore passed entirely unremarked, and it was merely reported that the Police had succeeded in recovering the stolen property hidden in the jungle near Bentong.

Chapter 10

MR. FARQUHARSON, A WELL-KNOWN RESIDENT of Singapore, high up in the Government service, had been passing through Hailam Street one day when his eye had been caught by a pretty little Chinese Nona. He had visited her and, after leaving, discovered that he had lost a most important paper which, unfortunately, he had had in his pocket at the time.

This paper was a very mysterious document, and even I was not informed of what it contained; but it appeared that its loss jeopardised the future position of its owner and it must be recovered at all costs, yet a knowledge of the contents was of no value to anyone else.

The circumstances of its loss being what they were, this gentleman naturally did not wish the Singapore Police to be informed of the matter, and it was therefore that I had been applied for, and took up the enquiry.

Mr. Farquharson could give me no particulars from which to start. He did not know the girl's name, nor even the number of the house, and the only description of her which he could give me was that she was short and dark, with a round face—which description, of course, would apply to any young female member of the Chinese race. The only other outstanding feature of her identity which seemed to have struck him, was that she wore "the trickiest pale-lilac-coloured trousers"! He would not consent to go through Hailam Street again, in the daytime, and try to recognize the house; so it was with this vague data that I opened my enquiry.

I appeared in Hailam Street as a half-caste Chinese hawker, selling a splendid line of face creams, powders, scents and cosmetics of all sorts. As these were supplied to me by the Federal Dispensary, on Mr. Farquharson's account, I could afford to offer tremendous bargains, and so was received with open arms by the little ladies of that quarter, where I speedily became popular.

Keeping my ears open and detailing what I alleged was the latest Malacca scandal, I encouraged reciprocal confidences wherever I went. After a few days of this, from the general gossip of the street I fixed on a young lady called Shi Shee as being the one I was in search of, so speedily gave her to understand that I had lost my heart to her. It was well for me that I spoke Chinese, for almost the only Malay words she knew were "ni atas".

I paid vigorous court to this girl, and she, knowing the brisk business I was doing with my cosmetics, looked on me, I have no doubt, as a most desirable suitor—I seemed to have plenty of money, took her rickshaw rides, gave her presents, and was most devoted. In this way I speedily captured her heart.

Whilst doing all this I learnt that she was the property of a wealthy Chinaman, Towkay Ah Chi, who had offices in Hop Yong Ti Street, and a bungalow along the Keppel Road. The Towkay had a nephew, who often visited her, and after we became really affectionate I learnt that it was this man, Poo Hup, who had stolen the paper.

I suggested to Shi Shee that, as doubtless this was a very valuable paper, it would be a good thing for us if I could steal it back again, and then we would make a great deal of money, and I would be able to buy her from the Towkay and marry her immediately. She fell in with my suggestion and we set about planning ways and means by which this could be accomplished. In the first place, of course, it was necessary to discover where the paper was kept, and she thought she could do this without much difficulty as she was frequently sent for to a flat which the Towkay had, adjoining his offices.

She was along at this flat again in two or three days' time, and when I met her the next day she told me that the Towkay kept the paper in the drawer of a cabinet, which was in the sitting-room. On the night following he was giving a big dinner party at his bungalow, so there would be no one at the flat, since all his servants were to be on duty at the party. This was quite definite, as she had heard these orders given before she left that morning.

We arranged, therefore, that she would get into the flat on the next night, through a small window, the catch of which she knew was broken, and there I would meet her at eleven o'clock. There was a back entrance in the narrow passage-way which ran down the side of the offices, and by this she would let me in; I would steal the paper and, after locking the door behind me again, she would climb out of the window. Nothing I could say would persuade her to steal the paper herself, she was too overawed by Ah Chi; but, as all this seemed plane sailing, I was looking forward to having accomplished my mission successfully in two days' time.

In due course I crept quietly down the passage-way at eleven o'clock the next evening, but, just as I reached the door, I was suddenly enveloped in a dark soft cloud. Before I realized that I had been trapped in a blanket, I had been lifted off my feet and was being carried swiftly into the house by many hands. When there, I was tightly bound with ropes without having the blanket removed, then carried out again and placed on the floor of some sort of vehicle, which immediately moved off with me.

Nearly suffocated as I was with the folds of the blanket, and suffering intense agony from the harsh binding of the ropes, I could make no guess at the direction we were taking. After a considerable time, however, when nature had begun to adapt itself to these new surroundings, I became more composed in my mind, so, when the vehicle stopped and I was again lifted out, I detected the sound of waves and realized that we were near the seashore.

I was carried down and lifted into a sampan, which bore me I knew not whither for about two hours; then I was again lifted out, and from the fact that I was carried both up and down a ladder I concluded that I had been taken on board a larger boat of some kind. I was not left long in doubt, for the blanket was soon cut from my head, and I found myself lying on the floor in the cabin of a junk.

Facing me was Towkay Ah Chi himself!

Lying bound on a divan to one side was Shi Shee, and the Towkay gave himself a lot of amusement by the things he said about us to each other. From his various remarks I gathered that Shi Shee had roused the suspicions of his nephew, Poo Hup, even before she had tried to find the location of the paper.

Poo Hup had been furiously jealous of me from the start; and a jealous man can generally see evil even where there is none, so when it in fact exists it must be extremely well hidden to avoid his attention. The placing of the paper in the cabinet, the story of the dinner party, and the orders to the servants had all been parts of the scheme to test whether Poo Hup's suspicions were correct or not.

The Towkay flourished the paper in our faces as he gloated over us. He was, however, curious to find out, if possible, why I wanted the paper, but I of course was very careful to give him no inkling of the truth, and denied the fact that I had wanted the paper or even knew of its existence. My story was that I had merely attended an ordinary lover's assignation, to spend the night in more luxurious surroundings than those to be had in Hailam Street.

This seemed such a reasonable story that I could see he was rather undecided as to its truth, and, I thought, rather sorry that he had been in such a hurry to talk about the paper, which I noticed he put under a blotting-pad on a table standing against the bulkhead. On the other hand, Poo Hup had no doubt whatsoever on the question of my veracity or otherwise. He assured his uncle that I was not speaking the truth, and guaranteed to make me do so, by the most horrible tortures if necessary. He enumerated these tortures to me in the greatest detail, hoping that the mere mention of them would, perhaps, be sufficient to make me confess.

After a lot of argument, the Towkay said that he would decide the matter in the morning, as it was now so late that, if they did not go to bed at once there would be no time for sleep. No one seemed to pay any attention to us as they walked from the cabin—they probably thought that we were sufficiently well tied to render escape impossible, and this certainly appeared to be the case. However impossible escape might seem, still I was determined to use my best efforts in the attempt.

When all was quiet, I wriggled across the floor towards the settee on which Shi Shee was lying and succeeded in reaching the side of it, then I whispered to her to roll off the settee on to me if she could. She was very cruelly bound, rendering her almost as stiff as a poker, but nevertheless she managed, in about half an hour, to fall over the edge, landing with her back on me and bouncing off on to her stomach beside me.

By dint of further wriggling I managed to get my mouth on to the rope which bound her wrists and, thanking God for a good set of teeth, I set to chew my way through it. After endless mastication I succeeded in freeing one of her hands, with which she speedily released the other, but, as a separate rope was binding her arms to her sides at the elbow, I had then to wriggle further up and place my bound feet into her hands, so that she could undo the knot. As my binding had been done by one continuous rope this was the only knot, and when she had undone it I was free, and taking out my knife soon placed her in the same situation.

All this had taken some hours, and I was afraid that dawn would break before we could escape from the junk, if indeed such an escape was possible at all. Not knowing in the least where the junk was, or how many men might be on her deck, the prospects of a complete escape did not seem very rosy; however, the first thing I did was to seize the paper from beneath the blotting-pad and fasten it securely in the pocket of my leather belt—meanwhile Shi Shee was rubbing her arms and legs to try and get the circulation back into them. I then cautiously opened one of the cabin windows, which looked out over the stern of the boat, and as my eyes had been accustomed to the darkness of the cabin in which we had been left, the starlight outside made things seem almost as bright as day to me.

I saw with pleasure that the junk was lying at anchor, only about two hundred yards away from the shore—the trees on which I could clearly distinguish against the sky. What shore it was, of course, I did not know, but I felt that any shore was a better position to be in than our present one on the junk.

I did not want to spoil the paper, especially after all the trouble I had been through to get it, and asked Shi Shee if she could think of any way in which I could protect it from the water, into which it seemed we would have to plunge if we were to escape. She remembered that she had seen a candle standing on a shelf and, sure enough, it had been left there, so I thoroughly greased the inside and the flap of my belt pocket with the grease of this and made, what eventually turned out to have been, a sufficiently watertight job of it.

All was now ready for our departure, though neither of us looked forward with pleasure to this early morning dip in unknown waters, probably infested with crocodiles; the nearness of which we would not even be able to see, owing to the darkness. The prospect of our landing on a mudbank, and actually making our first contact with *terra firma* by putting our hands on to a crocodile's slippery back, filled us with terror, and I had to pretend to be very brave before I could induce Shi Shee to accompany me. However, at last I did it, and we slipped as quietly as possible into the water down the table cloth which I had tied to the frame of the window.

Thank heavens it was not a long swim, for Shi Shee was no swimmer, and, equally thank heavens, we landed on a sandbank which appeared to be crocodile-free. In any case, we were not molested as we slipped across it and hid in the jungle edge to wait the short time before the sun rose. Waiting thus concealed near the vessel might seem a foolhardy proceeding, but it was a necessity. It would have been foolish to risk possible crocodiles by walking along the beach in the dark, and anyone who knows the jungle will appreciate the fact that it is practically impossible to make any headway through an unknown part of it in the dark, and a risky thing to attempt. It is quite bad enough during the day! In any case, having no parang, but only a small sheath knife, such an attempt was not to be thought of, so there was nothing for it but to wait where we were.

As soon as the sun rose we fought our way as quickly as possible through the jungle on a course parallel with the coast line. Since the sea was to the north of us, and knowing, from the nature of our surroundings that we were not on the island of Singapore, I concluded that we were on one of the many islands in the neighbourhood, and that, therefore, we might stand a chance of being taken off by one of the many fishing prahaus which frequent these waters. We kept peering out of the jungle from time to time over the sea, and when the junk was out of sight we made good progress along the sands. At last we came across some fishermen, who were busy repairing their nets on the beach, and, as I had plenty of money, it was a mere matter of moments before a bargain was struck, and we were off to Singapore before mid-day.

I took Shi Shee to the room in which I was living and, having changed my ragged garments, I reported to Mr. Farquharson, who I found at the club, and handed over his document to him. When he had heard my account of the manner in which it had been recovered, he generously arranged to have Shi Shee shipped back to China, where she had an auntie in Tientsin; where, of course, I promised to follow her so soon as my fortune had been made! It was as a result of my success in this investigation that I was promoted to the rank of corporal.

I noticed in the papers a few weeks later that the Singapore Police had cleverly succeeded in tracking down, and capturing, a Chinese vessel engaged in smuggling, and that a man named Poo Hup, who had been acting as the Singapore agent for the smugglers, was on board at the time of capture and was also a prisoner. Still later, I saw a small paragraph announcing the departure of Towkay Ah Chi, who was "retiring from business in Singapore" and returning to China. I had no official information on the subject, but it seemed to me that Mr. Farquharson had been dropping fruitful hints in the right quarters, otherwise the coincidences seemed remarkable.

Chapter 11

THE CATCHMENT AREA OF a water supply system must be kept free from inhabitants, so that the water is, as far as possible, uncontaminated even before it enters the filters. This being so, it follows that no mining leases are issued for work in these areas.

The water from one such catchment fell in a natural cascade, at the foot of which the waterworks were situated. The resident engineer had noticed that although there had been no heavy rains, yet the water was coming down impregnated with mud; which showed him that someone was working for tin in his area. If this was so, such work was illegal, and the workers were what might be called tin-poachers.

When he had gathered together a small troop of policemen, he proceeded to walk up-stream, tracking the muddy water to its source. As he reached the higher ravines he saw signs of tin-working on every side, but no sign of the tin-workers—which, considering the noise made by his booted police clambering over the rocks, was not exactly surprising.

After an arduous two or three days amongst the rocks and thorns, the expedition returned little or no wiser than when they had started out. Nevertheless, the poachers would have to be either captured or driven off; and in these circumstances I was sent out to see what I could discover regarding the personnel employed.

It is of course an unprofitable undertaking to wash for tin unless you can dispose of the tin recovered; so I thought that my best line of action would be to get on to the track of the parcels of tin being sent out of this area, and ascertain its destination.

My idea was that, when I had got this information, the police might possibly be able to seize some of these consignments as they passed, and they would certainly be able to close up the present means of disposal; then, even if it was impossible to arrest the actual workers—which from the nature of the country in which they worked seemed highly probable—this action would, by rendering their work valueless, as it were, starve them out.

It almost went without saying that these poachers would be Chinese, so I decided to tackle the job in the guise of a Chinese coolie; in which capacity I haunted the jungle edge at the foot of the hills for miles in each direction, seeking for news of the tin passing. I soon decided that this would lead to nothing, and that only penetrating to where the work was actually in progress would give me results. Collecting a suitable supply of food, I set out on my quest by following a stream, the source of which was on the outer side of the catchment watershed.

I estimated that this would bring me to the neighbourhood of the area in which the work was reported to be going on, by simply crossing the crest. This, of course, meant a severe climb uphill, and by the time I finally found myself over the watershed, I had decided that jungle work dressed as a Chinaman was too difficult, and that I would continue as an innocent Sakai.

Searching amongst the rocks I soon found a suitable shelter, under a huge overhanging slab, in which I could establish my headquarters, and I thankfully dumped my heavy load there. I soon made it quite a habitable little spot, and spent a not too uncomfortable night after my hard day's grind. In the morning I undressed myself for my new part, and although I had not the necessary adjuncts for the costume with me, by making do with what I had I managed to make a sufficiently life-like figure of a Sakai to pass muster, I thought, with the average Chinese coolie, who has no very close knowledge of them or their peculiarities. In this I was proved to be correct, when later in the day I came upon some of the poachers. There was no great difficulty in discovering their whereabouts, as the noises they made rang clearly from wall to wall of the valley.

There is a lot of noise in the jungle from time to time, as anyone who has heard the Wa-Wa monkeys' matitudinal chorus must admit; but even at its noisiest time the chink of metal on metal, or stone on stone, is quite clearly distinguishable above all else, and from a very long distance. I suppose that this is because all the other noises are the symphonic sylvan noises born of mother nature, whereas all metallic noises are the harsh artificial abortions of man's intellect.

As I had supposed, it was Chinamen who were at work and, although not actually hostile, they did not seem very pleased when they discovered my presence. It was a group of three which I first came across, and I trembled at the nature of their employment.

Burrowing down in the crevices below a mass of boulders, they were taking out the black sand from such pockets as they found, seemingly quite regardless of the fact that they were removing the foundations from the perilous pile of precariously-poised rocks under which they worked. I passed from this group, and in the course of the day came across five other groups similarly employed, till I eventually discovered the rough shelter in which they were evidently living and in which they doubtless stored their day's takings.

Here the cook was busy preparing rice, and I spoke to another man, who evidently was the headman of the gang. He spoke a little Malay, and as a Sakai, I spoke Malay with him, asking for food. He cross-questioned me to the best of his ability as to what I was doing here, and whence I had come; the answers I gave him were so voluble and complicated in their construction, and were furthermore given in such execrable Malay, that I was quite sure that he would be completely unable to understand them—in which disability he differed from me, who could thoroughly understand his remarks to the cook, concerning the barbarous savage. It was from this shelter, obviously, that the tin would be transported, so I decided to keep it under careful observation.

As I seemed to have been accepted at my face value (of a possibly inconvenient but otherwise harmless spectator of their labours) I decided that it was unnecessary for me to conceal my movements at all. Next day I quite established myself in the cook's good graces by bartering with him, for a ridiculously inadequate exchange of rice, the carcase of a large monitor lizard which I had been lucky enough to kill. This delicacy was a very welcome addition to their meagre fare, and I felt that my presence in the neighbourhood would now be looked on more in the nature of a blessing than a curse. Nightly I crept down and lay with my ears strained listening through the rough attap wall of their hut, trying to pick up from their conversation any clue as to the destination of their tin—and a long, wearisome job it was. These Chinamen seemed never to sleep, and would go on talking till all hours of the night.

However, at last I got my information on the third night, when I learnt that they would be moving their tin two days hence. I could now afford to give myself two days' holiday from the constant watch on their headquarters, and I decided to employ my time by finding the track which would be taken by the tin stealers through the jungle.

I had a lazy morning, and did not set out till well after seven o'clock. After having followed several false trails, which were apparently the result of prospecting investigations, I at last struck one which was obviously that which I was searching for, as when it penetrated further into the jungle, it became a clearly-defined and thoroughly well-trodden path. It emerged from the jungle tortuously over flat rocks amongst the tumbled masses of boulders, and I considered myself fortunate to have come upon it as I did, early in the afternoon. Although I felt quite sure from its appearance that this was their route, it seemed to lead in entirely the wrong direction if the tin was to be delivered according to what I had overheard. I thought it necessary, therefore, that I should follow this path as far as possible to find out whither it led.

It was, as I have said, a good path, and I had no difficulty in hurrying along it at a rapid pace. After leading diagonally along the hillside it rounded a shoulder and, entering the next valley, took the direction which I had expected it to take in the first instance. Obviously it had been taken by this roundabout route to make the gradient easier for the heavily-burdened coolies who used it. By the time I had decided definitely as to the final direction taken by this pathway it was late in the afternoon, and although it was a good path, it was anything but a straight one, so if I did not want to find myself left to negotiate its windings in the dark, it was time for me to turn back. I had misjudged either the time or the distance, however, for darkness fell before I had reached the neighbourhood of the hut which I now knew so well. Once there, however, I had no difficulty in finding my way to my rocky home.

As I approached my little shelter something struck me violently on the shoulder, and I had been struck twice more before I realized that I was being attacked by the Chinamen; by that time, however, and it was merely an instant of time, the forest rang with their cries as they struck. I immediately dropped to the ground, and had the satisfaction of hearing two Chinamen attacking each other with their chunkols over my head as I cautiously crawled backwards from them. I found myself in sad case. My right arm hung useless, and I had other wounds, the extent of which I only dimly realized at the time. As I crawled off I was pleased to hear, from the free fight which was going on, that my absence had not been discovered, each of the Chinamen seeming to think his neighbour was me.

I realized that my position was extremely serious, since the smell of my fresh blood, which I had no means of staunching, would attract any tiger or panther in the neighbourhood, against which I was utterly unable to put up any sort of a fight should either come. I hauled myself painfully, but with the energy of despair, down the hill as rapidly as I could, till I reached the stream at the foot of the ravine up which I had originally entered the jungle.

Bathing my wounded body was a painful operation, but the delightfully cold water refreshed me greatly, and I was relieved to think that it was rapidly removing the smell of fresh blood, which I feared so much to have with me. This stream, I was pleased to find, was running on what seemed to be bedrock, and was apparently free from boulders, so I decided that to follow down its bed would be my quickest line of retreat.

It descended by a series of shallow waterfalls, in some cases there being no actual fall at all, but merely a smooth chute. Helped by the current, I scrambled, flopped, and floated my way down-stream for I did not know how long, but it was daylight when I at last realized that there was a house on the bank, and to this I crawled, crying for help.

I knew no more till I found myself in the hospital at Kuala Lumpur, but it appeared that I must have recovered sufficiently, at some time or other, to have told my rescuers that I would pay handsomely for immediate removal thither. As soon as I was sufficiently recovered to realize where I was and what had happened, I gave the attendants no peace until I had seen the white doctor, to whom I confided who I was; through him I sent a message to Major Ritchie, giving him the information I had obtained. If the Chinamen did not, like the Kilkenny cats, succeed in killing each other completely, and were carrying out their programme, the next night would be the one on which the tin was to be transported to the little adit mine, run by some half-dozen Chinese, near Bukit Langsam, as the production of which it would be sold.

I am glad to say that my information reached Police headquarters in time. A careful ambush was laid near the mine, and seven Chinamen, including the headman, were caught carrying the washed tin to the mine. Needless to say the licence was taken away and the mine closed down. After this the stream ran clear over its fall near the waterworks.

I was in hospital for nearly three months, and even then was not fit for duty for another month after this disastrous expedition. When the whole matter had been thoroughly sifted, it appeared that the Chinese kapalla had been suspicious of the lonely Sakai, and had been spending a good deal of his time in trying to find out where I was living. He must have succeeded in doing this at very much the same time that I had discovered their pathway. As soon as he found my cave he would, of course, see my Chinaman's outfit and, as he would most certainly overhaul everything, he would not have failed to look over the bundle of chits, in the jacket pocket, recommending me as a gardener. Several of these were in Chinese, but even without that he would see enough from my general 'Barang', my tinned meats, and so on, to show that I was certainly not a Sakai, and to confirm his worst fears. He had therefore brought up his coolies and arranged the ambush into which I fell.

It was by the merest good fortune that I had my Police badge with me that day, and I have never been so near giving myself away when in one of my disguises as I was on that occasion. Apart from the scars, I suffered no permanent injury from this savage attack.

Chapter 12

WHEN THE GREAT WAR BROKE out, and the disturbances occurred at Singapore, I was rushed off there immediately, before it was known to what extent the operations might extend. Of course I had hardly arrived before the whole thing had fizzled out, so although being present at its closing stages I can hardly claim to have taken any part in its suppression.

As an aftermath of it, however, I was busy for many weeks in trying to trace out the subversive influences which had led up to the outbreak, and as a result there were a number of arrests made, some of them being even so far distant as at Amritsar. In all this work there was no incident of any general importance, the whole enquiry being routine work of the stodgiest variety. It was, however, whilst so engaged that my attention was called to Fung To and Ah Ping, two Chinamen who appeared to be comfortably off, but whose source of income seemed vague.

I had reported them as being suspicious characters, without being able to state precisely in what direction these suspicions pointed, and when the enquiries on which I was engaged were completed, I was ordered to make a report on the doings of these two men.

They lived in very good style in a Chinese hotel in Princep Street, and whatever their business was it rendered them extraordinarily restless beings, as they were constantly on the move. I managed to scrape an acquaintance with them, but beyond learning that they had come from Shanghai in July, and hearing a reference from which it appeared that they had been at Tsingtau before that, I could learn nothing of their business. This, of course, might mean nothing, but still, Tsingtau was a German fortress, and there was always the possibility that they were German agents of some sort. On thinking things over, their doings seemed to support this theory to some extent. It might have been all perfectly innocent, or it might have been by base design, but it was undoubtedly a fact that one or other of them always seemed to have the harbour and anchorage in view, and they were constantly taking trips to neighbouring islands.

Secretly following them on these trips was not a practicable proposition, as it is impossible to conceal yourself on the sea; and visiting the islands immediately after their return, which I did on several occasions, taught me nothing. I came to the conclusion that these visits meant nothing in themselves, but were only used as a pretext for a thorough survey of the surrounding waters, made with an idea of determining definitely whether any Naval units were lying in anchorages concealed from the view of Singapore.

One or other of this couple would frequently leave the other, as it were, on watch at Singapore, whilst he visited Malacca, and sometimes even so far afield as Penang. All this pointed to Naval espionage, but Naval espionage is of no practical use unless the knowledge obtained can be communicated, and I could not discover in what way they were passing on any news which they might have, so their whole endeavours, if my suspicions were correct, seemed to be entirely useless.

One morning, however, they set off together to the station, each with a suitcase, which in itself was strange, as heretofore their journeys had been taken singly, so I determined to travel with them. With a tremendous scurry round I just managed to catch the train, and not knowing whither my quarries were bound, booked to Kuala Lumpur. They had evidently done the same—at any rate they did not leave the train until we reached there.

On arrival at Kuala Lumpur, I noticed that they did not give up their tickets, so concluded that they were booked through to Penang. I kept them in sight, as during the hour's wait they spent their time in a restaurant in High Street, and then I followed them back across the river to the station, where I took my ticket to Penang also.

When next morning we arrived at Prai, I came very near to being discovered. I was so sure that the pair were bound for Penang, that I was not prepared to find them not taking the boat, and very nearly ran full tilt into them as they made their way for the station exit. They and a porter were all carrying very bulky luggage, which had evidently been sent to the station in advance of them at Singapore, and I wondered if this meant that they had definitely given up residence there, and had all their belongings with them.

I followed them down into the town, where their proceedings became even more mysterious. They put their packages into a bullock cart which was standing empty at the roadside with the unyoked bullocks tethered to the near-side wheel. Having seen them safely started with their breakfast in a water-side eating-house, I returned and learnt that

Fung To had hired this cart and its Afghan driver to be at the roadside at the spot at which it now was, and on this particular morning, when he had visited Prai on his way from Penang three weeks ago.

It was certain, therefore, that whatever journey they were about to undertake it was the result of no sudden decision, but had been part of their scheme of movement for some time. I felt rather like a draughts' player suddenly set down to a game of chess. My opponents knew all the erratic moves and their meaning, whilst I, seeing the move made, was left groping as to whither it led. My bewilderment was not greatly enlightened, as you may imagine, when the couple, having finished their breakfast, set out in a sampan. As I have explained, keeping on the track of criminals when they are proceeding in a small boat cannot be done secretly, and all I could do if I did not wish to rouse their suspicions was to keep an eye on their boat from the shore.

I would be a poor organizer, however, if I did not arrange to be able to keep them in sight wherever they might go, so, needless to say, I had immediately hired a motor boat in which I could pursue them if the sampan went out of my sight. As a matter of fact, however, this precaution turned out to be unnecessary—the sampan merely cruising about, rather aimlessly, in the straits between Penang and the mainland. Evidently they were prospecting the shipping lying in the roads, and again I was left racking my brains as to their purpose. How on earth could any information which they could thus gather be made use of in the enemy's interest?

I had plenty of time to cogitate on this question, as it was not until after three o'clock that the sampan returned. My persistence in watching their movements was richly rewarded. When it came back the boat avoided the landing-stage from which they had started, and discharged its passengers far along the foreshore. If I had not had them constantly under observation, I could not have blamed myself if I had failed to recognize my two gentlemen in the couple who then landed. Gone were the smart European clothes, the straw hats, and the well-polished brown shoes, and in their place were the loose white jackets, the baggy black trousers, and the heel-less slippers of a typical couple of middle-class tradesmen. As it happened I had thought it advisable to make some slight alteration in my own appearance, and it was in my true colours as a native Malay—in place of the half-caste Chinaman in which they knew me—that I followed their bullock cart when it made its way along the road north.

Bullock carts do not travel at any excessive speed, and following one in such a way as to remain unobserved in that occupation exercises one's powers of restraint rather than one's agility. There is, however, a tirelessness in the bullock, with his slow steady plod, which I had never before fully appreciated. When we finally stopped, about two-thirty in the morning, I was considerably more tired than I would have been if I had run all the way.

I was not familiar enough with the district to know exactly where we were, but I estimated roughly that we were a few miles short of Kuala Muda when the passengers alighted from the cart I had been following for so long, and each taking what appeared to be a very heavy package in either hand, left the track by a path leading to the left. It was less than two miles along this path when we emerged on to a tiny patch of sandy beach, which stood up like an island amongst the surrounding mangrove swamps. As I crept cautiously out from the under-growth, I saw that Fung To and Ah Ping were busily engaged unpacking their packages on the dilapidated veranda of a deserted fisherman's shanty. It had been a crazy affair at its best, and in its present condition swayed ominously beneath their movements.

I now began to have a suspicion as to their true purpose, and therefore was not surprised when, with a hissing splutter, they managed to get an old-fashioned limelight apparatus under way and eventually commenced signalling out to sea. They were using ordinary Morse, but evidently in a secret code, as I could make nothing of the jumble of letters which I could read. Having seen this I had completed my mission, there being now no doubt as to these men being enemy agents. Leaving them at their work, I returned with all speed to Penang in order that the Police there might arrest them with the signalling lamp in their possession, thus providing sufficient evidence for their conviction as spies.

Before I reached Prai, however, the result of their signalling was conveyed to me by the sound of gun-fire from the sea. When I got to Penang I learnt that the German cruiser *Emden* had sunk the Russian cruiser *Femtschug* which had been lying at anchor in the roads, and the French destroyer *Mousquet* which she had met just to the north of the island.

It was evident that these two spies had been telling the *Emden* that all was safe for a raid. They were arrested as they re-entered Prai in their bullock cart, complete with their lamps and their small, surgeon's gas bottles. At the subsequent enquiry it turned out that they had both been foremen in the German Imperial Dockyard at Tsingtau, who had been taken from there to Shanghai by a Captain Luring just before hostilities broke out, with the object of furthering the enemy's intelligence. Needless to say they met the deserved fate of spies.

* * *

Later on in the War, when it was decided to employ labour battalions of Chinese in road-making and similar labouring occupations in France, it was arranged that I should accompany these contingents to keep an eye on them—or perhaps it would be more correct for me to say keep an ear on them—with a view to the possibilities of espionage or mutiny which might occur amongst their numbers.

Needless to say, I was delighted at having been chosen for this special duty, which was not only a compliment to my efficiency but gave me a chance, which I had long hoped for, of seeing something of Europe.

I was to be in sole charge of the Secret Police attached to these detachments, with the rank of sergeant; and had under me five Japanese, kindly loaned to us by our Allies, through the good offices of the Chief of the Tokio Police. These were all men who had been used to mingling with the Chinese working classes in Korea and elsewhere, and were quite indistinguishable from the coolies themselves. With this team to lighten my labours, I felt quite confident that nothing would happen amongst those under my charge without our having full information beforehand.

Of the voyage across the Indian Ocean, the stay at Colombo, the strange spectacle of the parched hills of Aden, and the sandy wastes bordering the Suez Canal, I could write a lot; but all these places, which were so new and seemed so strange to me are, of course, well known and commonplace to the peoples of Europe for whom I write, so I reluctantly forego any description of the voyage.

Immediately on our arrival at Marseilles, I was ordered to leave my present duty and take up a special enquiry on behalf of Scotland Yard. It appeared that the number of Chinese in the East End of London had been greatly increased owing to the shortage of labour caused by recruiting, and that the smuggling of opium by these men was reaching serious dimensions.

Scotland Yard, with its numbers also seriously reduced, both as regards its actual personnel and even more so in the matter of its special sources of information, found itself with its resources strained to the utmost unable to cope with this flood of Asiatic drug-smugglers. They had, therefore, arranged with the F.M.S. Government to borrow my services in the preparation of a concentrated attack on the receivers and distributors. When I heard of this proposal, as I did from a Colonel Gore at Marseilles, I told him that it was no good my proceeding to London via Havre and Southampton as he had arranged, since were I to do so I would have no standing amongst the Chinese when I mysteriously arrived amongst them.

It was therefore arranged that I should board a vessel at Marseilles and arrive in London as a stowaway deserter from the Chinese Labour Corps. This was done, and on my arrival in London I was led ashore by the Police, where I in due course appeared at the Thames Police Court under the name of Tom Mah, a Chinese half-caste, charged with stowing away on a British vessel.

Mr. Challenor kept a particularly straight face as he solemnly passed a sentence of ten days' imprisonment—though I have no doubt that he had private information as to the farce which was being enacted.

It was very necessary to my success that this scene should take place, for at that time an agent of the opium traffickers was present at every sitting of the Police court to overhear the cases involving their underlings there, and arrange for the payment of the fines. To be presented before the eyes of this important personage as a culprit against the law was, therefore, the best introduction I could possibly have to their good graces.

Having been driven away in the prison van, I ultimately found myself enjoying a not very needful but extremely enjoyable holiday of ten days at Droitwich.

I was met at the station when I arrived there, and found that comfortable European quarters had been provided for me in a bedroom and sitting-room at the house of an English police sergeant, where I was surrounded by every luxury.

When I was having tea the next afternoon, I was surprised and delighted by Colonel Munroe walking into my room. He had retired and was living only a few miles away, at Malvern. It appeared that it was as a result of a conversation he had had with the Chief Commissioner that my services had been applied for. He had arranged my present quarters for me, and had now come over to see if I was comfortable or if there was anything else he could do for me. I was very grateful to him for thus remembering an old servant, and was extremely touched by this great kindness which he showed me.

I was very much interested in walking about the quiet little English town and in seeing, for the first time, the actuality of English home-life—with the reflection of which I was so well acquainted. I now realized that the reflection I had known was but a pale picture. The Eastern mirror had not shown true. Probably its bright background had dulled the colourings, even as its atmosphere had distorted the image.

The Salt Works were, of course, the most interesting feature of the place, and I need hardly remark how astonished I was to find that it was impossible to sink in the swimming baths. I made an excursion, guided by my kind host, to Worcester where, through his official influence, he arranged to have us shown all over the Royal Potteries in which place the King's chinaware is made. We saw all the processes, finishing up with seeing the artists, many of whom were young ladies, painting designs on cups doubtless soon to be graced by the touch of Royal lips.

On several days Colonel Munroe sent his car, the driver of which had instructions to show me the beauties of the English countryside. In this way I travelled through the beautiful Evesham Valley which is so famous for its orchards, and passed many of the stately homes of the nobility nestling in the seclusion of their high-walled parks.

On one occasion I was taken to his house and had the honour of having tea with him, his wife, and his daughter—the latter of whom I had not seen since she was a very small girl some twelve years before. His two sons, both of whom I had known so well as children, were fighting in France, which made me realize, I think more than anything else, how the years had rolled on. The Colonel, aged as he was, was nevertheless engaged on some sort of war work—I think something to do with recruiting. It was a great pleasure to me to talk comfortably in my own language once more, and that sunny afternoon at Malvern remains one of the pleasantest recollections of my life.

Colonel Munroe, alas! is no more, but I take this opportunity of paying my final respects to one who, by his invariable kindness and justice to me, taught me what a perfect being a man can be.

What a change it was after this pleasant holiday when I had once more to don my greasy workman's clothes and appear in the East End of London as a discharged prisoner!

On the tenth day of my 'imprisonment' I was visited by Superintendent Gilcrest, who told me that I was to be working under him and that he had come through to tell me what he expected of me. He then explained his methods of work. In the first place I was to take up my quarters in a Chinese lodging-house in the neighbourhood of the West India Dock Road, and he supplied me with the addresses of several such establishments.

When I was so established I was to report my address to him through a small tobacconist's shop in Trinidad Street, the address of which had not been written down but which I had to memorize. I was to introduce myself to the tobacconist by asking for two 'Sailors' Whiffs'. If there were other customers in the shop, or circumstances were otherwise unsuitable, the tobacconist would tell me that he "thought he had run out of them, but would look again in a minute if I would wait", otherwise he would merely say: "Sailors' Whiffs. Yes". When he said this I was to hand him the note giving my address and he would hand me two cheroots wrapped in any message that there might be for me. This was to be the only method by which I was to communicate with the Superintendent. I could call at any time at the tobacconist's, leaving a written message for him, which he would be sure to receive before midnight that day. If I had any urgent message to send, I was to ask for three or four 'Sailors' Whiffs' according to the urgency of the message, when the tobacconist would take steps accordingly to have it delivered forthwith.

The Superintendent impressed on me the importance of giving no verbal messages to the tobacconist. I could talk to him as much as I pleased about the weather, the cigars, or anything else I liked, but so far as Police matters were concerned no words were to be used except the formula prescribed. He explained that it had taken a long time to establish this shop as an unsuspected Police post office, that the 'shopkeeper' had been fined several times for betting on horse races, and so was now considered a perfectly 'safe' person by all the criminal fraternity. It was therefore vitally important that nothing should be done to raise any suspicions regarding his integrity.

Mr. Gilcrest told me that he did not expect me to produce results for some weeks yet, as it would take me some time to find my feet in London. I quite realized that it is impossible to do Police work in any place where you are not familiar with both 'the lie of the land', local customs, and available means of transport. But I had worked in Singapore and Penang, had visited Rangoon and Calcutta, seen Marseilles and Worcester, and although realizing that London would be a larger city than any of these, still I did not doubt but that I could feel moderately at home, certainly within ten days. The Superintendent laughed and said that he hoped that I was right, but that I should let him know when I felt ready.

He had given me full directions as to how I was to reach West India Dock Road, and seemed very amused at the explanation he had to give me of the underground railway, which I was to take at Praed Street and by which I was to travel to Aldgate station. He seemed to think that a policeman who had never heard of an electric underground railway could not know much about anything, but he was very kind and helpful in the very full advice and descriptions which he gave me to help me on my way.

Having wished me luck, and telling me not to be shy about asking him for anything I might want, he shook me by the hand and left me to follow him by the next train to Paddington.

I had, up to this time, seen nothing of London save the short walk from the Docks to the Police station. One gets no view from the inside of a 'Black Maria', and it had been night-time when I was smuggled out of Pentonville in a closed car and hurried to Droitwich.

I do not suppose it is possible to tell you just how lost I felt as I emerged from the railway station at Aldgate, after the strange and noisy experience I had just undergone in arriving there. Feeling quite sure that it is absolutely beyond my powers of description, I shall make no attempt to do so. Pulling myself together as I stood outside the station entrance, I turned to the left and set forth to find my new home. To my surprise I immediately found myself passing along a squalid array of butchers' booths, which gave me an impression of the capital of the Empire such as I, to say the least of it, had never expected.

This was, however, after I had succeeded in crossing the road.

You who live continually in their midst do not seem to appreciate the wonders which surround you, and in this I speak not only of London but Paris, which I subsequently came to know. The constant rush of traffic, which to me at that time was so amazing and bewildering, flies past you and you never even give it a glance. Every moment accidents are avoided by a mere hairsbreadth before your eyes, yet you never even gasp! You are so sure that the impending accident will be avoided, and you seem to feel no wonder that it should be so!

Immense vehicles crowded with your fellow-men fly along, hurtling them as it seems to their doom. Only a miracle it seems can save them, and you stand idly by, serenely confident that that miracle will take place, which of course it does—but to one unused to such sights, your serene confidence itself is another miracle. To me, standing at the corner of the Commercial Road facing the frowsty frontage of a Turkish baths, the scene had all the thrill of a gladiatorial combat. The tense expectation of witnessing a catastrophe, alternating with the relaxed relief when each was avoided, became almost unsupportable; and I felt quite weak as I boarded a tramcar which was pointed out to me by an obliging pedestrian as being one which would take me in the direction of West India Dock Road.

I duly made arrangements for myself at a Chinese boarding-house in West India Dock Road; at the first of the addresses which Mr. Gilcrest had given me, as a matter of fact, to which I applied. I then set out and, looking round the neighbourhood, found the tobacconist of whom I had been told without much difficulty and bought my two daily 'Sailors' Whiffs'—leaving my message and receiving one from the Superintendent simply saying: 'Good luck'.

During the next few days I tramped the district wearily—from Barford Street to Broomfield Street, from Three Colt Street to Leven Road—miles and miles of squalid streets, in every direction. I realized that it would take me weeks to memorize all the names—and this was only a corner of London! At last I understood why Superintendent

Gilcrest had laughed at me. Nevertheless, after a day or two I did begin to appreciate the general lie of the land, and could find my way back to my lodging-house without having to enquire.

When I felt fully confident and fairly conversant with my immediate neighbourhood, I next started taking buses and threaded London from end to end. From Ilford to Hanwell, from Golders Green to Purley I explored in this manner till I could find my way by bus more or less easily, and knew at any rate the general direction of the main arterial routes and something of their general appearance. I explored the underground railway system from station to station, coming to the surface at each station in turn and taking a short walk round before buying my ticket to the next one.

In this way I had in my mind a picture of how each station was situated, and how to approach it from the nearest omnibus routes. But there is no need to enlarge on the various methods I employed to accustom myself to my new surroundings. It is sufficient to say that, after three weeks' hard grind, I felt myself sufficiently at home to seriously undertake my mission.

During these three weeks I did not, of course, devote my entire time to wandering about London; I had also been establishing myself as a known individual amongst the Asiatic population in the midst of which I was situated. Tom Mah, as I was called, was, as a large number of people could soon have told you, a mother-o'-pearl cutter seeking employment which, since pearl-shell was not being imported during the war to any large extent, he was not very likely to find. He was, moreover, also a 'picker-up of unconsidered trifles', and at this appeared to be either extremely clever or extraordinarily lucky.

Whichever it may have been, he certainly always appeared to have half a crown between him and his wants. He had been jugged by the scoundrelly Police merely for stowing away on a British vessel, and the things he could and would say about these professional persecutors of mankind excelled in vituperative point most of the curses which might be heard in that neighbourhood—a district where the art of cursing has reached a high state of perfection. He was a good fellow, and with a little persuasion would entertain a new friend generously, albeit in a modest way.

Thus I became known to a gradually widening circle of acquaintances, selecting them carefully with an eye to their social status. Starting with the dregs who shared my modest lodgings, by the end of these three weeks I was on nodding acquaintance with several of the local Oriental tradesmen and shopkeepers. Following my old plan I arranged for Superintendent Gilcrest to supply me with an assortment of 'stolen property', and when opportunity offered I would receive not only my 'Sailors' Whiffs', but a conveniently small packet.

In this way I often had a watch and chain that I was anxiously trying to dispose of on the most advantageous terms, with no questions asked; rings, cuff-links, and other small pieces of jewellery made a variation in the articles of my commerce. By this means my reputation speedily became established and I was a tolerated, if not a popular, customer, in three or four of the largest eating-houses. I had also made two purchases of opium during this time, both from men who, from their penurious condition of life, I knew could only be of the very lowest in the scale of distributors, but as I was only establishing myself as yet, I made no attempt to investigate their connections further.

Chapter 13

THIS, THEN, WAS THE POSITION of affairs when I seriously tackled the job for which I had been brought over. Since the opium was being brought ashore from ships, it was obvious that I had better try to get employment which brought me in contact with the crews, and I tried several boarding-houses with a view to being engaged as a 'runner' for them. Eventually, however, I found something better, obtaining a part-time job as assistant to the 'water-clerk' of a Chinese ship-chandler who had a store on the Causeway.

It was this man's job to go on board all vessels which had Chinese crews, as they came up the river, when they anchored at Gravesend, and endeavour to obtain their orders for his master. It was to be my job to act as his deputy when there was a second vessel coming up at the same time, but in the meantime I was to accompany him to learn the business. Nothing could have suited my book better, as in this way I was left free to mingle with the crews whilst my superior was discussing business with the officers or the steward.

I had only been engaged on this work for three days when I was approached by a man named Long Li. When you saw him you understood whence he had got the name of 'Long', for he was certainly the tallest, and I think the thinnest, Chinaman I have ever seen, with a face which looked like an accident to a cemetery. He introduced himself to me one evening whilst I was having supper, and he was so chatty and friendly that I was at once suspicious. When, later on, he suggested entertaining me with a seat at the cinema, I was more than suspicious, in fact I felt quite certain that the fish were about to nibble at the bait of my disreputable personality.

During the evening Long Li asked many casual questions, the drift of which I have no doubt but that he thought I did not appreciate, though as a result of my equally casual replies to them he acquired a mass of details which fully supported the past history of his companion which was in general circulation. Of course my story was absolutely unassailable, since, being a half-caste born in a back street in Malacca, I had never been to China, and my ignorance of that country was perfectly natural, whereas he had never been ashore in Malaya except for a few hours in Singapore, though I found him well primed on the subject of life there. Beyond putting me through this enquiry no move was made that night, and we parted with mutual expressions of esteem, having arranged to meet again the following evening.

At the first meeting our conversation had been entirely in Cantonese, but when I met him next evening Long Li was accompanied by a friend of his whom he introduced as being a wealthy merchant. This man, Song Moy, tested me very carefully during the three or four hours we were together by passing remarks in Kheh, which seemed to be the natural dialect of these two friends. Several times they would carry on a short conversation in Kheh, and then, continuing it in Cantonese, bring me in, and after a sentence or two refer to the opinion one or other had just expressed in Kheh, which I had to be careful to remember that I had not heard.

It was all very cleverly done, but I had had too many similar experiences in my lifetime to be caught off my guard. In fact, the practice of exhibiting ignorance of conversations which I thoroughly comprehend has become almost second nature to me. So much so that sometimes even when I have been talking to my official superiors in Malay, and they have addressed a remark to me in English, I have found myself paying no attention to it, and it often has taken quite a mental effort on my part to force myself to reply in these circumstances.

During the evening the conversation was led round to the ever present question of the Police, whereupon I gave my famous representation of a man consumed with hatred of all authority, the intensity of which seemed to impress them favourably. I was satisfied that such was the case when, before parting, Long Li told me that from time to time his friend had some slightly illegal dealings in which I could perhaps assist him, if I would care to do so; and I was quite sure that the eagerness with which I accepted any chance of outwitting the despised Police thoroughly convinced them.

We three met repeatedly during the next few days, and I was evidently at length accepted at my face value, the proof being that I was taken to Song Moy's establishment. This alleged merchant lived in the three upper rooms of a house in Amoy Place, the ground floor of which was an eating-house. As there was a door from the restaurant into his passage-way, and an entrance from the basement kitchen into the backyard, by which means also the staircase could be reached, this was a very useful position for anyone to occupy who did not wish his various visitors either to be kept tally of or to be quickly remarked. On the other hand, the quarters were not exactly those in which one would expect to find a merchant prince established: I realized that though I might be on the right track, I was at any rate only putting my foot on the first step of it.

In due course it came out that this merchant dealt in smuggled tobacco, which I was to bring ashore for him. Being by this time well known to the Customs officers and the Police at the dock gates as a ship-store clerk, I could generally pass without examination. In fact, if the business was quickly settled, I could leave the vessels whilst they were still at Gravesend and, landing at any one of a dozen private quays, or even on the mud bank, reach the ferry without meeting anyone in authority at all.

This being the case, Song Moy asked me to approach a member of the crew in a vessel which was due the next day and ask him for the "packet for Song Moy", which would contain the tobacco in question. For this small service he was willing to pay me the quite extravagant price of ten shillings—so I was quite certain that my suspicions had been correct. Having duly received the packet the next day and realizing that, if it had indeed been tobacco, its total value was less than the ten shillings which I was being paid for this transport, I had the curiosity to open it before delivering it at Amoy Place. Having done so I was mildly surprised to find that it contained six slabs of hard tobacco each neatly done up in tissue paper. Evidently my friends were being particularly careful and still subjecting me to the testing process.

It was not until I had carefully opened four such packages that their confidence in me was apparently complete. The fifth package, when unwrapped, proved to contain a wooden box which, without opening, I guessed to be some of the opium which I was in search of. Having definitely laid my hands on one end of the string, it now became my duty to unravel its tangled skein until I could find the other. This I now set about doing.

Being in more or less regular employment and receiving these extra payments for the package carrying, I was justified in spending some money on improving my appearance, thus making me a more presentable companion for the gentlemen in the superior status of Long Li and his circle. Needless to say I discussed these delicate points quite openly with him and Song Moy. These two quite agreed with me, but urged me to make no change in my appearance for the present for, as they said, I might be of yet more use to them—in some mysterious and unnamed way!

After a day or two Long Li told me that they had been thinking over what I had said about improving my position, and as the first step in this direction they had arranged a new lodging for me, which he was sure would be to my liking. This lodging was an attic room in a house in Swaile Street, which was a quiet *cul-de-sac*, in which to live, and, having also a room to myself, it seemed like heaven after the crowded noisy lodging house life. The house in which my new room was possessed a peculiar advantage, in that, by descending to the basement and going along a passage which led under the backyard, one could come up again into a house fronting on Nankin Street, another *cul-de-sac*, and so emerge into Pekin Street. This second entrance, however, was not a matter of common knowledge to the other tenants of the various rooms, and I myself only came to learn of it later on.

As our friendship ripened Song Moy suggested an outing 'up West' one evening, and this was the occasion on which I learnt of the second entrance to my lodging. He explained to me that I must smarten myself up for the West End outing with new clothes giving me more the appearance of a clerk than my usual shoddy outfit. He then showed me the secret passage under the backyard leading to Nankin Street, and told me to be careful never to appear in Swaile Street in my new finery, using always this other entrance when so attired. In this way the Police would never be able to connect my new West End personality with the humble water-clerk of the docks.

He arranged that we should meet outside the Eastern Tavern in the West India Dock Road, which we did, and boarded a No. 23 omnibus, in which we journeyed to Tottenham Court Road corner, where we alighted. To my surprise Song Moy led me across the road, and we entered the ornate foyer of Frascatti's restaurant.

There was no pretence about the discomfort I displayed when I found myself following my companion to a table in these palatial surroundings; glittering with gilt, blazing with electric lights, princely vistas surrounded me on all sides through the unending mirrors.

Not the least surprising thing to me was the way Song Moy seemed to fit in with his present surroundings. His black clothing, which had been dingily inconspicuous amongst the mottled throngs of Pennyfields, seemed smartly unobtrusive here. His slow walk, which in the East End had seemed to be somehow stealthy, here appeared merely the sign of dignified confidence. He was the same man, his manner was unchanged, his movements identical, the tones of his voice unaltered, and yet in some subtle way he had become an entirely different individual.

Doing my best to suppress my surprise I took my seat, facing him across the spotless table to which the deferential waiter had led us.

I had, of course, seen such places before, though none perhaps so blatantly bedizened with exotic ornamentation, but this was the first time I had ever entered one as a customer; and I was glad that it was in keeping with the character which I was portraying to express my delight and wonder at the novelty of my position.

Song Moy was thoroughly at home, and even seemed to be recognized as a regular customer by the waiter. He was quite delighted with the surprise he had caused me, and pointed out special features of the restaurant with a pride which was almost proprietory. I do not now remember what we had to eat, but from subsequent experiences of the excellent cuisine of this hostelry, I am quite sure that it was something exceptionally appetising. In any case we ended our meal by having a special coffee, which was served to us from a barrow by a man with whom Song Moy conversed in a language which I did not know; the only word used which I recognized was 'cigarette'.

In making payment for this coffee I noticed that a small packet changed hands, and for the first time I realized why we had visited this place, and that the evening's outing was not entirely a pleasure jaunt on the part of my friend; he was, it seemed; bent on business as well!

On leaving the restaurant we crossed the road and sauntered through Soho Square, in which place another packet changed hands, this time to a man who had been leaning up against the railings there presumably waiting for our arrival. When he saw us coming he straightened up and offered matches for sale, of which Song Moy took a box and then immediately returned it, saying that after all he did not want any. He had not been quick enough, however, to stop me seeing that the box he returned was not the box he had lifted, and looking back over my shoulder as we passed on, I was in time to see the match-seller removing the returned box from his tray and pocketing it.

We called at a small restaurant in Frith Street, where Song Moy said he wanted to make enquiries about a friend. At another, on some other excuse, and finally found ourselves at a music hall in Leicester Square. Here it was quite impossible for me to keep track of all Moy's doings without arousing his suspicions, but I saw enough to satisfy myself that he was meeting a large number of friends.

We finished up the night in a club, held in a cellar practically next door to the music hall, which seemed to be a popular resort of those who make up the night life of a great city. These 'votaries of Venus' and 'believers in Bacchus' thronged the small tables and crowded the diminutive dancing area which they surrounded.

I could easily see that it was intended to be a scene of lighthearted gaiety; the intention, however, was so insistently obvious that it did not achieve its object. The scene remained merely one of thwarted intention. The winsome smiles and arch coquetries of the young ladies were forced and unnatural. The light badinage lacked spontaneity. The laughter rang hollow, and the crowd moved, in the lifeless smoky atmosphere of the place, with no more real animation than so many marionettes.

The only bright sparks of real vitality were the animal cries and aimless antics of a few young khaki-clad men who were uproariously drunk. These few, at least, were genuinely enjoying themselves for the time being, yet, strange as are the workings of the human mind, though these few alone attained consummation of the joviality after which all were so painfully striving, they were looked upon with great disapproval by the others and were speedily hustled out.

Here also Moy seemed not only well known, but welcome, and retiring 'behind the scenes' doubtless effected his distribution in those discreet purlieus. Whether this was so or not, of course, I could not see, but a considerable number of people made inconspicuous visits to the same quarter, so he had every opportunity to do so.

This was my first experience of an evening up West, but it was the first of many. Eventually my discretion was approved of, and perhaps the excellence of my English had something to do with it, but whatever may have been the reason I was soon initiated into a part of the secret of the organization. In the first place I got a tremendous surprise when I found that it was not the opium traffic—which I had been deputed to find—that I was dealing with. Song Moy was dealing with cocaine.

I reported this as an urgent message to Superintendent Gilcrest, and received the reply that I had to stick to it, as it was even more important. For my first job as distributor I was given a district in the neighbourhood of Victoria Street, where I had a circle of some twelve agents to whom I must deliver packets twice weekly.

It was part of my duty to do up these quantities of cocaine in packets which, accorded with the fancies of the recipients—and an extraordinary collection of parcels they looked as I set forth on my round. In some cases a plain packet was all that was required, but these were in the minority. There was a red-faced, jovial-looking man whom I used to meet in the saloon bars of one or other of a half-dozen public houses alternately, according to the arrangement.

He was, I think, a bookmaker, whose fancy it was to receive his cocaine packet disguised as a cigar, and for this purpose I was provided with a number of paper fans which shut themselves up into an imitation cigar, out of which I had to rip the fan and substitute a long packet. Twice weekly this man and I went through the solemn farce of offering each other a cigar, and on every such occasion he would say that "this was too good a cigar to smoke outside", and putting it in his pocket he would "save it up to smoke at home".

A lady at whose house I used to call in Wilton Road—she was one of those ladies who had a number of young ladies staying with her— always had to receive a box of a well-known face powder. At a chemist's shop I had always to return a box of Beecham's pills, explaining that it had been "Carter's Little Liver Pills which Lady Dives had ordered", and the chemist would always promise to send them on the morrow. From a flower-girl in Buckingham Palace Road, who was a plain-packet customer, I always bought a buttonhole, which I as regularly gave away to the young lady sitting at the next table in the Pillar Hall restaurant, where I dined.

It was some time before I realized that I was being followed on my rounds by another, more tried, agent. This evidently served the double purpose of keeping an eye on me, with my valuable cargo, in case I should take it into my head to do a little private business of my own with it, and he also collected immediate payment from my clients for the goods just delivered.

By dint of careful watching I discovered that there were three of these gentry who, from time to time, followed me round, two of them being Chinamen and the third an Italian. I decided that the man who finally received the money would be the head of the organization, and that, if I followed this Italian, he might lead me to the headquarters where the leader could be found.

Choosing my opportunity, therefore, one evening when he was following me round, I delayed things until it was nearly eleven o'clock before my last delivery had been effected, for which late call I chose the lady in Wilton Road. Leaving her house after I had made my delivery, I continued along the pavement as if making as usual for the underground station, but turning along Gillingham Street I ran round by Berwick Street and St. Leonard Street, the corner of which I reached just in time to see my friend leaving the house.

He turned along New Street, and crossing Vauxhall Bridge Road entered a block of flats in Carlisle Place. Not wishing to be seen from the windows, I walked up and down in Francis Street. It would have been too conspicuous to stand still at the corner, and as the door he had gone in was close to my end of the street, there was no risk of him disappearing by the other end of it whilst I was at the extremity of my beat, which I felt could safely be as far as to the back of the Cathedral.

It was as well that I had adopted this method of watching, since before many minutes had passed I was surprised to see my Italian coming down the steps from Morpeth Mansions, in the next street. How he had gone from one building to the other I could not at this time understand, but I have since discovered that there is a gangway connecting the roofs of these two terraces, for use in case of fire. Evidently the man I was following was taking every precaution, and I felt sure that he would lead me to someone important.

Crossing Victoria Street, I kept up the chase past the front of Buckingham Palace and on to the long straight road of Constitution Hill. This was a very difficult situation to handle, since I could not afford to let my quarry be far ahead when we reached Hyde Park Corner, and yet there were not sufficient people about at that time of night to conceal me if I attempted to follow him closely. There seemed only one thing to be done unless I was to lose him altogether, and thanks to the subdued lights I was able to do it successfully. Climbing the railings on the right I raced across the park almost to the Piccadilly side, and then swerving round, reached the triumphal archway in time to be sauntering past it as he, quite unsuspectingly, overtook me and crossed into Hyde Park.

Following him in Hyde Park was, of course, child's play to me, though I am afraid my clothes suffered somewhat in the process. He used all the old dodges to ensure that he was not being followed, turning suddenly and walking smartly back along his track, standing still immediately he had rounded a tree, and so on. He eventually decided that he was now safe from pursuit and made straight for Bayswater by the Victoria Gate, from there taking no precautions as he walked hurriedly westwards.

Luckily there were no taxicabs to be seen, for had a lonely cab appeared and he taken it, I would undoubtedly have lost him. As it was I followed him to a house on the south side of Princes Square, which I subsequently discovered to be a private hotel, and watching from across the gardens, almost immediately saw a light go up in one of the upper rooms, which satisfied me that he was safe for the night. I then sprinted for the District Railway, at Queens Road station, where I just managed to catch the last train to Aldgate.

Next morning I appeared bright and early at my ship-chandler's and cried off work for the day—to his intense indignation. However, I was firm about it, and eight o'clock found me once more in the neighbourhood of Princes Square, but this time dressed in my seediest working clothes, determined to keep my eye on this Italian at all costs, feeling certain that he would lead me, at any rate, a step further on my journey if not to the headquarters of the system itself.

Needless to say I had been keeping Superintendent Gilcrest fully informed of my various movements from day to day. In fact I had met him once or twice, in the following circumstances. One day when I was buying my regulation 'Sailors' Whiffs', I found that the instructions with them were to the effect that I should return at 6.15 p.m. and ask for two more of them.

This I did, and instead of getting my usual cheroots was immediately ushered into the back room of the tobacconist's where, to my surprise, I found the Superintendent waiting for me. He explained that the back door of the shop opened into an alley-way which led from Salter Street to Grenade Street, and that in the latter thoroughfare was a pawnbroker's shop with a back door also opening into the same alley-way. By visiting the pawnbroker's, which is a thing the Police are constantly doing in search of stolen property, he could thus enter the tobacconist's unobserved by any followers, and it was in this manner that he had come to our meeting.

In this way, and by the reports I had handed in, he was kept up to date both as to what I was doing and what were my opinions of the people I met, and of their doings. I interpose this short explanation here so that those who are not conversant with the Police methods may not think that I was running a 'lone hand' search, such as I had from time to time undertaken when my duties led me far into the jungle.

So long as it is possible for him to do so, it is a policeman's duty to keep his superiors informed minutely as to his doings. I had, therefore, you will understand, already bought my two 'Sailors' Whiffs' that morning and left the news of what I intended doing.

I managed to fill in the morning by calling at every house in the square, except the one in which I was interested, making enquiries for an imaginary Mr. Parsons. By dint of speaking the very worst of broken English—and my worst broken English is a language to wonder at!—I managed to prolong each of these doorstep interviews to sometimes incredible lengths, and I thus whiled away the time doing nothing though being apparently fully occupied.

Still there was no sign of my gentleman appearing, and at about twelve o'clock I was lounging past the end of the square for the third time, realizing that if I continued this I would become conspicuous and racking my brains for some other method by which I could appear to be busy, when I was accosted by a man, in shirt sleeves and a livery waistcoat, who was leading two little dogs on the end of long bright-red leather straps.

This man remarked on the weather and listened with interest to my reply to this. He then astonished me by saying, "That's all right, Sergeant Nalla, I have been sent to take over this watching job from you." He went on to explain that Superintendent Gilcrest, realizing that it would be difficult for an Asiatic like myself to hang about a square in the West End of London doing nothing, for any great length of time, without rousing the suspicions not only of the local Police but also of the neighbouring inhabitants, had sent him to relieve me.

In any case, he said, it was a job which needed a constant change of watchers, especially in circumstances like the present, where the person watched was suspicious of surveillance. As I had just reached this conclusion myself, in my cogitations, I was only too glad to give my strangely garbed relief a minute description of the Italian, and leave him to his stately parade giving milady's dogs their airing. His final instructions to me were that I was to see the Superintendent at once at the Hyde Park Police station, whither I departed.

When I saw Mr. Gilcrest he told me that I had been very foolish in attempting to carry out this watching at all, and he hoped no harm had been done. I explained to him that I now quite realized the impossibility of such work for me in London, but that I had so often spent days of successful watching in Malaya that I had started my morning without appreciating the tremendous difference there would be and the handicap I would be working under. He quite saw my point and, congratulating me on my last night's work, dismissed me to continue my job in the East End.

I met Song Moy that evening and, as we were having supper in the eating-house below his rooms, Long Li entered. Sitting down at our table he said to Moy in Kheh, "This pig has been reported. He has been spying. I am to take him to the Chief," to which Song Moy replied, "He will make short work of him." This conversation sounded very ominous to me, but on the other hand I was glad to hear that I was to be taken to the Chief—since it was his whereabouts that I was chiefly in search of. But if Song Moy's gloomy prediction proved true, it appeared that when I had acquired this knowledge it would be of little use to me!

I was not surprised, therefore, when after we had finished our supper Long Li suggested a trip up West with him, and I agreed to the suggestion with the greatest enthusiasm. I thanked Li most effusively for his condescension in deigning to accept my company, and appeared to fall in with the suggestion with the utmost relish. I hurried off to change into my West End costume—not forgetting to buy two 'Sailors' Whiffs' on my way.

Within half an hour I was back at the table, eagerly asking Long Li whither he proposed taking me. He said that, as it was now after ten o'clock, he thought it was too late for anything but a night club, and that he knew of one such club which he was sure I would like to see, and of which he was a member, at 114 Draycott Avenue. From the way that he said this I thought it probably was the real address of the house to which he was taking me, and felt it highly important to advise Superintendent Gilcrest of my destination.

In order to accomplish this I explained to Li that I had been intending to call round at my employer's store to tell him that I would be back at work tomorrow. When he arrived with his flattering proposal it put the matter right out of my head, but if he would not mind we could walk round that way now and I would deliver my message.

He was quite agreeable to this, so we walked down to the Causeway and I left my message at the store. Whilst standing there doing this, I wrote the address to which I was being taken on a page of the notebook in my jacket pocket, and tore the page off as we turned the corner into Trinidad Street. As we approached the tobacconist's I suddenly "remembered that I had no smokes", so we went in and I ordered six 'Sailors' Whiffs'. I managed to pass over the address which I had ready in my hand, quite unobserved, whilst making payment.

The tobacconist seemed to me to be a little surprised at the extent of my order, following so swiftly as it did my previous purchase of the customary modest couple, but he did not display this feeling openly. I felt very relieved when this tricky business had been successfully carried through under the very nose of my companion. Writing notes in my pocket was an accomplishment which I had assiduously practised, and which had proved of the greatest use to me on many occasions when I wished to write unobserved, but never before had it been of such immense importance to me.

Leaving the underground railway at South Kensington station, Li and I strolled down Draycott Avenue, which proved to be a street of tall imposing houses, each with a heavily-pillared portico, and I was duly impressed (for Li's benefit) by the impressiveness of my surroundings. The door of No. 114 was thrown open to us by an immense flunkey, and I followed Li through the lavishly-furnished hall to a cloakroom on the right, where a second flunkey took our hats and coats from us. We then walked up a broad staircase, and I was told to wait on the landing whilst Li disappeared into a room on the right. Whilst I was waiting there, with a flood of music, a door in front of me opened and a laughing party of young ladies in the most stylish evening dress, accompanied by their khaki-clad gallants, came out, thus giving me a glimpse of a large and magnificently furnished room, on the parquet floor of which some dozen or so couples were dancing.

The young folk who had come out passed me with hardly a glance and made their way upstairs, laughing and chatting in anticipation of some unmentioned treat which awaited them in the regions above.

When Long Li had returned, it appeared that we were also to ascend to that land of promise. I followed him up several flights of stairs, and finally into a small bare room which contained an iron bedstead immediately behind the door, a chest of drawers against the left-hand wall, two Windsor chairs, and a washhand stand beneath the low window—through which I could see the balustrading of the roof.

Playing my part of ignorance, I expressed surprise at our coming to a room like this, and asked why we were not joining the gay throng downstairs. Li was very affable, and explained that he had brought me up here as he wished to introduce me to a very old friend of his, and by coming to this quiet room we could be sure of having our conversation uninterrupted. He seemed very anxious to put me at my ease, and I think he was rather afraid that I might 'smell a rat' and use some personal violence towards him.

Though he did not know it, nothing would have been easier than for me to do so, for I had in my pocket my very excellent knuckleduster, which is a silent weapon of defence that I had specially manufactured for me—its three-quarter inch spikes being specifically designed to grip the cutting edge of any weapon with which I might be attacked—when a turn of the wrist would disarm my opponent. This of course could also be used as a powerful weapon of attack should necessity demand. However, until I knew definitely whether this was, in fact, the address of the mysterious Chief, it did not suit my book to be otherwise than compliant.

After a few minutes there entered three men, who took up their position sitting on the bed, beyond the foot of which Li and I were sitting on the chairs facing the chest of drawers. One of the men was the Italian whom I had followed the night before, another was a very fat, very smooth, very smiling Chinaman—who, by the way, is the only Chinaman I have ever seen who was completely bald—and the last, a man whose nationality I could not guess. He was a commanding figure of a man, and I estimated his age to be about fifty; he had cold, almost dead-looking blue eyes, with raven-black eyebrows, but iron-grey hair and moustache, and one of those predatory noses which make you think of a hawk. I immediately realized that he was, indeed, the Chief.

As I did not understand the language in which he spoke to his Chinese companion, it was some time before I could take any interest in the conversation, and I filled in the time by innocently asking Long Li to introduce me to his friends. Needless to say his manner had entirely changed on the arrival of these others, and he insolently commanded me to be silent.

Presently the bald-headed Chinaman, whose name I gathered was Tung, spoke to Li (in Kheh) asking him more or less what the charge against me was. Li went into a long explanation of my employment, finishing up with the fact that he had heard from the Italian of my attempted espionage that morning, and had brought me along as ordered. All this Tung seemingly translated to his Chief, who then cross-examined the Italian in his native tongue which, though I did not know it, I recognized; then, seeming to have satisfied himself on the facts of the case, he dismissed him.

After the departure of the Italian, the Chinaman, Tung, commenced to question me as to my doings. It appeared that the Italian had recognized me from a window, as I called from door to door on the other side of the square, and had consulted Long Li by telephone as to the reason for my appearance in Princes Square. The latter, of course, knew no reason why I should be there, so on putting two and two together they had realized that I must have tracked the Italian home the night before. Owing to the nature of their business, they had immediately jumped to the right conclusion and reported the matter to headquarters—with a result that I was now there to give an innocent explanation of my doings if such were possible. Needless to say I found it quite impossible to give any explanation which covered the facts that they knew, and at the same time sounded at all reasonable.

This is not to say that I did not give any explanation at all. On the contrary, I launched into an interminable story of how I had noticed this man following me on several occasions and had become suspicious of him, thinking that he was an emissary of the law, and so, wishing only to protect my superiors in the business, I had undertaken the task of shadowing him; but how, after having hung about till mid-day round Princes Square, I had felt myself so conspicuous and the policeman had looked at me several times so suspiciously, that I had been compelled to come away without having seen the Italian again at all.

I made the story as long as possible and full of countless unimportant details, while the two on the bed listened to me patiently—not so, however, Long Li. He kept interrupting and being silenced and, immediately I had concluded my tale, he demanded to know why, if all this were true, I had not told Song Moy when I met him that evening? I explained again at as great length as possible that my reason was that I hoped, by keeping the matter to myself, I might yet solve the mystery of this Italian, and by thus gaining credit with my superiors, would perhaps obtain advancement in the organization. Here the bald-headed Tung took up the interrogation and, pointing out the weakness of my reasons, intimated that they did not believe a word of it!

He was in the midst of a regular homily on the iniquity of curiosity, when the Chief interrupted him by demanding from me, in English, whether or not I was working for the Police? Before I had time to answer him, he answered himself, and told me fiercely that it was the last time I would work for anyone, as he would see to it that I disappeared forthwith.

He spoke English with hardly a trace of a foreign accent, and although speaking quite quietly, the threat in his voice was more terrible to hear than any threat I have ever heard shouted or screamed. There was an icy-cold menace in his voice which made shivers run down my spine, and I wondered if, indeed, this was to be the end of all things for me. He spoke a while with Tung, and then left me with the two Chinamen.

Tung passed on his orders to Long Li, which were that I was to be kept where I was until the party downstairs had dispersed, when I was to be taken down to the cellar "to be dealt with". They were talking in Kheh and, of course, were quite sure that I did not know what they were saying. Tung said that he was now going to rejoin the party, and would immediately send two men up to help Li keep me in charge.

Li asked what was he to do in the meantime, as he had not even a revolver? To which Tung replied that it was quite all right as I did not know that, and breaking into Cantonese for my benefit, he finished up by saying "there is no need to have the two men on the landing brought in, if you object to their company. They will come if you shout, and in any case you have your revolver." He then left the room and said a few words to the imaginary men on the landing before I heard his footsteps disappear.

I realized at once that this was the moment in which to save myself. I had already put my hand in my pocket and now, quickly slipping my fingers through the knuckleduster, I said I would like a drink of water from the carafe on the washhand stand, rising to my feet as I said so. Long Li foolishly glanced at the washhand stand to see if, in fact, there was any water there, and, in the moment of his glance, I whipped out my right hand, which met his face just as he turned back.

I had meant to hit him on the temple, but owing to his turning back my blow became a rolling one and punctured both his eyes, as I could tell by the quantity of vitreous juice which ran down his face and over his clawing inquisitive fingers. He sat there with his face screwed into the very mask of agony, and screamed horribly—till my second blow got him in the windpipe, which effectually silenced him.

Leaving my now helpless enemy I made for the window and, scrambling over the washhand stand regardless of the falling crockery,

I made my escape into the gutter. Here I found that windows to the right and left of me also opened on to this gutter, and I at once realized that it would be unsafe to remain there, so scrambled up the tiles to the ridge of the roof, along which I proceeded to make my way at my best speed. Whilst doing this I became aware of the fact that there were two roof ridges to these houses, between which ran a valley along which progress would be much quicker. I therefore slid down the tiles into this valley and started running thus between the roofs. I had not gone very far when I ran full tilt into a uniformed constable, who immediately collared me and told me to consider myself under arrest. He made quite sure that I realized my condition by handcuffing me, in spite of my explanation that it was unnecessary to do so.

In due course I was handed over to another policeman, who had joined his companion on the roofs, and passed from one to another down the stairs through a neighbouring house, and so to the Police station. It was only after the arrival of Superintendent Gilcrest that I was released.

The opportune arrival of the constables was entirely due to the importance placed on my very urgent message, on the receipt of which Mr. Gilcrest had organized the raid, completely surrounding the house with Police. This raid was entirely successful in capturing all the headquarters members of the organization. It was discovered from papers found there that they had been dealing not only with drugs but also opium. The Police were able to make a large haul that night, as lists of the distributors and agents had been carefully kept at Draycott Avenue—and all were rounded up before daybreak. Long Li received a lighter sentence than would otherwise have been the case, owing to his having been completely blinded by my fortunate blow.

The London Police were very grateful to me for my services in this connection, though, as Superintendent Gilcrest pointed out to me, it was really owing to my foolish mistake in trying to shadow the Italian that success had been achieved, and that if it had not been for the perfect organization of Scotland Yard disaster would have overtaken me. My mission having now been accomplished, I returned to France.

Chapter 14

I FOUND MY UNIT BILLETED near the town of Bethune, living in long Nissen huts, which looked like half-submerged drainpipes. The reports which I received from my Japanese assistants showed that they had succeeded in weeding out one or two undesirable characters during my absence, but were really of very little interest. The next day I was with a detachment who were renewing the foundations of a road which had been made leading across the fields to a new bridge over the La Bassee Canal. This wooden bridge had been built here to be out of rifle range from the Germans, and to relieve some of the night traffic from the ruined and repaired Pont Fixe at Cuinchy. The Pont Fixe was in any case a dangerous crossing owing to its proximity to the front line. All that prevented snipers making it impassable to daylight foot traffic was the sacking screen, suspended from the one undamaged iron girder, which prevented them seeing their targets. In these circumstances this new bridge was little short of a necessity.

During the morning I was surprised to be addressed in Malay, and turning, found myself confronting no less a person than Colonel Munroe's second son Arthur, who was a Lieutenant in the Artillery. He had heard from his father of my present employment, and had been more or less on the look-out for me whenever he saw Chinese labourers at work. Needless to say I was overjoyed thus to meet him and see that he was so far safe. He was on his way to an observation post at Givenchy, but told me to come and see him the next afternoon at his dugout, the situation of which he pointed out to me from where we were standing.

The prospect of this visit cheered me up tremendously, and next afternoon I gave myself leave and made my way to his dugout in the fields near Annequin. This habitation was miscalled a dugout, as it was really only one-quarter dugout and three-quarters built up. It was impossible to dig deeper hereabouts without finding water, owing to the nature of the ground, and to get sufficient head room sandbag walls had to be built. This one stood at the edge of a field quite near to a small farmhouse, and was disguised as a manure heap—as Mr. Munroe humorously pointed out!

We had a long talk, and I had tea with him. His battery of guns was situated at the front edge of a wood nearby, and his mess was in one of the houses in the neighbouring village. It was a very pleasant afternoon, and not the least pleasant part of it was his promise to show me something of the front line from their observation posts on the morrow. I was to meet him at the wooden bridge at seven o'clock.

Next morning we started off from the bridge and, passing a large engineers' dump behind an estaminet on the canal bank, entered a communication trench which led us tortuously to the ruined village of Givenchy. This was my first close view of really extensive ruination, and you may well easily guess how amazed I was by the sight. Better pens than mine have described such scenes, so I will not attempt any description of the devastation which surrounded me. It is sufficient to say that our course led us through part of the ruins, and then by a trench, roofed over with hurdles, which had been cut through the graveyard to the church. This roofed trench was an awe-inspiring path. Sticking out of the walls on either hand were the crumbling remains of coffins and their contents, which had been ruthlessly cut through in its formation; thus showing that the stern necessities of war had brought home to man a fact which in times of peace he is apt to overlook, namely, that the preservation of the living is more important than the sanctity of the dead.

I thought of the lesson of this trench when I heard of the serious chill which the King-Emperor had caught through standing bareheaded at the Cenotaph in London; and I sorrowfully realized that mankind, however civilized, is slow to benefit from the lessons which experience has taught him.

We came out of this trench behind the one remaining buttress of the ruined church wall, and found ourselves at the mouth of a dugout situated between this buttress and the shattered remains of the tower. In this haunted spot the officer on duty at the observation post, together with his staff of telephonists, spent their nights: and it was with a shiver that I contemplated these doings—sharing the mould, as they did, with their ghastly mouldering companions through the dark hours—and was glad that the nature of my services did not impose this grim experience on me.

At the foot of the tower a hole had been broken through the wall to the staircase. Ascending the few remaining steps we passed through a trap-door in a wooden platform on to which we mounted, closing the door beneath our feet. We were now in the artillery observation post, the outlook from which was made through a telescope that was suspended in a small funnel-shaped hole which penetrated the wall. Looking through this opening a wonderful view lay before my eyes. Arthur Munroe pointed out the various objects of interest to me.

In the immediate foreground was our front line trench, separated from that of the Germans, who were only a few yards distant, by masses of barbed wire. Through the telescope the German trenches seemed so near that it was as though one was sitting in the circle of a theatre and seeing them on the stage. In the distance, to the left, was a pinkish patch of broken ground which, I was told, was the village of Violanes. Nearer, a row of jagged, torn tree stumps, which were called the Cantileux Fringe. In the middle distance, straight to our front, surrounded by the seemingly empty fields of rank, coarse grass stood the ruined wayside shrine which was suspected of being an enemy observation post; and to its right the tall tree trunk which, from its indestructibility, was thought to be a disguised mast of steel used for the same purposes. Immediately below us there was the crater between the front lines, for the possession of which so many lives had been sacrificed on both sides, and which was now a pit completely full of rusty wire.

Even two German snipers' posts were pointed out. As I watched one of them, a hand rose into view and took down a can which had been standing behind some sandbags on a plank bridging the sap which formed the post. Evidently the sniper was thirsty! Mr. Munroe told me that he had seen both of these snipers so repeatedly that, if he met either of them after the war, he would be able to recognize him at once! For the purposes of reference he had christened them, in his lighthearted way, Hans Voglestein and Fritz Steubler respectively.

Either of these men could have been shot from this observation post with the greatest of ease, but he explained to me that if an observation post was used for any such purpose, it would certainly not be permitted to stand. It was only by leaving it a matter of doubt, to the Germans, whether a building was being used for observation purposes or not, that buildings could be so used. Once it was a matter of certainty, they would suffer such a bombardment that they would no longer be of any service. Shooting from them would definitely label them to the enemy as dangerous structures, and therefore could not be permitted in any circumstances. He had, however, spent a long time with the machine-gun officer of the infantry holding the line, in trying to get the machine-guns trained on to these two snipers from other positions, so far, unfortunately, without success.

From Givenchy we had a long walk, through the second line trenches, and here I saw my first casualty; and a sufficiently grim one it was, being two dripping sandbags on a stretcher, containing all that was left of a soldier who had been the unfortunate recipient of a direct hit by a trench mortar bomb.

We came out on to the canal bank just beside some lock gates, across the back of which a footbridge had been constructed, and, crossing this, we were soon in the next observation post, which was known as the "Cowl House". This building had been a brewery, and a large part of it lay in ruins, but one corner remained more or less intact.

Mounting by the staircase, and finally climbing a wooden ladder, we found ourselves amongst the rafters of the roof where, by stepping in front of a piece of hanging canvas, we looked out through the broken slates over the field of battle. We were not so near the front line here, but having nothing but the flimsy red tiles between oneself and the rifles of the Germans gave one a feeling of insecurity and discomfort which one had not experienced behind the sturdy walls of the church tower.

Here again I had the objects of interest pointed out: La Bassee far across the fields; the railway triangle with its ruined rolling stock; the indestructible brick stacks on our right, which Mr. Munroe assured me were honeycombed with observation posts, and yet which no amount of artillery fire would obliterate; and on our side the tremendous sandbag fortification forming a strong point by the canal bank.

While we were here one of the Captains of Mr. Munroe's battery arrived to 'do a shoot', and I was privileged to watch the process of a British battery registering a target. The process consisted of sending curt, cryptic corrections over the telephone after each shell had exploded. It was a grand sight there in the sunshine to see the columns of black earth, mixed with debris of all sorts, thrown up by each succeeding shell.

The magic words "Register. Target No. 52. A 1.6, B 4.1. North end of solid line of trucks" were only sent over the telephone after we had witnessed a most marvellous spectacle. Suddenly, from the black line of railway trucks sprang the usual tall column, but this time, instead of it being enveloped in a cloud of tawny smoke as usual, it expanded into a sheet of rolling flame which spread wider and ever wider. Upwards and outwards it spread, further and yet further, this appalling canopy of fire till, aghast, one felt that it would envelop the whole horizon. I thought the shell had hit a store of the enemy's ammunition, but they explained that it was merely the burning of the dust thrown up by the shell from a coal-laden truck which we had seen. Practically we had just witnessed in the open air of a summer's morning a demonstration of the physics of that dread catastrophe, a coalmine explosion.

This "Cowl House" was used by a number of batteries of all calibres, and when we came downstairs again Arthur Munroe took me into the cellars to see the night quarters of those on duty there. The cellars were dotted with mattresses and furniture retrieved from the ruined houses. The most incongruous adjunct to this scene of discomfort was a large and decorative piano, which he told me was a 'perfect godsend' during the evenings, when, with plenty of candles burning, this gloomy vault became one of the gayest cabarets in France—where all sorts of unexpected talent was displayed.

We left this place through a small orchard at the back of it, and again diving into the trenches we made our way to a house standing at the side of the Bethune-La Bassee Road. Before entering this house we passed a tremendous sandpit, the significance of which I did not realize until we had passed through the back door. Here we were fronted by an immense pyramid of sandbags occupying the whole interior area of the house.

We climbed the back of this pyramid by a ladder, and on its flat top, under the slates, found a little three-sided room also constructed out of sandbags. The back wall was missing to form the entrance, and across the front wall ran a narrow slit, from which we could look through the badly broken slate roof in front of us over to the German lines, which were here also a considerable distance from us. Mr. Munroe explained that the front of the house was very largely a ruin, and that leaning against the pyramid of sandbags were the various floors, this disguising the solidity of the present structure from German eyes.

Here he again pointed out features of the landscape. Between the opposing front lines here was a broad strip of 'no man's land', which increased in width from left to right of our view. Over there were the remains of the British aeroplane which had crashed on this dangerous strip. Far to our right was 'Mad Point', a German stronghold of some note. The buildings of Auchy lay straight in front of us, and were all considered worthy targets; owing to the distance the view from this observation post presented but little of detailed interest to an outside spectator like myself. From this post he sent me back, with a telephonist as guide, through the communication trenches to my working party near the canal.

I describe this day's outing in some detail, not only in grateful memory of Mr. (now Captain) Munroe's kindness, but also because it was the most comprehensive view of a section of the front which I ever had.

* * *

Whilst we kept our coolies concentrated in their camp area so far as possible, they were not of course prisoners, and parties of them were more or less continually on leave in the evenings visiting the local estaminets, and could even wander so far afield as the town of Bethune. Here lay the danger of espionage. Working as we were, constantly either on the roads or handling stores and ammunition, an intelligent man in our gangs could accumulate in a very short time a vast amount of information regarding both infantry units and the number and nature of guns in our area.

There were quite a number of our Chinese who had worked in Saigon, and who consequently spoke French fluently. This language was completely foreign to both my Japanese helpers and myself when we first landed, and this rendered our work doubly difficult as regards these men, but by dint of studying hard we rapidly came to understand it, and even became fairly fluent speakers.

We soon noticed that these men were in the habit, when in Bethune, of frequenting a house near the railway station with what seemed suspicious regularity; but on having the matter sifted by the military police, a perfectly reasonable explanation was provided and the patriotism of the inhabitants vouched for—though their morals were hardly so unassailable.

Work went on very peacefully, and apart from unexciting investigations such as the above, and occasionally being shelled whilst at work by the pictorially named 'woolly bears' or the onomatopoetic 'crumps', nothing that would be of interest to the general reader occurred. Every now and then we were moved from place to place as occasion demanded. Sometimes we were engaged on constructing light railways near the front line, sometimes far back handling ammunition and stores—but our various moves and employments would make a wearisome catalogue.

* * *

For some time I had been suspicious of an exceptionally tall and well-built man, by the name of Ah Sing. From time to time he had seemed to me to display an intelligence far superior to his apparent status, yet on further conversation he would appear to be as ignorant as his fellows. I drafted my Japanese, one after the other, into the same working party as this man in an endeavour to find out more about him, but it was not until the third of them had been working with him for over three weeks that I first heard anything more definitely suspicious concerning him. All that I then learnt was that he had once been employed, in some capacity unnamed, in the batteries at Kiao-Chau.

We were at that time working hard at getting up artillery and stores for another advance, and in consequence it was even more important than usual that secrecy should be maintained; I decided, therefore, never to let this man out of my sight, and endeavour to trip him up should he actually be engaged in espionage. Unfortunately, circumstanced as we were, it was well-nigh impossible to do this without raising his suspicions, and this, as it transpired, I undoubtedly did.

At the time I did not realize this important fact, and it was by the merest good fortune that I succeeded in thwarting him when it came to the point. At that time Amiens was our nearest town of any size, and each of our men got a chance of visiting it, according to the leave roster, about once in every three weeks. It so happened that Ah Sing had missed his last visit owing to a disciplinary punishment inflicted by the officer in charge of his company, and since then he had been daily trying to arrange to substitute himself for one or other of the men whose turn it was. Needless to say a quiet word from myself, or one of my subordinates to the authorities, was sufficient to ensure that he should not succeed in this endeavour. His anxiety struck me as unnatural and, as it increased daily, I became more convinced that this detention was preventing him from keeping an appointment with a German agent that he had been due to meet in Amiens, and to whom he wanted to pass over the valuable information he had doubtless acquired.

This, then, was the position when one evening I watched him making up a bundle from the contents of his ditty bag, and followed him as he left the hut with this tucked under his arm. He strolled into the local estaminet, and there not only had a drink but made several purchases, which he stuffed into his pockets. Coming out he turned to the left down the village street, and was some three hundred yards or more ahead of me when he suddenly jumped on to a despatch rider's motor bicycle which was standing at the roadside, and flew off along the road leading to Amiens.

He thus put me in a quandary, and I started running after him, reaching the corner just in time to see him take the first turning to the left from the direct Amiens road. At this corner I was lucky enough to find a Triumph motor cycle standing, which I hastily commandeered for my own use, setting off in pursuit. Following him into the side road, I found that it was in no condition for speedy work; being nearly bumped off the saddle before I realized that it was a case of 'more haste less speed', and slowed down. I could not see Ah Sing, but could hear his machine thudding away ahead of me, and as we got into the country I had no doubt but that I could keep on his heels with ease unless his bicycle proved very much more efficient than my own, which seemed to be practically a new machine.

I did not know the geography of the district very well, but realized, from the direction he was taking, that it was not Amiens that he was making for, and after we had been twisting and turning through endless side roads, I began to think that he was making for Paris. At one place we came out on to a long, straight, well-paved road; here, as I bumped along the side road, I heard the fugitive speeding rapidly along till I feared he would go beyond my hearing.

When I reached the corner I stopped my machine in order to listen better and, to my dismay, could hear nothing of him, so mounting again I raced down the road for some miles and again stopped to listen; still there was no sound of the bicycle whose note I had already learnt to recognize, and I had almost come to the conclusion that he had either outdistanced me completely, or had hidden himself at the roadside as I sped past—though I had been careful in my look-out lest such a trick was practised on me.

Almost despairing with these gloomy thoughts, I sat on my silent machine wondering what I should do next, when to my joy I heard his machine start off again, only a comparatively short distance ahead. Evidently he had had some sort of a breakdown, owing to overspeeding, which he had now put right. Once more the chase continued. Sure enough, it was Paris he was making for, and we entered the outskirts of that city before midnight.

Here again I mysteriously lost track of my quarry, and had to stop at the city gates completely baffled. I realized that it was perhaps five minutes ago since my ear had lost the regular beat of his machine, and I carefully thought over all that I had seen on the road during the last mile or so. The only picture which seemed to mean anything was that of a French officer of the Chasseurs d'Afrique standing in the lighted doorway of a garage. Like a flash it came to me that this was Ah Sing! The bundle he had taken with him under his arm had contained this disguise, and the spell of silence on the road was when he had been quickly changing! Doubtless his Labour Battalion uniform was now lying in the ditch at the roadside! So soon as I saw the truth I dashed back to the garage where, beyond confirming the fact that this Moroccan officer had bought petrol for his bicycle, they could only tell me that he had taken the road to Nogent.

Hastily buying a tin of petrol, I tied it on my carrier and broke the record along the same road until at last I heard the familiar sound away in front of me. I immediately stopped and altered the sound of my machine by kicking the end of the silencer almost flat. Then feeling safe from recognition, I speeded up and drew fairly close, though do what I could I found it impossible to overtake the man in front of me.

We drove all through the night in this manner till, just as day was breaking, he put on a spurt in which I found myself being gradually left behind, so much so that eventually I lost the sound of Ah Sing's bicycle in the distance at about six o'clock. I was not at all sure whether this was because he had passed beyond my hearing or because he had stopped again. I raced on madly, keeping my eyes busy on the roadside to see if he had turned off anywhere, but saw no signs of this as I flew along.

Presently I turned a corner into a small village, where I was surprised to find the road blocked by having a farm cart drawn across it from side to side. Jamming on my brakes fiercely, I just managed to stop as I reached this obstacle, and was at once surrounded by an excited crowd of peasants, who immediately seized me and dragged me from my machine. They hustled me roughly into the garden before the largest of the miserable houses which composed this tiny village, and here I was confronted by a rustic decorated with a tricolour scarf, who proclaimed himself to be the Maire.

As everybody was talking at once, it took me some time before I got a clear idea of exactly what had happened, and why I was being treated thus. At length, however, I understood that Ah Sing had stopped in the village and told them that there was a deserter coming along the road on a motor bicycle, whom they must seize and hold for the military authorities. He had superintended the placing of the farm cart across the road, and then said that, in order to save time, he would hurry off to Dijon which, it appeared, was the next large town along the road, and arrange for a military escort to be sent out for me.

Nothing I could say would convince the Maire of the real truth. "Had he not himself received orders from a Capitaine in the armies of glorious France, and who was this queer foreigner who accused Monsieur le Capitaine of lying?" This seemed to be his line of argument. My police pass, and other papers which I had with me he brushed aside with contempt, hardly, deigning to look at them. Indeed, I strongly suspect that, in spite of his official position, this bucolic dignitary could not have read them even if he had tried!

"He had been ordered to keep me in custody, and keep me in custody he would. Those in authority, who were coming, would investigate all these matters which I was referring to. In the meantime they were none of his business, and in any case they were probably all lies. Prisoners always told lies, and I was a prisoner, was I not?" therefore, obviously, what I was saying was nothing but lies. This argument was entirely convincing to his rude mind, and I found all my protests unavailing.

To be perfectly fair to the man, I certainly must have appeared a fishy customer. I was obviously of an entirely unknown nationality, wearing an entirely unknown uniform and talking a French the accent of which I have no doubt proclaimed me as something exotic. In view of all these circumstances I can sympathize with his action when I look back on it, but at the time I was merely exasperated by his besotted foolishness.

I was duly haled off and incarcerated in a small outbuilding, which by its smells and stains I took to be the village slaughter-house. It was an oblong chamber of about fifteen by ten feet, against the end of a farmhouse. In the stout rafters of its lean-to roof were hooks, which confirmed my original impression of the uses to which the building was put, and on the three outward sides alternate bricks had been removed from the walls, in a diamond-shaped pattern, to act by way of ventilators and windows combined.

This little room stood at the entrance to the farmyard, one of the gateposts being, in fact, fastened against the right-hand corner of its wall. From the right-hand ventilator I looked out on to the village street, from that on the left I could see my motor bicycle standing forlornly beside a manure heap, and from the front openings I viewed the gateway beside which my guards were standing. The door was a substantial affair, and appeared to be bolted on the outside. Very little examination convinced me that it was useless to attempt breaking out by this exit.

That the peasants did not mean to be unkind was proved when, after I had been shut up for about half an hour, one of them appeared bringing me a bowl of quite passable coffee and a larger crock containing a sort of hash, from which I made an excellent breakfast. After this very welcome refreshment I turned my attention seriously to the matter of escape. I preferred to return to my unit, unsuccessful though I was, by my own volition rather than being taken back ignominiously as a suspected deserter!

From the conversations I had overheard through my airy ventilators, I had learnt that only one man could be spared from the fields to guard me, and by observation I noticed that the whole place seemed to be deserted, except for a few children and the rustic, armed with a billhook, who sat on the top bar of the open gate in front of my door. From his position he could only see the front of the building, and I therefore commenced carefully digging out the top brick of the left-hand ventilator pattern.

I found the mortar quite soft, and with my penknife I managed to remove the brick quite silently in a very short time. Once this had been done the removal of the other bricks was almost as easy as if they had been merely laid there without mortar at all. I removed them all carefully, and was then left with a diamond-shaped opening more than sufficiently large for me to clamber through. However, it was no good my climbing out whilst my guard remained where he was, as I should have been instantly spotted.

Replacing the bricks carefully in their position so that all appeared normal, I then turned my attention to the roadway. Here I saw some children playing on the other side of the road almost directly opposite my prison. Knowing what children are, and having in my pocket a number of bright new ten-centime pieces, I threw one of these into the dust across the road, as far to my right as possible. This having been successfully accomplished without having drawn any attention, it was followed by three or four more. I then commenced to lay my trail. The next couple of coins I threw not so far to the right; a few more at still less an acute angle, and finally one or two just to the right of the children. This exhausted my stock and I sat down, patiently waiting to see whether my ruse would succeed.

Sure enough, after about a quarter of an hour one of the little ones found a coin. Like hens running to corn, the others immediately gathered to the spot, and there were soon joyous cries as more coins were found. As I had expected, the mention of money attracted the attention of my guard, who vacated his position and hastened across the road to join in the search. Before he had even left the gate I was hastily dismantling my brick pattern again, and by the time he was half-way across the road I dived through my opening into the farmyard.

Quickly examining my bicycle and flooding the carburettor, I quietly pushed it as near to the gate as I dared, close to the wall of my prison, and then, risking all, ran it as rapidly as I could diagonally out on to the road, and mounted with a flying start. I was too busy scorching to look over my shoulder, but I have no doubt that it was a very astonished sentry who picked up the remaining coins.

I was now once again following the road taken by Ah Sing, and expected to find my way to Dijon without difficulty, whence, I thought, I might as well take the train back to Amiens. I entered the town in well under an hour where, as my chase had been fruitless and I had had a very tiring night of it, I thought that I might as well have a sleep before enquiring about the trains. I turned into the first side street after I had reached this decision and commenced looking for a suitable small hotel, till I presently found myself outside the Belle Savoyarde.

Leaving my bicycle in the street, I had no difficulty in engaging a room here, and was told that I could wheel my bicycle through the archway to the left of the hotel, where I would find an excellent stable in which to house it. This I did and, to my amazement, found the stable already occupied by a motor bicycle which I was almost sure I recognized as that of Ah Sing. Hastily entering the back door, I asked the landlord to whom the other bicycle belonged. He told me that it was the property of a Captain of the Chasseurs d'Afrique who had arrived that morning and was now asleep in room No. 3.

You can well imagine my surprise and delight at thus having kept on his track entirely by accident! At last I had him! I hurried out of the hotel, to make my way to the Police station. As I bustled along I suddenly bethought me of my morning's experiences; supposing Ah Sing had really done what he had promised to do? Suppose that he had been to the Police station and had denounced me there as a deserter? What would be my reception when I turned up with my story, demanding his immediate arrest? In any case, would they not probably detain me whilst they enquired into the genuineness of my credentials, thus giving Ah Sing time to disappear again?

I decided that it would be unsafe for me to approach the Police here, where possibly Monsieur le Capitaine had got his word in first, and as I felt quite sure that he would now be resting, in the firm belief that he had successfully shaken off all pursuit, I decided to keep on his heels until we reached a place where I could be the one to give the first word of accusation! I stood still as I reached this conclusion and, by a strange coincidence, found myself in front of a shop displaying motorists' equipment.

Nothing could have suited me better, so I entered forthwith and bought a pair of goggles mounted on a broad leather strap, and a light blue waterproof hat-covering which had a flap at the back which folded down and fastened across the chin; of the same material they had also waterproof overalls, a suit of which I added to my purchases, together with a pair of large gauntleted gloves. When I was dressed in these, only a small part of my nose and mouth would be visible and, as it would be quite impossible for even my best friend to have recognized me, I felt sure that Ah Sing would be unable to do so.

That he might recognize my bicycle, however, was possible, but I considered it extremely unlikely since the only view he had had of it was when I had passed him, in the dark, outside the garage near Paris. I decided that it would be perfectly safe for me to risk recognition on the road, but I thought it would be unwise to leave my mount standing where he could examine it closely when getting his own machine—the mere fact of it being a Triumph was enough to arouse his suspicions.

So, on returning to the hotel, I pushed my bicycle into a small room which had doubtless been a harness-room in coaching days, but had now sunk to the position of a general lumber room, and I had to remove a litter of gardening tools, boxes of earth, flower pots, and the like, before I could make a clear space on the floor on which to stand it. Closing the door carefully I then went to my chamber, which I was pleased to find was one overlooking the yard. Having reached the seclusion of this room without having been seen, I decided that it would be foolhardy to risk a casual meeting and recognition by appearing in the public rooms, so I ordered up a meal, which I ate in privacy.

Before seeking my sleep, I still had something else to do, however. The room which had been given to me was No. 5, and was immediately across the corridor from that occupied by Ah Sing. If I was to sleep peacefully I must first arrange some method of knowing when he left his room. As both our doors were the last in a corridor which ended in a window, it seemed extremely unlikely that anybody would be passing them. I felt inclined merely to fasten a thread to his door handle, the other end of which I could attach to my toe and thus ensure being awakened when his door opened. This would have served, but I realized that he might notice the jerk of the breaking thread, and seeing the remnant attached to his door handle, would become suspicious; I therefore arranged things differently.

I went down to the lumber-room and brought back a flower pot. I then fastened one end of a thread to the nail which held back the curtains of the window, passed the thread over the handle of Ah Sing's door and back along the wall to the window, immediately outside of which I suspended the flower pot by it, closing the window again to within less than half an inch of the bottom. In this way, when the thread was broken by the opening door, one end of the thread would fall amongst the folds of the curtain and the other be drawn through the open window by the falling flower pot.

As I am a very light sleeper and have, moreover, trained myself to waken at any expected noise, I felt quite confident of being roused by the flower pot shattering in the yard, just round the corner from my open window. At the same time, the noise caused being seemingly so far away from him, it would not seem at all suspicious to my enemy. Having arranged this, I threw myself on my bed and enjoyed my well-earned sleep.

When I woke again it was with the crash of the flower pot still sounding in my ears, and looking at my watch I saw that it was a quarter-past six. I at once put on my blue motoring costume and fitted my hat cover. As things turned out, however, I need not have been in such a hurry, for the gallant Captain was merely ordering a meal, and I had to sit on my bed till almost seven o'clock waiting for him to finish. Eventually, however, I heard him talking to the landlord in the yard, and was pleased to hear him enquiring his way to Besancon.

This confirmed the idea, which had been growing upon me, that he was bound for Switzerland; not only this, but he had thus made it very much easier for me to pursue him, since I could now make my way to this city direct, without actually keeping on his tracks and, at any rate as far as possible, there was no need for him to see anything of the blue bird which would be flying after him!

Waiting until I heard his machine starting off in the road, I descended the stairs, and having received a packet of sandwiches which I had ordered from the landlord to be ready for me, I settled my account and set forth once again on my pursuit. It was my intention to reach Besancon if possible before Ah Sing, and have the Police there waiting for his arrival. I had heard the landlord directing him to go by Montmirey Road "since, although longer, it was a better road than that past Pontaille", so I decided to take the latter route, and, pressing forward, make certain of reaching Besancon first.

I sped along the road at a grand pace, and finding nothing to complain about in its condition, laughed to think how out-of-date the landlord's information evidently was. At the rate I was covering the ground I felt that I would have no difficulty in far outdistancing anyone who had taken a longer way. After leaving Pontaille, however, I was not quite so amused, for the road became steadily worse and worse, till it degenerated into one which would not have been tolerated in any part of the back-of-the-front which I have seen. Unless I risked breaking my machine at every yard, I did not dare to travel at more than what seemed to be a veritable snail's pace, and my hope of forestalling the fugitive became less and less with every bumpy mile I covered. This bad patch seemed to go on interminably, and it was nearly ten o'clock when I again reached a good surface on the outskirts of Besancon.

Passing directly through the town, I started making my enquiries for the Moorish Captain at the eastern exits, and after about half an hour's anxious and very delicate questioning, learnt that he had taken the road to Pontarlier. I lost no time in pursuing him, and risked my neck momentarily by flying along a road which was entirely unknown to me, at a speed which would have been risky on a race track. However, I arrived safely at my destination and again heard that my quarry was ahead of me, but this time only by a quarter of an hour. He had evidently stopped somewhere in the town, either to refill or have another meal.

We were now nearing the frontier, and I pressed on anxiously along the road to the north-east which Ah Sing had taken.

Making an 'S' bend downhill, the road turned at the foot over a hump-backed stone bridge, and as it climbed again at the far side I noticed, as I flashed past, a white patch on the wooden railings which here formed the left boundary of the road. I had gone some distance up-hill before the possible meaning of this became a conscious thought. When it did so I stopped my machine and returned to investigate. My unconscious mind had registered this impression correctly; for I found that the white patch was, indeed, the newly-broken end of a rail, and on closer inspection I saw the tracks of a motor bicycle which had been wheeled through the gap thus formed. Parking my machine carefully amongst the trees on the other side of the road I followed these tracks, which led me to the brink of a cliff.

I scrambled down the bank where it was less precipitous, and returning along the bottom found the motor bicycle lying in the bed of a stream, where it had evidently been thrown from the rocky bank above. Sure enough, it was my old friend, but there was no sign of its rider. Once more I was on the right track, and this time in circumstances which were much more congenial to me. The thick woods with which the valley of this stream was clothed were but a feeble imitation of the jungle I knew so well, and it was child's play to me to find Ah Sing's booted trail where he had entered the timber at a spot near to the place at which I had parked my bicycle.

Before starting to follow him I stripped off my blue coverings, my goggles, and my boots, and made a hasty bundle of these impedimenta, which I strapped to my machine. I also took off my revolver belt from its position under my trousers, strapped it round my tunic, and saw that the revolver was fully loaded and ready for immediate use. Then I took up the trail. He seemed to be making straight up the valley, and I concluded that the frontier-line must run along the watershed from which this stream flowed. I had always understood that the frontiers were very closely guarded, and intended, therefore, to try to find these guards and make such a disturbance with Ah Sing in their neighbourhood, that both of us would be arrested by them.

Having reached this decision I determined to take the risk of possibly losing Ah Sing, and pressed rapidly forward without making any attempt at following his footsteps—hoping to get within hearing distance of him by this means. My method was to hurry forward for perhaps a quarter of a mile, then stand still and listen. After I had progressed up-hill some miles in this fashion, and was beginning to fear that I had risked too much by doing so, I was gratified to hear undoubted signs of him. These noises came, however, from the other side of the stream, which he had evidently crossed lower down. The valley had by now narrowed down to almost the dimensions of a glen, and his progress was clearly audible through the still night.

As he was making steadily up-stream, I felt justified in going forward and meeting him when he emerged from the head of the ravine. Since I was going barefooted I could afford to do this without any danger of warning him of my presence, so I proceeded to put this plan into execution. It was a steep climb up the hill, and the timber petered out before the sides of the gorge closed in on each other, the stream continuing upwards at the foot of a bare rocky chasm.

It was a bright moonlight night, and it now became necessary for me to take every precaution against being seen. We were evidently nearing the watershed, and I anxiously scanned the crags ahead in the hope of seeing the expected frontier posts. Up and up I went, from time to time halting and hearing the noise of hobnails scraping on rocks behind me. Ah Sing was evidently doing as I had anticipated, and I felt quite satisfied that I could lead his way for him. The linn in which the diminished stream now ran rose higher and higher, steeper and steeper, till finally it reared itself on end and the trickle became an attenuated waterfall—and still no sign of the frontier posts.

The climbing soon became almost perpendicular, and the stream's bed a mere cleft in a precipice. The moon was almost setting when at last I saw the lights of the guard-house for which I had been keeping such an anxious look-out. I went forward until I was within about five hundred yards of the post, and there I sat down to wait for the spy. I had evidently far outdistanced him, as only the faintest noises of his advance reached me where I sat. The moon had set, it was completely dark, and nearly five o'clock in the morning before at last I heard him labouring up the final climb. Soon he evidently saw the lights, as I had done, and he was instantly silent. Presently, however, he was on the move again. His time of silence had presumably been occupied in taking off his boots, and from the nature of the noises which I now heard bearing off to my right, I judged that he was proceeding to do the remainder of his journey on hands and knees.

I crept silently to my right and took up my position behind a rock directly in the path he seemed to be taking, and there I waited his approach with my revolver in my hand—I was going to run no risks of his escaping! Sure enough, he came quietly on and crept past the end of my rock, little knowing that I was within a foot of him. I watched his cautious progress with interest, and when his feet were on a level with me, reached forward and, pressing the trigger firmly, blew off his right heel.

The sound of this shot caused great excitement amongst the guards, as I had expected, and guided by the agonized shrieks of the disabled scoundrel at my feet, some three or four of them ran towards us holding their rifles at the 'ready'. Not wishing to be shot I ran to meet them, calling to them in French that I had wounded a spy. Needless to say they made a prisoner of me, but I did not mind that since Ah Sing was also taken into custody. The guards took sufficient notice of what I said to strip us both of all our papers and possessions before doing anything else.

Later on that morning we were both taken down to the Commandant, where on investigation I was of course released, and where sufficient evidence was found amongst Ah Sing's papers to prove that he was a German spy. As a result of which he received some more bullets—but this time not in such a safe place as his heel.

When I returned to my unit I found myself under arrest for purloining the motor bicycle, which I had brought back with me. It was, of course, a merely formal affair and entirely secret. But I was nevertheless duly court-martialed and the verdict given that, in the circumstances, I had been entitled to act as I did. If my mission had not ended successfully I wonder whether this decision would have been given by the court?

Chapter 15

LIFE IN THE LABOUR CORPS went on as usual, with the customary petty enquiries and investigations regarding thefts and other small crimes which had been laid to the door of my iniquitous flock. It is a strange thing, but nevertheless true, that if there is a labour battalion of Chinese billeted in a district, all these misdemeanours entirely cease amongst the other units in the area! Any crime which is reported is one which has been committed by the Chinks. If there is a hundredweight of corrugated iron missing from a goods yard—the Chinks have got it! If there are eighty standards of four-by-four timber short on the waybill—the Chinks have got it! These same malefactors will also have stolen bags of cement, loads of gravel, planks, coils of barbed wire, wheels, bandages, and even motor lorries!

If these reports were all true, the Chinks had collected enough material in my area alone to build a second Pekin in northern France. However obviously untrue such a charge was, it had nevertheless to be investigated and reported on, all of which kept me and my assistants busy. Many of the charges of course dealt with foodstuffs—cases of bully beef, Tickler or Maconochie; tins of biscuits, sacks of potatoes, and the like—in which cases the charge was as often as not proved to be true, and a lot of our time was spent in ferreting out the culprits. There were also a number of cases dealing with infractions of the moral law which required, if anything, even more delicate investigation—but of these I do not wish to speak further.

This employment, though of serious enough importance to me (for of course it all had to be done without letting our fellow-workmen know from whom the authorities received the information on which they acted), nevertheless is not the sort of material which is of use to an autobiographist—the petty details of his daily employment being the last thing which the public wishes to read about.

Of the panic which occurred in the labour ranks when the Germans broke through in 1918, I do not propose to write. The happenings in my surroundings, though of intense interest to me, were only a microscopic part of a whole which I did not know then, and which has been described in detail so ably by others since, that even if I had seen it all, any attempted description by me would be a mere 'painting the lily'. It is sufficient to say that I had the greatest satisfaction of shooting down several Germans, from a shell hole which I occupied during a long evening in company with a dead British soldier whose rifle I used for the purpose, before following the mass of my fleeing companions when darkness fell. Situated as I was, I could not appear to be different from my fellow-workmen without destroying my usefulness.

I have always been grateful to the Germans for breaking through as they did on that occasion. Had they not done so, I would never have had any opportunity of shooting one. There is no denying the fact that however useful to your country your work may be; however many lives you may save by your exertions; however many secrets you may protect inviolate from the enemy, there is no satisfaction in the knowledge of these things to equal the glow of triumphant exultation which you feel when you actually can see your enemy's warm blood run red at your own hands; and I am eternally grateful that I was permitted to have this supreme satisfaction, without which I would have felt myself to have been robbed of something during the War.

* * *

When the Allied advance had definitely started I was once more sent for by Scotland Yard, where I reported myself to my old friend Superintendent Gilcrest. He introduced me to Detective-Superintendent Jones of Cardiff, who had come up to London to give me my instructions.

It appeared that there was a large Asiatic population in the dock district of his city, and that the Police were convinced, from signs which they had noticed, that some plot was hatching in this quarter. Several ships had been sunk at the mouth of the Bristol Channel shortly after leaving Cardiff, and though these losses had been put down to submarine activity, nevertheless the Police were not definitely satisfied that they had not been caused by explosives concealed amongst the bunker coals. On the other hand the plotting which seemed to be going on might be in connection with the drug traffic, or again, might portend a civil uprising.

In spite of their utmost endeavours the Police had been unable to lay a finger on anything definite enough to point them in the right direction. The whole conspiracy seemed to centre round a Chinese launderer who had of late risen to mysterious affluence, but beyond this they had learnt very little about it. It was decided, therefore, to appeal to Scotland Yard for assistance in order that the investigation might be taken up by individuals definitely unknown to the local populace. Thus it was that I had been called in.

Superintendent Jones and I discussed the matter at great length and arranged that I should give up the character of Tom Mah, the half-caste Chinese, in which I was still working as a member of the Labour Battalion, and do the work simply as a Malay. There are quite a number of Malays in Cardiff, and by retaining my own nationality I need not profess a knowledge of any Chinese dialect at all, and would thus, perhaps, have an advantage in overhearing any remarks which might be made in my presence. It was therefore to be as Mat Jowa, able seaman of Malacca, latterly from South Shields, that I was to appear on the scene of my operations.

We discussed our method of communication, but as the Cardiff Police were not organized for this sort of work, there was no previously arranged scheme which we could employ, and it was necessary for Jones to return to Cardiff and see what he could arrange extemporarily. This fitted in very well, as it gave me an opportunity of dashing up to the North and becoming, at any rate superficially, acquainted with the town from which I was supposed to have reached Cardiff. Needless to say this opportunity of traversing England from end to end delighted me.

I was surprised on leaving the train at Newcastle to find that the bleak, cold North which I had expected appeared in no way different from the South which I had just left. The bright, sunny evening air was as balmy as any I had met with elsewhere in Europe, and considerably warmer than any of the days during the winter I had spent in 'sunny France'. I was almost disappointed not to find myself shivering in an icy blast.

I had been provided with a letter of introduction to the Newcastle Police, to whom I reported. I was there introduced to Sergeant Atkins, who was to act as my guide and instructor in my intensive study of South Shields. He suggested that we should start work on this in the morning, and in the meantime took me along to the room which had been engaged for me, in a hotel near Barras Bridge. On the way there he learnt how anxious I was to see as much of this northern country as I could while I had an opportunity, so he kindly offered to take me in his sidecar to see the nearest seaport town that evening.

When we had finished the meal to which I invited him at my hotel, we set off at about seven o'clock to visit Sunderland. I had not, of course, done any motoring through the country roads of England since I had done so in Colonel Munroe's car from Droitwich, and I looked forward keenly to another such delightful experience. Crossing the river, we proceeded through the slums of Gateshead, and it was not until after some two miles of this unsavoury introduction to our outing that we reached green fields at last. The country here, I found as we sped along the bumpy road, was very different to that which I had seen. In no matter which direction we looked, the grimy buildings or unsightly pitheads of a coalmine spoilt the view. Atkins was a splendid guide and pointed out all these objects of local interest almost with a touch of pride, naming each in turn—names, which, alas! I cannot recall.

Presently we passed through the pretty village of Boldon, which provided us with the only picturesque view we were to enjoy on our trip. After passing here Atkins pointed to the left, and following his indication I obtained my first view of the North Sea, seen over flat, intervening fields. We soon reached Sunderland, and passing through the main street Atkins dismounted and led me to the top of a cliff in Mowbray Park, from which eminence the whole town was laid out beneath us, and we had a view far out to sea beyond the docks and piers.

He pointed out numerous places, the names of which I have forgotten, and at my suggestion then took me down to study the dock area. Passing down Mowbray Road, and through Hendon, we passed under some railway arches and found ourselves on the dockside, which we traversed, and presently left to visit the Town Moor, the Ferry Landing in Low Street, the Shipping Office, and other places with which I as a seaman would be expected to be familiar. Climbing the steep slope of High Street, we were soon crossing the bridge on our return journey.

It was an interesting experience, and one which I thought would be of value to me in talking to the water-side population with which I would soon be mingling—though, for the purpose of pleasure only, there are places which I would rather visit. Even in the cheerful evening sunset it looked a dreary spot. I was back at my hotel and in bed by eleven o'clock—having arranged for an early start with the friendly Sergeant Atkins in the morning.

In order to let me see as much as possible of the Tyneside during the short time at our disposal, we travelled down to Tynemouth by the electric train, and Sergeant Atkins could thus give me a hasty view of this pleasant, old-fashioned town and its sordid neighbour, North Shields, before taking me across the ferry to the squalid town I was supposed to have been staying in.

Passing up Ferry Street we found ourselves almost immediately in the Market Place, but I will not weary the reader with details of our depressing wanderings. The Golden Lion Hotel provided us with our breakfast, and the Royal gave us an excellent lunch—the two cheerful moments of the day. Meanwhile we were tramping the town from end to end. Westoe Lane, Imeary Street, Fowler Street—but why go on? It is a town of mean streets, and we covered them all. In the late afternoon we went on to the neighbouring slums of Jarrow which, it appeared, anyone who had lived in South Shields would be sure to know something about. From here we took the train to Newcastle, where I bid my kind guide goodbye before packing up for my return to London, which I reached next morning.

Meeting Superintendent Jones once more, I learnt that the best arrangement he had succeeded in making was with a local ship-store merchant, a man named McPhee, whose busy store was being constantly visited by all ranks of the Merchant Marine, and to whom, therefore, my visits would be completely unremarkable. As his store could be entered from either of two streets, it was an even more suitable point for our purpose.

This man, a tall raw-boned Scotsman with ginger whiskers, whom I had no difficulty in recognizing, was a well-known character about the docks, with a catholic circle of acquaintances, and I could therefore accost him at any time in the streets without the incident appearing at all suspicious. He had agreed to pass on all messages between the Police and myself, and altogether the arrangement, at a moment's notice, was a good one—though it was far from perfect from my point of view.

In Paddington Station once more I was amused to compare my present self with the almost frightened individual who had awkwardly traversed its evil-smelling length, in search of Praed Street District Railway Station, not really so many months ago, though looking back it seemed years, so full of new sensations and impressions had the intervening interval been.

I had certainly seen life since that day. In the East End of London: crowded life—a Superintendent of a mere district in London held more life under his protection than did the Chief of the whole Federal Police at home. In the West End: leisured life—the like of which simply does not exist in Malaya. In France: concentrated life—stupendous masses of life gathered together, shaken and pressed down as it were into a uniform measure, before being poured out in red streams as a libation to the gods of war.

Life! What had I seen of it before? The crowd which made the streets of Singapore seem like a seething ant-hill would, it seemed, barely furnish forth a miserable labour battalion. In the busy mining district of Taiping—one of the most densely-populated parts of my country—there worked a number who would, I suppose, form a bare division—

and I had seen endless battalions, countless divisions, passing before my eyes daily! Thinking of these things, and wondering what new experiences were to be mine in the commercial capital of Wales, I kept myself entirely to myself in the corner seat which I had been lucky enough to get in the crowded compartment, as I was hurried to this new country.

It will not be necessary to tell British readers what a disappointment was mine when I saw this so-called capital city. It is sufficient to say that I was glad I had been prepared for the shock by my previous visits to the Tyneside. I found a room here in the "Tiger Bay" district. When I say I found a room, it would perhaps be better to explain that I found only half a room—the other occupant of the apartment being one Achmed Ali by name, a Somali.

This man, thanks to having worked as a boatman in Aden, spoke very fair English, in fact he spoke better English than the horrible 'pidgin' which was all that I admitted being capable of. He was a friendly soul, and was most useful to me in showing me the local ropes, and giving me short and remarkably pithy character studies of the more notable characters of the district. The fact that I appeared to be well in funds may, of course, have had some influence on him, but I feel sure that he would have been equally friendly had I not been in a position to entertain him as I did. As it turned out, had I not had the benefit of this man's guidance as I did, my mission to Cardiff would probably have ended disastrously before I had accomplished anything, as will be seen.

It was about ten days after my arrival, and I was beginning to find myself established amongst the motley throng, drifting daily to the shipping office in the pretence of looking for a ship, when one evening I entered Ben Said's restaurant. I call it a restaurant for so it was labelled, but as a matter of fact 'eating-house' would have been a much better description of this converted shop. The proprietor was an Arab, also hailing from Aden, and it was on Achmed's introduction to him that I first visited the place, which was a popular resort even amongst the Chinese.

On this evening, however, I was alone, and took my place at the smaller of the three tables, which was one running across the end of the room farthest from the door. I sat, as is my custom whenever possible, with my back to the room but facing a mirror. In this case the mirror happened to be a circular one, advertising I remember "Jeyes Fluid", but still, better than no mirror at all. The place was not very full when I went in, but it speedily filled up and became crowded. Amongst the customers were a few white women with their coloured paramours. Quite a number of the latest arrivals were more or less under the influence of drink, and the noise of the high-pitched conversations, in a dozen different languages and dialects, was indescribable.

It was with difficulty that I realized that I was being addressed, and I rose to my feet just as my chair was snatched away by a tremendous West African negro, who went by the name of "The Parson". Thanks to Achmed, I knew something about this man already. He claimed, probably without any foundation, to be a properly ordained priest of the Methodist Church. According to his story he had been educated at a mission station, and finally been put in charge of a small station of his own, after which, for reasons which he never clearly explained, he had given up the whole thing and gone to sea as a fireman.

When he accused me of having been 'making eyes at' the white slut who accompanied him, I was not surprised—for "The Parson" held the whole district in terror, with his immense strength and his callous brutality. He had gathered round him an international gang of sycophants who, terrified of his ferocity, were prepared to take part in any cut-throat enterprise at his mere command, depending on him for protection against reprisals. Had I not known his evil reputation I would doubtless have entered into an argument with him, for the absurdity of his claim was obvious to all; sitting facing the wall as I was I could 'make eyes' at no one—even if I had wished to do so.

Argument, however, was out of the question. "The Parson" had his regular routine of "beating up" all newcomers to the shop, to establish his authority; nothing I could have said would have averted this, but on the contrary would have merely provided a better excuse for his display of force. On this occasion, being slightly drunk, it looked as though he would make a more formidable attack than usual. I therefore said nothing, and merely shrugged my shoulders as I turned back to the table, the edge of which, however, I grasped very firmly in my hands. Looking in my mirror I saw him pull a razor from his upper waistcoat pocket. Achmed had told me that razor-slashing formed his favourite method of subjugation, so I had been on the look-out for this.

I watched him step up behind me, with an evil grin of anticipation on his sweating face, and when he had reached the appointed spot I launched my attack. With all the force which my arms, body, and leg could give it, my heel took him fair in the pit of the stomach. Letting fall his razor, he collapsed almost without a sound, and bedlam instantly broke loose.

Now, dearly as I love a fight, it is no part of my duties to run needless risk of being incapacitated for my work. Indulging myself in this respect unnecessarily is almost equivalent to absenting myself without leave.

In the circumstances in which I now found myself it was my duty to avoid further combat if possible, and it was for this reason that I dropped to the floor as soon as I saw that my blow had taken satisfactory effect. I crawled along, practically out of sight under the table, till I reached the service door, and before two minutes were past I was safe in the back lane. For some time "The Parson's" gang carried on a free fight with Ben Said and his supporters, but finding that their leader continued *hors de combat*, they were surrendering by the time the Police, who I had at once called, arrived on the scene.

After this incident I was considered rather a hero, and was made much of by everyone in the neighbourhood, especially those whose lives had been made a misery to them for so long by this bully. Until I left Cardiff "The Parson" was still in hospital, suffering from a ruptured spleen. I sincerely hope that he found this severe lesson which I had given him of benefit to him when he was well enough to rejoin his companions. This was undoubtedly the best introduction I could possibly have had for the furtherance of my enquiries, since the story of "The Parson's" downfall quickly spread, and I became, as I have said, an established favourite, being welcomed in any circle.

It did not take me long after this to get on the track of the mystery. Sure enough, there was something going on, and I would hear mysterious references to 'messengers', 'parcels', 'casks', and 'cash' almost anywhere I went amongst the Chinese, but it was a long time before I got further than this.

Mah Chang, the launderer whom the Police suspected, was particularly grateful to me for the removal of "The Parson", to whom he had had to pay a weekly subsidy under the threat of having his laundry smashed up and his customers' clothes ruined. I was therefore excellently placed to thoroughly investigate his doings, without causing him any suspicions. The extraordinary thing was that I often met Chang at Mr. McPhee's, and at first I thought that this was because he suspected me, and he was perhaps keeping me under observation, but I soon learnt that the real reason was that they could be of mutual assistance to each other in their business. Sometimes McPhee would introduce Chang as a reliable man to the captain of a ship he was storing, and sometimes Chang would be able to obtain a stores' order for Mr. McPhee from a captain whose linen he was washing.

Things seemed to have reached an *impasse* so far as I was concerned, and I regretted having given up my Chinese character. The whole thing seemed to be entirely confined to the Chinese, and they appeared to be determined to keep it, whatever it was, amongst themselves. Friendly disposed though Chang was to me, he showed no inclination of using me in any way in his schemes. I determined therefore to make a bold bid to learn more, even at the risk of my neck.

One night I prolonged my visit to the laundry, sitting chatting to Chang and his friends in his back room, and drinking the half bottle of brandy with which I had arrived, until the shutters were put up, his workpeople left, and the shop empty. Bidding them good night, I walked through the dark shop, opened the front door and slammed it again, then creeping behind a work-bench, I started to bury myself in a pile of dirty clothes which had just been delivered.

Whilst concealing myself here, a cry was almost wrung from me as I nearly blinded myself on the corner of a heavy box, over which the pile of clothes had been carelessly thrown. As I did not know Chang's routine this was an extremely risky thing to do, for all I knew he and his wife might yet come to carry these clothes to the boiler. There seemed, however, nothing else to be done if I was to make headway, and as it turned out I remained undisturbed sufficiently long to hear that a 'parcel' was to be delivered at twelve o'clock the next night to somewhere called "The Hollies", which from the conversation I gathered was a house some miles along the Penarth Road.

This seemed sufficiently definite, and would give the Police a chance of, at any rate, finding out what the parcel contained and from it what the conspiracy was—if nothing else. I therefore contented myself with this piece of information and waited for no more. Fastening the Yale lock back, I quietly let myself out of the front door, leaving it fastened by the handle only.

Next morning I handed my message to Mr. McPhee the moment he reached his store, and told him it was extremely urgent. At about eleven o'clock I was surprised to be hailed by him as I was crossing the dock bridge at the end of James Street. He had an urgent message for me from Superintendent Jones, and had been "looking all over the place for me", he said. The message which he handed me was to the effect that I must on no account tell Mr. McPhee the news I had gathered. I had never dreamt of telling him anything about my business at all, and on his side he had never expressed any curiosity, being apparently quite content to enact the role of a mere post office, as which I had used him. This message, coming after all this time, was entirely inexplicable to me.

I had determined to be a witness of what happened at "The Hollies", and thought that, since the road from Cardiff would be already fairly full of pursuers and pursued, it would be better for me to approach the house from the direction of Penarth. With that object in view, I took the train at about five o'clock to that salubrious resort, where I whiled away a pleasant evening. I started out before darkness fell to have a preliminary reconnaissance of the scene of the midnight operations.

I found "The Hollies" to be a large house standing in its own grounds, which sloped up acutely from the left of the road. The house was separated from the road by two ivy-grown banks, with a grassy terrace between them, and a broad drive, entering at the left corner, rose steeply to a wide gravel sweep at that end of the house, on to which the garage and the front door both opened. Behind the house were flower and vegetable gardens, which a brick wall separated from the fields beyond. I did not dare to approach too closely, but decided to take up my position in a small coppice crowning the slope on which the house stood, and from which I could approach the gardens silently over the fields when operations commenced. By a wide detour I made my way to the top of the hill, and entering the little wood, worked cautiously through to its front edge, from which position I overlooked the house. Here I slept for a couple of hours, and woke refreshed well before midnight.

Taking off my shoes and stockings and slipping them into my pocket (I always have my pockets sufficiently large for this purpose), I crept quietly down the hill, and in due course heard the unmistakable creaking of a policeman's boots as he shifted his weight from one leg to the other, in his post at the left-hand corner of the garden-wall. Leaving him to his lonely vigil I moved round the garden to the right, and so approached the drive entrance, passing three more watchers on my way. There was evidently a party of eight surrounding the house, but I found no difficulty in climbing the wall and taking up my position in the shrubbery across the gravel opposite the front door of the house. Here I felt that I was well placed to see all and hear all that went on, which proved to be the case.

I had not been established long in this position, in fact, having drawn on my shoes I was in the act of fastening the second lace, when a disturbance started at the gate. A high-pitched sing-song voice raised in protest, mingled with gruff monosyllabic grunts in a lower key, told me that a Chinaman was in the hands of the Police. Immediately both voices were raised, and by the scuffling on the gravel I gathered that the prisoner was attempting to escape. A whistle blew, and voices sounded from all round as the watchers proceeded to clamber over the wall and close in on the house. These sounds had not passed unnoticed from within. A light flashed up in the hall, the front door was thrown open, and a figure brandishing a stick ran rapidly across the gravel. As this figure passed me on its way down the drive, I was astonished to find it was no less a person than the Police recommended Angus McPhee.

Now I understood the meaning of Superintendent Jones' note of that morning, which had surprised me so much. Of course he would know that the address I had given him was that of his 'safe' post office. And I laughed to think of his feelings when he opened my report. Having seen all I wanted to see at the moment, I crept away quietly and reached the road just as the police were leading the astonished McPhee and the crestfallen Chang into the former's house. I made my way back to Cardiff and went to bed, feeling highly amused at the turn events had taken.

In the morning I called along at Mr. McPhee's store, expecting to find it in the hands of the Police, but great was my astonishment to find everything going on as usual. McPhee led me into a small room in which he usually entertained captains, the door of which he closed carefully, then giving me a cigar and a glass of whisky, he entered into a long and almost apologetic explanation.

Not to make a long story of it, the facts were that Chang had a relation in Dublin, from whom he had been in the habit of receiving presents from time to time, which took the form of farm produce. When the war-time restrictions were imposed, Chang and his cousin realized that there was a chance of making a profit out of their relationship; starting in a small way they had gradually built up quite a large business in unrationed butter, in league with the stewards of several small boats which traded from Ireland to Cardiff. Chang would bring the butter ashore concealed in the centre of a pile of washing and arrange for its distribution, always in the dead of night—to avoid detection. With the Chinaman's customary love of secret societies, he had surrounded the whole business with such an air of mystery and intrigue that it had, naturally enough, killed the trade instead of protecting it as was intended.

The Scotsman was merely one of his regular customers, and on the previous night Chang had been engaged in no more nefarious work than delivering four pounds of the best Irish butter. In these circumstances the Police had agreed that, whilst reporting Chang to the Food Controller, they would keep McPhee's name out of it, and he was very anxious that I should do the same. However, the story of the terrible Chinese conspiracy in Cardiff was far too funny for me to make any such promise, and the best I could do was to promise him that I would not mention his name in connection with this affair in any quarter where it would do him an injury—I knew that my friend, Superintendent Gilcrest, would never forgive me if I kept such an amusing tale from him. Time, however, heals all wounds, and as the principal actors in this "life and death drama" are probably dead or dispersed about the world, I feel justified in now giving the main outlines further publicity.

Needless to say this concluded my stay at Cardiff, and returning to London I found that I had in no way underestimated the pleasure which my story gave to my superior officer. It is still a pleasant memory to recall his jovial face wreathed in smiles when I parted from him—as I left to catch the leave train at Victoria Station.

Chapter 16

TAKING UP MY DUTIES AGAIN in Malaya after the war seemed strange. The proportions of my surroundings seemed all wrong, and it took me a long time to properly orient my mind again.

In my new vision, my big cities had shrunk to small provincial towns, towns to hamlets, and my hamlets to mere farmsteadings. In the same way, buildings which had been tall and imposing to my eyes, were now but ordinary structures, and the smaller houses appeared so diminutive as to seem almost like those from a child's playbox. I felt like Gulliver amongst the Lilliputians. Even the busiest streets no longer seemed crowded, and the silence which seemed to lie over the whole country was almost painful.

I found many changes in the officers of the Police, well-remembered faces had gone from our ranks never to return, but I was glad to find my old friend Major Ritchie still in command, now with the rank of Colonel. This officer seemed to appreciate something of my feelings, and gave me three months' leave on full pay during which to readjust my mind; after which I took up the threads of my work again, quite in the old style.

* * *

Now, however, a new difficulty was added to our task by the continued attempts of the Bolsheviks to sow dissension amongst the various races which make up our population. Their agents came from every point of the compass; from China, from Australia, from India, from Burma, from Siam, from anywhere. They had agents of every nationality, and from every walk in life. Hunting these agents, and obtaining sufficient evidence of their activities to justify their expulsion from the country became, as the months went on, a serious hindrance to our normal Police duties, and in course of time I was employed almost exclusively on this class of work.

As I am now approaching the most immediate past, I must choose my material for this history with a still greater discretion. It behoves me to tread even more warily over the quaking bog of crime. I must step cautiously from tussock to tussock, and pay the greatest attention to my footholds, lest my track be too clearly blazoned to the keenly-watching eyes on the look-out for it. Events are so recent, newspaper references to them are still in the mind of many, and the people concerned in them are still amongst us—all of which considerations forbid my dealing with many of the more outstanding cases in the annals of our crime during the last decade.

Were I to attempt it, thoughts of the public interest, of renewed publicity brought to suffering, innocent relations, and of, need I add the law of libel, would cling about my pen. They would restrict the flow of ink, clogging it even more closely as the years approached the present; and I would have to mantle my history with an ever-thickening cloak.

I can reveal, however, something of what has been going on below the surface by dealing only with the one or two matters which both obtained no publicity at the time of their occurrence, and which I can handle without risk of exposing anything of the secrets of our organization. To those of you who feel disappointed in not learning something of the inner history of events about which you have read in the papers, I offer my apologies, and point out to you that this is entirely due to the exigencies of my service.

* * *

Papers captured in Singapore seemed to indicate that Bolshevik agents were being trained by a 'cell' established in Siam, and I was despatched to the Siamese border to see what confirmation I could obtain of the existence of such an organization, and, if possible, locate its whereabouts, with a view to the Siamese Government being asked to enforce its dispersal.

I realized that to do the job properly this meant my once more working in the guise of a Sakai—a prospect to which I did not look forward after such a long interval. Duty must be done, however. So I broke myself into the rigours of the life by joining a gang of Sakais who were felling jungle on contract for the new railway in Perlis.

As it turned out I could have done nothing wiser, for this gang was what might be described as a 'scratch team'; in that, on a nucleus of a regular band, it was built up of Sakais from tribes scattered all across the country. My arrival, therefore, was unremarkable, and in the evenings' conversations I learnt the names and general territories of nearly all the Sakai headmen frequenting the border jungles. After a month of this life I not only felt myself sufficiently acclimatized once more to the Sakai mode of life, but had amassed a store of information concerning life on the border which I felt to be invaluable.

I had been sharing a hut with, and made a very good friend of a man called Shri, who came from a band living near the border at the source of the Sungei Padang Terap. Shri had been working at this railway job for some weeks before I arrived, and when I suggested to him that this regular employment was becoming monotonous, he heartily agreed with me and decided to rejoin his tribe forthwith, taking me with him. We made leisurely progress through the jungle, rarely spending more than two nights away from one or other of the Sakai clearings, at each of which we were hospitably entertained, and at most of which we spent two or three days before continuing our journey.

We were passing practically along the border, and in this way I made the personal acquaintance of all the Sakais inhabiting that district. Most of the headmen, of course, I had already heard of by name, and it was at few clearings that Shri and I were unable to deliver messages from members of the family with whom we had been working. Needless to say I led the conversation, whenever possible, in the direction of my principal enquiries, but no one in this district seemed to have heard anything at all helpful, and we reached the clearing of Dato Mdulla, for which we were making, without my having heard a single word in any way pointing to Bolshevik activities.

I felt quite sure that this was not because anything was being kept from me, but was because no one whom I had met so far had any information on the subject, and it was plain that I would have to push my enquiries further eastward. It was necessary, however, that I should identify myself with Mdulla's band first, to use it as a jumping-off place for my next move, and as an introduction.

It was whilst staying with these people that I witnessed what was, I suppose, not only the most terrible fight it has ever been my good fortune to see, but was also a confirmation of an event in natural history long suspected but heretofore not confirmed as a fact. I had been out for a long day of hunting with Shri, and as we were making our way home by the side of a little mossy-banked stream, we suddenly heard the most appalling screaming and snarling break out on our right. We recognized the voice of a tiger, and that of a panther, and we realized that something unusual was happening. Shri whispered to me that the noise came from an old clearing, and beckoning me, led the way rapidly by an almost overgrown pathway till we reached a tall guttapercha tree, the trunk of which was nicked for climbing.

Swarming breathlessly up this, we soon found ourselves on the first large branch overlooking the deserted clearing which had, up to a year or two ago, been Shri's home. Perched high up as we were, we looked down on the roughly circular patch of lallang grass, in which now a contest was taking place, the ferocity of which was awe-inspiring. A tiger and a black panther were engaged in mortal combat.

At our first view of them they were separated by about five yards in an arena which was already trampled flat. Both, crouching low to the ground, were snarling forth their hate of each other. Presently the tiger sprang, but with a lithe movement the panther avoided his huge bulk, and lashing at his flank as he passed, inflicted a ripping wound which stretched from his shoulder to his rump—at the same time bounding to the opposite side of the trampled arena and again facing his enemy.

It was only now that I noticed the cause of the combat. Seated some twenty yards distant, with her head and shoulders only showing over the lallang, was the panther's lady—an interested spectator of the battle. If a panther can be said to have such an expression, her face expressed gratification that her favours were being sought by two such magnificent swains.

The fight again called my attention, however. This time it was the panther who was the aggressor, and with his usual choking cough he made a magnificent running spring, with the evident intention of landing on his adversary's back. The tiger met this attack by rising on his hind legs, with a result that they met face to face and for a second looked like a couple waltzing, only for less than a second though, for with clutching forepaws and snapping mouths they fell to the ground, while their hind legs tore at each other's entrails.

The sight was magnificent, and the sounds terrifying in their appalling mixture of intense hate and acute agony. Locked thus the animals rolled far and wide, a kaleidoscope of black, orange, red, and white, in which it was impossible to tell which had the advantage. Weight and length of limb, however, told in the end, and it was a blood-soaked tiger who at last dragged himself wearily from the prostrate corpse of his disembowelled enemy, and sat giving himself a preliminary lick over in the centre of the ring.

Shri and I sat on our perch petrified with delight at the extraordinary scene we had been privileged to witness; but with feelings far otherwise when we realized that darkness would soon be upon us, and it would be impossible for us to make our way home with this infuriated beast almost at the foot of our tree. The tiger walked across to the body of the panther, and gave it one or two pats with his forepaws. Then digging his claws in, threw it with a violent jerk about six feet along the ground.

Having evidently satisfied himself that life was extinct, he slowly made his stately way to the lady in the case who had been sitting all this time motionless, but who, as we had only noticed when the noise of battle ceased, was singing a low crooning song of love and delight, which in some ways sounded like the singing of a kettle.

Complimented though she doubtless felt by the battle which had been fought for her, nevertheless when the conquering hero approached she greeted him with a snarl and a quick scratch on the face, before coquettishly springing away from him. He seemed to take this unmerited attack all in good part, however, and followed her steadily as she made her way, looking coyly over her shoulder from time to time, into the jungle on the far side of the clearing.

This exit of the live members of the caste came as a great relief to Shri and myself, and hastily descending our tree, I was returning along the path by which we had come when Shri stopped me, and I had to wait till he had carefully cut off the whiskers of the dead panther, with which treasure he joyfully led the way home. This incident definitely establishes the fact that cross-breeding between tigers and panthers does, on occasions, take place naturally.

I had been three weeks with these people, and had arranged to leave them in two days' time with the intention of proceeding farther south along the border, when at last I heard news which I thought might lead me in the right direction.

Three young Sakais who were on their way to seek employment at the railway came to the clearing. They came from the district between the two rivers Sungei Tepa and Sungei Jeneri, and from them we heard that their headman was at present sheltering fugitives from clearings to the east of them, which had been raided by a bandit called Mohamed Abdulla, who was supposed to have his headquarters somewhere on the banks of the Sungei Patani, over the Siamese border.

The tales the fugitives had brought of this man's doings were, in themselves, sufficient justification for Police investigation, but apart from that I felt that this might have some connection with the Soviet school which I was in search of. I therefore determined to make for the clearing nearest to the scene of action, which was that of Dato Suliman, father of one of our visitors, and where I was assured of a welcome.

This old man was pleased to have news of his son when I arrived, and made me welcome in his band, who all rather had the 'wind up' (as we would have said in France) by the possibility of being raided in their turn by Abdulla; and they felt that the more men there were the better. At the time of my arrival things were far from harmonious, and Suliman was having a very hard time of it to keep the peace. The facts were that he had had with him for many years a noted Pawang named Hadj, and one of the fugitives who had sought his hospitality was also a Pawang, by the name of Musa, who was the sole survivor of one of the tribes who had been raided. This visitor was the source of the trouble. Being used to exercising the chief authority, he could not settle down under the authority of a rival practitioner!

By insidious means he had attracted a following, which faction were all in favour of vacating their present clearing and moving into the now empty site on a very large clearing which Pawang Musa knew of— the amenities of which were, according to him, immensely superior to those of Suliman's present position. It was one of the clearings the inhabitants of which Abdulla had exterminated, and Musa argued that the place having already been raided, it would now be left undisturbed. It was the old argument that 'shells do not land in the same place twice', the fallacy of which, of course, I knew by personal experience— but I could not very well tell them so. The Dato, Pawang Hadj, and their following, on the other hand, all felt that they were very comfortable where they were, and that by moving as suggested they were merely putting themselves within more comfortable striking distance of the bandits, and inviting attack.

It was into these troubled waters that I had fallen and I was approached by both sides, each of which wished to add to their numbers, soliciting my support of their opinion on this momentous question. Remembering the solution which Solomon suggested when two women propounded a similarly difficult point for his judgment, I proposed that those in favour of going should go, and those in favour of staying should stay.

I gave this as my opinion, not because I thought it would be a good thing to be done but because I was quite sure that it would suit neither party. As things were they had a force of eighteen men with which to repel any attack, but if my advice was followed there would be two parties, one of eleven staying where they were and the other of seven moving off. This latter party would have to rebuild the houses and replant the new clearing—which, from what I heard, was too big to be properly looked after by such a small number.

By taking up this standpoint I avoided taking any side in the question, and became, as it were, a third party of one whose favour was sought by the opposing factions—thus occupying a position very similar to that of your Mr. Lloyd George at the present moment.

Every evening resolved itself into a debating society's meeting, and in the course of two or three days the 'home' party, as one might have called them, began to win over adherents until Musa had only a party of three, and they were very shaky supporters at that—Pawang Hadj's magic was obviously proving the stronger. Musa knew, of course, that I was a stranger like himself, and seemed to think that I was more on his side than against him, so from time to time he said things to me which caused me to think that he was more concerned for his own position than for the general good.

I was not surprised, therefore, when, with his party falling from him, he approached me and suggested that we should both join Abdulla's band, which he seemed to consider was the winning side at present. I did not quite see how this was to be done, but Musa seemed so confident of his ability to arrange for our friendly reception that I began to suspect him of being a secret agent of Abdulla, even as I was of the Government. His endeavour to split Suliman's band into two smaller parties now took on a more sinister aspect, and even his miraculous escape from the massacre, which he put down to the power of his magic, fitted in well with this view of the case.

Joining Abdulla's band suited my book exactly, so I easily allowed myself to be persuaded by Musa's insistent arguments. After all, perhaps he really did look on me as a suitable recruit, and this certainly seemed more reasonable than to suppose that he was wanting to lead me to them as a possible victim. I considered that it was quite impossible for him to have the faintest suspicion that I was a Police agent, and for no other reason could Abdulla think it to his advantage to murder me. Unlike the people whom the bandits had already killed, I had no possessions, no house to be rifled, nothing but what I stood up in; and what I stood up in was merely three twisted pieces of filthy cloth, a yard or two of string, my parang, and a dart quiver!

To be sure, this latter was rather more than it seemed. It contained a roomy compartment, concealed by a false bottom, in which I kept the more civilized and private of my possessions—but Musa certainly did not know of this. To all appearances I merely carried it, as I said, pending the day when I would once more be in the possession of a sumpitan, and I was by no means the only man thus carrying a quiver during the temporary loss of his blowpipe. This and my gunny-sack formed my only luggage. To all appearances I was a wanderer in the wilds, far from my home with Dato Mdulla, a veritable tramp of the jungle whom it was worth nobody's while to rob. I felt therefore quite safe in following Musa.

After I had agreed to go with him, he fully confirmed my suspicions by suggesting that, before leaving, we should kill both Pawang Hadj and Dato Suliman as they slept. He had two excellent spears, and his proposal was that we should arm ourselves with these and, creeping under their huts just before dawn, should take up our positions beneath their sleeping mats; then, at a signal from him, we would both drive our spears up through the interstices of the split bamboo flooring, thus transfixing our sleeping victims above.

It was with the greatest difficulty that I persuaded him from this bloodthirsty scheme, but I at length managed to make him see reason when I pointed out to him that we had a long jungle journey in front of us, which would be difficult enough to negotiate without pursuit and almost impossible if we murdered our hosts; when we would most certainly be pursued so relentlessly that we would inevitably be overtaken and slain. It was therefore with very doubtful feelings regarding my companion that I set out with him next day on our journey to the south-east.

Of the feelings of those who we left behind, however, there was no doubt. Both Hadj and the Dato frankly expressed their delight at being relieved of one whom they had come to consider an incubus; whilst everybody else seemed to experience relief, which was reflected in the many gifts which were heaped upon us; indeed, so plentiful were the offerings of food for our journey that we would have required a coolie to carry it had we taken it all. Needless to say we did not announce our prospective destination. We were supposed to be setting out to risk a journey through the raided districts to an imaginary uncle of mine in Upper Perak. Nearly everybody contrived a chance of telling me privately how grateful they were to me for taking Pawang Musa with me—so little did they realize that the position was the direct opposite.

That I mistrusted my companion goes without saying, and I determined to be constantly on the watch in case I was mistaken, and he knew more about me than I thought he did. After all, he was a man possessed of remarkable powers and it might well, be that, by some obscure psychological process, he had penetrated the secret of my disguise.

It was therefore up to me to give him no opportunity of taking advantage of our lonely situation. I could very well carry out this programme without acting suspiciously, by merely leaving him to assume the position of leader, thus keeping him in front of me. I not only flattered his vanity in this way, but lost no opportunity of flattering him directly by adulatory remarks. I was very much the humble follower of a much-admired chief!

After a couple of days of this close companionship, I was quite convinced that Musa intended me no harm, for had he done so, unavoidable opportunities had occurred during this time when he could have disposed of me with the greatest ease and safety, and this conviction of mine made our subsequent travelling much pleasanter for me. We were by this time over the border and penetrating the jungles of Siam, and I noticed that, not only did Musa seem to be making for a definite objective, but the further we penetrated the more open he became in his disclosures, showing his knowledge of Abdulla and his followers. Several times he referred to individuals by name, as being with Abdulla, and as we approached that Chieftain's quarters he made no disguise of the fact that he was a trusted henchman.

Needless to say, acting my part as an ignorant Sakai, I concealed the fact that his remarks had revealed his secret to me, and not until he openly avowed his attachment to the band did I display my gratified astonishment. Shortly after this revelation he told me that we would very soon be reaching our destination, and sure enough, as we went along the track which we were then following, an armed Chinaman suddenly stepped into the path before us and barred our passage. This man was evidently a sentry, and he passed us freely when Musa had given him a password which I did not hear.

Our way now led us by a winding, rocky path, which appeared to be bordered by precipices on either hand. We had followed this track for perhaps two hundred yards when further progress was prevented by a massive stockade. Here again Musa had to give some form of password before the gate was thrown open and we were admitted.

It was a motley throng who crowded the encampment, all the races of the East seemed to have supplied their outlaw recruits to swell the ranks. I was immediately led to the mouth of a cave within which I was brought before Mohamed Abdulla who, I was surprised to find, was a Chinaman.

With Musa acting as interpreter, for of course I spoke nothing but Sakai, the Chief put me through a lengthy cross-examination, to which I replied stumblingly and in a stupidly voluble manner. This seemed to satisfy him, for turning to his lieutenant, a strapping Afghan who stood at his elbow, he remarked that whilst I was not intelligent enough to be worth teaching, nevertheless I would be a handy servant to have about the camp and might be useful as a guide later on.

I was compelled to swear secrecy and loyalty, under dire threats, both from Abdulla as regarded my body, and Musa as regarded my soul—but as I was only swearing by the spirits—Pelsit and Bajang—I did not feel myself unduly bound by these oaths! Musa took my parang from me and I was then made free of the enclosure.

Leaving the "august presence", I inspected the encampment, which I found was situated on the rocky shoulder of a hill jutting out far above the valley of the Sungei Patani. My first impression of this lair was that it was a veritable fortress, and subsequent examination proved this to be literally true. On three sides the ground fell away precipitously to the valley floor, in many places by perpendicular rock faces of sixty to eighty feet high, rendering these fronts completely impassable. On the fourth side entrance was prohibited by the constantly guarded stockade which ran from precipice to precipice across that front, rendering the whole impregnable.

The encampment itself was on a flat shelf overlooking the valley, from which, however, it was completely hidden by a narrow belt of jungle which had been left growing round the periphery. Behind this ledge the ground rose to a jagged, jungle-clad hill, by a cliff in which there were a series of caves all of which were being made use of.

On the flat, cleared area in front of the caves stood three long huts, at a distance of about forty feet from the cliff face. They looked similar to coolie lines, and it was, in fact, in these that the rank and file of the band were quartered. One of them was a sort of communal room, with the kitchen fires at one end of it. Of the other two, one was inhabited exclusively by Chinese, whilst the other housed a motley collection of Siamese, Tonkinese, Malays, Javanese, Burmese, and even Arabs and Afghans. On closer acquaintance I discovered, what had not at first glance been apparent, that there were in fact but two representatives of each of these latter races.

It was in this hut that I was told to take up my quarters. Nobody seemed to welcome my arrival, and I appeared to be the only Sakai there with the exception of Musa, who I discovered lived in the caves— which exclusive quarters were reserved for the use of the leaders only. I comported myself, as becomes an ignorant savage from the wilds, with due humility, and was allotted all the menial tasks of the camp, my taskmasters being the two Malays whose language was the only one I dare acknowledge having any acquaintance with, and I professed only a slight acquaintance at that.

The majority of my room mates seemed to speak English, and it was the lingua franca of the hut. They all seemed rather proud of this accomplishment, in fact they would even address their fellow nationals in it rather than in their mother tongue. None of my companions seemed very warlike, and at first acquaintance I found it hard to picture them having taken part in the deeds of rapine and murder of which I had heard—the reports of which had led me here.

After a few days, when I understood the organization of the camp more clearly, I came to realize that, as a matter of fact, not only had they not taken part in these raids but they did not even know that such massacres had occurred! These people were merely the students, and the raids had been carried out solely by parties of the twenty Chinese who lived in the other hut, keeping themselves very much to themselves. These Chinese were employed as a sort of camp police. They provided the sentries and stockade guard, and appeared to be the true bandits.

The students were daily harangued by one or other of the leaders, of whom there seemed to be six. Abdulla himself may have harangued the Chinese, but during my stay with them I never knew him to do so. His lieutenant, on the other hand, held the classes of Afghans and Arabs. Musa would occasionally attend to the Javanese and Malays. There were also Burmese and Siamese teachers, the latter of whom lectured his own nationals and the Tonkinese. These latter, and a Chinaman who appeared to be polyglot, were the most busily employed of the lecturing staff, as all of them gave lectures in English to the whole school.

I was, of course, not supposed to be included in the classes, but I heard many of these lectures as I went about my humble duties—and amusing farragoes of nonsense they were. The temptation to interrupt, and try to drive some common sense into the muddled heads of these fanatics, was at times almost irresistible!

How I longed to point out to them that a name was merely a name, and that, whether it was King or kommisar, colonel or capitalist, sergeant or soviet, made no difference, the fact remained that the name represented authority in any case.

I would nearly burst with the suppressed desire to make these 'pudding heads' understand that, if society was to be organized in any way at all, someone must be in authority to see that the rules of the organization were carried out; that it mattered not at all what label was attached to that someone; that whether he was sultan, rajah, shah, king, czar, president, emperor, generalissimo, dictator, or kommisar, his functions must be the same in any case; and that only in complete anarchy, where might alone was right and no social organization of any kind existed, could there be a state without a paramount ruler. With thoughts like these running through my head, I would hasten out of the lecture room and busy myself at a distance until I had mentally cooled down again.

Needless to say that, having discovered the whereabouts of the school I had been sent to seek, my mind had been occupied, from the moment of enlightenment, with the question of how I was to carry the information I had gained back to my headquarters. This was a problem which required considerable study, more especially as I very soon found out that we of the students' hut were not permitted to pass the stockade unless escorted by one of the headquarters' staff, who alone seemed to know the password. I was also engaged in a close study not only of the terrain with a view to possible escape, but of the organization of this post.

I had, from the moment of my arrival, done my best to efface myself and become the most insignificant member of the community—and I must say that I was given every assistance in doing so. The fellow-occupants of my hut looked down on me, with almost disgust, from the eminence of their 'little learning'; the Chinese in the neighbouring hut looked down on the students, from the height of their muscular brutality, with a disdainful and scarcely veiled contempt; whilst the inhabitants of the caves looked down on all, from the altitude of their admitted leadership.

While this state of affairs amused me tremendously—as an illustration of the 'freedom', 'brotherhood', and 'equality' of practical Bolshevism, here in the very home of its professors—nevertheless it aided me in my submergence in a way which a more bourgeoise organization could never have done; and I was therefore duly appreciative of Mr. Lenin's doctrines from this point of view. For putting a man in a position where he is considered as less than dirt, I can confidently recommend the Soviet regime!

The Chinese in the camp seemed to be mostly Hokkien, and from scraps of conversation which I picked up I learnt that, in the raids of which I had heard, they had overstepped their instructions. The intention had been merely to frighten the Sakais from the district, with a view to leaving a broad corridor of completely uninhabited jungle through which agents could pass unobserved to the river Ketil. This was the shortest and most convenient highway to the Federated Malay States, and was one from which agents could proceed inconspicuously either by road, rail, or water, to spread themselves in the Federated Malay States.

Musa, it seemed, had been an early student at the school, and had marked down the clearings to be visited. Once the Chinamen had got going, however, led by this bloodthirsty savage they had proceeded along the usual lines of terrorism, which resulted in the excesses I have already referred to. Their action had certainly led to the desired result so far as emptying the jungle of inhabitants was concerned, but Abdulla feared it would call more attention to his doings than was desirable. The Chief was very angry with Musa for having led them into these outrages, and the Chinamen were wondering what his punishment would be. Evidently I had been brought to the camp as a sort of peace offering. All the supplies for the encampment, I learnt, came up the river Patani and, so far as the Siamese were concerned, care was being taken that nothing should be done on this side of the border to show that Abdulla was anything other than the prospector he pretended to be.

I seized every chance which was offered of examining the caves, but found it very difficult to do so; though from time to time my duties took me into their guarded depths in my capacity as a 'hewer of wood and drawer of water'—though general dustman would be perhaps a better designation.

At night-time a Chinese sentry was mounted at the entrance to the cave which formed Abdulla's living quarters, but at the neighbouring cave in which the lecturing staff lived the door was merely locked. It was this cave which I first entered, and I found that it was, in fact, a series of caves leading one from the other in a confusion of rough staircases, passages, and different sized chambers.

Taking advantage of an opportunity one afternoon when I was alone in this cave, I subjected the whole system to a thorough examination, and discovered that by climbing nearly to the roof in one of the innermost rooms, which was used as a sort of storeroom and in which were piled stacks of literature, I could hear the voice of Abdulla coming up through a sort of chimney, which evidently connected with the neighbouring cave system. This chimney was an opening at least two feet in area, which ran down almost perpendicularly from where I clung to the tough wall, and as it seemed to me sufficiently large to form a passage-way, I determined to put this to the test whenever possible.

As night-time would give me my only possible chance of inspecting Abdulla's private quarters, I absented myself from my usual place in the hut that night and slept under a large rock in the narrow strip of the jungle which separated the front of the clearing from the precipices. Next morning no one seemed to have remarked my absence, and therefore during the next four days I slept three nights away in the same manner, and found that no one took the least interest in my having done so. Having satisfied myself on this point, the next thing was to discover a means of concealing myself in the lecturers' caves in such a way that I would be locked in for the night.

Musa had by this time disappeared, in fact the personnel of the lecturing party had undergone one or two changes, and the manner in which these changes had been effected seemed so mysterious that I was exercising my wits as to what had actually happened.

Musa was, of course, the one in whom I took the most interest. The way he had vanished was so simple. I had seen him enter Abdulla's cave three days ago, but had never seen him come out again! It was not merely that I had not seen him come out, but that I was perfectly convinced of the fact that he had not, indeed, again emerged. I had been most careful in my watch and was certain that, unless he had slipped out whilst I slept, he was still there. On the other hand, no more food was being prepared and taken into the cave than usual. What then had happened? Was Musa dead? These questions I determined to find an answer to if I could.

It was whilst pondering on this problem that I realized, with something of a shock that, so far as my recollection carried me, identically the same thing had occurred to the Burmese and the Siamese lecturers, both of whom had been replaced within the last day or two. As I thought the matter over, it appeared to me that I had no recollection of ever having seen the two new lecturers admitted through the stockade. As most of my time was spent about the clearing in full view of the entrance, a considerable proportion of it in preparing firewood for the kitchens from a pile of timber which lay directly opposite the gate, I had a fair idea of the general comings and goings, yet, think as I would, I could not remember any incident of their arrival.

The meaning of these various phenomena slowly began to dawn on me, as they collected together in my mind, and what was merely a dim suspicion gradually crystallized and took form, until I became convinced that there must be a secret entrance leading to Abdulla's cave from outside. The idea more than ever confirmed me in my determination to explore the possibilities of the chimney which I had discovered, and as it was now quite clear that my absence from my usual sleeping place caused no suspicion, I turned my attention entirely to the matter of my safe concealment in the far cave.

Owing to Musa no longer being there, and to my being an accepted identity to the new members of the staff, this problem did not now present the same difficulty as it would have done three or four days ago. A fire was lighted every evening in the large central cave of the staff quarters, and it was one of my duties to see that sufficient wood for its replenishment stood in a convenient alcove, which, was in the right-hand wall just inside the door, and I fixed on this spot as being the best suited to my purpose. There had never been anything in the nature of a store of wood kept here, merely a meagre sufficiency for the night's use was daily thrown into the recess.

Displaying any excess of zeal in this regard might have proved suspicious, but by dint of gradually increasing the supply which I daily brought, I gradually formed a pile of firewood which I stacked neatly, and by the end of the third day it had reached quite reasonable proportions. So much so that I decided that after tomorrow's supply there would be enough to enable me to make the attempt during the following night.

Next day I was even more assiduous in heaping up the pile in a compact stack, sufficiently far away from the back wall of the alcove to leave a narrow chamber in which I could conceal myself. I took care to leave a supply of wood lying loosely and conveniently near the front of the recess, which would be more than sufficient to last out the night's requirements—I wanted to run no risk of being discovered by having my concealing wall drawn upon by any would-be stoker!

Seizing an opportunity when there was nobody in sight of me, I slipped into the chamber I had thus prepared at about six o'clock that evening, and as I had what I hoped would be a long night of investigation before me, I at once settled down to a four hours' sleep and spent an undisturbed evening. When I woke up conversation was still going on round the fire, and it was painful for me to lie there listening to the misguided enthusiasm for their rotten cause which these deluded visionaries displayed.

As I listened to them, the conviction was borne in upon me that this enthusiasm was not, in fact, genuine, but was being 'put on' for the benefit of their auditors. They were each afraid that the other was a spy, who would report to their superiors any backsliding of theirs from the original ardour which they had displaced on their conversion!

No matter to what extent their eyes had been opened to the falseness of the millennium they preached as a result of their short practical experience of the working of their doctrine, nevertheless they dared not but continue to pay enthusiastic lip-service to it! My opinion on this may, of course, be entirely wrong, but to me the voices stealing along the rocky cavern seemed redolent of knavery and deceit; they sounded as hollow and empty of conviction as that of a bachelor expressing to a young mother his intense admiration for the beauty of her two-months-old firstborn! It was with relief that I heard the party break up and retire for the night.

With their first movement in this direction, I started taking down the timber wall of my prison, in the doing of which I was bound to make a certain amount of noise, which, though unnoticeable whilst movement and conversation was going on, would have echoed through the vaulted chambers had I put it off till all was still. As it was, I had my exit all prepared almost before the last man had reached his dormitory grotto.

I waited until the fire was nothing but a mass of glowing embers before I silently threaded the maze of corridors to the chimney I had discovered, and when there, commenced to solve the real problem which this concealed cleft in the rock presented. The questions were: For how far down did the chimney continue to be of the same dimensions? Was it possible for me to traverse it at all? What was at the other end of it? For all I knew it might open directly above Abdulla's bed—and I had no fancy for alighting, all unarmed, on to a newly-wakened Abdulla! Or perhaps the other end of the chimney was actually in the roof of a cave, and on emerging I would find myself without support, in which case, if I did not break my neck in the fall, I would at any rate be unable to regain its shelter and would be discovered in the morning.

These last two considerations seemed the most vital and, as I had already given them considerable thought, I was provided with the means of settling, at any rate these questions, definitely—which I proceeded to do forthwith. I unwrapped the long length of string, which I was carrying round my waist, and attached a small stone to the end of it, then, climbing to my chimney, lowered this improvised sounding-line gently down, carefully measuring the depth as I did so by counting the knots I had made in the string at each yard.

The stone came to rest at a point very little lower than the floor of the cave to the wall of which I was now clinging. I lifted it slightly and swung it as far as possible in each direction, lowering it at the end of each swing, but in every case it indicated the same level. At the same time I could hear the gentle click it made as it landed on rock, and it was therefore clear to me that it was nature's, and not Abdulla's, bosom on which the stone was resting.

I hauled the string up again and, after carefully untying my stone and replacing it quietly on the floor of the cave, I re-wound it once more about my waist, then proceeded to find the answers to my other conundrums. I decided that the safest method of procedure would be for me to go down head first. By doing this, not only could I feel my way with careful fingers and ensure that I did not dislodge an avalanche of stones, the noise of which would call attention to my proceedings, but, making frequent halts, my ears could tell me much from whatever noises might come up the thus unobstructed passage. Another consideration in favour of this method was that the broadest portion of my body would be going down first and, should the passage taper narrowly, I would have sufficient warning not to become wedged in it—one can bend one's arms and obtain sufficient leverage for a lift in a space which would render one's legs entirely useless.

I therefore slid over the edge quietly and hung, waist down, till my anxious exploratory fingers told me that the walls of the chimney so far as I could reach were safe and smooth. I slipped further over, and was presently hanging by my toes to the lip. The opening appeared to be a natural cleft in the solid limestone; to the left and right were numerous horizontal cracks, but it seemed to be smooth slabs of rock which were at my back and front. This formation made it a simple matter to lower myself by shifting my hands alternately from crack to crack, and I realized that if it continued to the bottom in this way, climbing up again would be almost as easy as mounting a flight of stairs.

Slowly, slowly, I descended, my hands carefully exploring every inch of the surface before I dare lower myself to the next grip, but at last my searching fingers came to the opening which I knew to exist. This was on my right-hand side, and lowering myself so far as I could, depending on a grip with my left hand only, I was presently able to extend my right arm to its full extent and explore with it what seemed to be the roof of a narrow passage leading in that direction. I now found myself in an extremely awkward position. I had been quite unable to calculate the distance I had climbed down, so had no means of knowing how far this opening was from the floor on which my stone had rested.

I was holding myself propped against the right wall, with my left arm stiffly extended, the side of my left hand being firmly jammed into a crack which gave a good hold. My right shoulder was below the opening, but in no direction could my right hand feel anything on which to lay hold and give me support. If I lowered myself further, by bending my left arm, the wedging action which it was now exercising would become inoperative, as the lintel of the passage would cease to press against my ribs and come to my waist—altogether things were looking far from rosy for me.

I decided that it was necessary to 'take a chance' and, by supporting my weight so far as possible with extended legs against the sides, dive what I hoped were the few remaining feet. I knew that in any case the distance could not be excessive, and hoping for the best, extended my right arm in the diving attitude over my head and let go with my left.

I had nerved myself for this desperate plunge, so I felt particularly foolish when my hands met the floor almost before I had started sliding. I suppose, as a matter of fact, I dropped about six inches! Needless to say it was not long before I was sitting up and letting the blood run back from my poor congested head. I found that making this effort had taken more out of me than I had realized during the excitement of its actual performance, and when I finally rose to my feet, not only was the blood drumming in my ears to such an extent that my sense of hearing was completely occluded, but I found myself trembling and twitching like a man with the palsy.

When I had recovered somewhat, I explored the narrow passage which I had felt leading to the right, and found that it extended for only a very few feet in that direction. At the end of it there was a hole close to the floor, through which it was evident I had heard Abdulla's voice. It was a ragged-shaped opening, but was at any rate, so far as I reached, of a size sufficient to form an entrance to Abdulla's quarters.

Owing to my condition I decided to leave further exploration until the next night, and returned up my chimney with comparative ease— had I not been so exhausted it would have been quite as easy as I had anticipated. The only real difficulty which I found was in negotiating the turn which had to be made on emerging from the opening, situated as it was high up in the wall of the cave. However, even this was successfully accomplished, and with a sigh of relief I finally completed the silent building-up of my firewood wall, and slept peacefully until I was awakened by the opening of the cave door about six o'clock.

As it turned out, things could not have been better arranged, even if I had been omniscient and planned them myself. During the morning I overheard Abdulla telling two of the Chinamen that they would have to accompany him, in the afternoon, on a journey he was making. He told them they must take sufficient food with them for an absence of twenty-four hours, as it was quite likely they would be delayed over night.

The beauty of my position was, that these people would carry on their conversations in my presence quite openly, so sure were they that I only knew Sakai and a smattering of Malay. In this case, for instance, the conversation was in Hokkien, which is a dialect with which I am perfectly familiar; and the news was very welcome to me, as it meant that I could make my preliminary search of Abdulla's cave that afternoon, with the assurance that it would remain unoccupied during my visit.

I therefore witnessed the locking of his door, and his departure shortly after the mid-day meal, with the greatest satisfaction, then, after giving him half an hour's grace, made my way to the chimney, taking a bamboo broom with me into the cave as an excuse for my presence. I hastily collected a heap of rubbish into a small pile near the entrance, looking all ready for removal, before I finally slipped into the storeroom and, climbing the now familiar wall, slipped feet first through the hole and descended my secret stairway quite rapidly.

I took with me a box of matches and a small oil lamp, the using of which I felt would be perfectly safe in the circumstances. Even if my light happened to be visible from the doorway, the sentry posted there would be quite unable to see it against the glaring sunshine, unless he was peering closely through the crack, a thing which I had never seen any of the sentries do; and in any case I did not intend to have my lamp alight anywhere within view of the door if I could avoid it.

Lighting my lamp, I thrust it through the opening I had discovered at the end of the short passage, and for a moment could hardly realize what it was that I was seeing. In front of me was a curving wall of glistening white, which seemed to close the end of the five-foot-long passage in which I found myself. As I crawled along, however, I saw that this wall was at least two feet away from the rock in which my passage was formed, and on closer examination I realized that what I was looking at was the upper portion of a tremendous stalactite.

The opening through which I was peering was high up in the wall of a chamber, the floor of which was, according to my string, some twenty-three feet beneath me. The stalactite, hanging as it did close to the wall, formed a comfortable means of descent. I found it quite an easy matter to walk down the rough cavern wall with my back leaning against its smooth surface. I then found myself in a tremendous subterranean vault, in the centre of which was a pile of packing-cases.

It was a magnificent chamber, with a high arched roof, and on all sides the walls were screened by a fringe of these massive, centuries old stalactites, making it look like the pillared nave of a cathedral. On the packing-cases and leaning against them, were piled a motley assortment of arms of all kinds, lying on the top of which I was pleased to see my parang—when I made my escape I would at any rate know where to lay my hands on this indispensable weapon, without which progress through the jungle is well-nigh impossible. On closer inspection, I found that one of the packing-cases had been broken open and, to my surprise, found it nearly full of automatic pistols and packets of ammunition. Evidently this was Abdulla's armoury.

I did not linger long over these investigations; in fact, though it takes long to write, all these things were noted as I made my way to the middle of the room immediately after my entrance. Leading from the packing-cases, a well-marked path showed me the way which evidently led to Abdulla's quarters. I went behind the screen of stalactites and examined the walls of the solid rock carefully all round the cave, but found only one other passage-way leading into it. Leaving this till later, I decided to investigate the one which appeared to lead to the front first.

Climbing up a rocky slope, I made my way through a large passage, or a series of small caves, till I found the way blocked by a heavy wooden barricade, in which there was a locked door. This door having been designed to prevent approach from the other side, however, the lock was in front of me. The iron socket into which the massive bolt entered was attached to the doorpost by four screws. These yielded quickly to the persuasion of my parang, which I lost no time in bringing, into action.

Passing this barricade, I found myself in Abdulla's living quarters. Here was his office, evidently; a large desk was littered with papers, and in an oaken case standing to one side were neatly arranged ranks of files. Had it not been for the uncouth surroundings, I might have been in the counting-house of a prosperous city business! I realized that before me lay information which would be of priceless value to the authorities. The hasty glance I was able to give to the documents told me nothing, as all seemed to be written in Chinese, which language, though I can speak it, is one the reading of which is beyond my powers. I had no doubt, however, that there would be official lists of students, and perhaps agents, amongst these papers which I was looking at. It was all too orderly for records of this sort to be lacking.

Heading to right down this cave, I passed into a luxuriously furnished sitting-room, the walls and ceiling of which were formed by Indian or Persian carpets, which completely hid its troglodytical character. It was a chamber which would not have disgraced a palace. There was no difficulty in finding the other entrance to this chamber, as the arrangement of the furniture indicated clearly which hanging should be pulled aside to reach it; so, passing through, I found myself in the front portion of the cave where I had been interviewed on my arrival and which I had, from time to time, had the pleasure of sweeping out.

I was glad to have reached here, as I could fix it as a datum point from which to plan out the 'lie' of this system of caves in my mind, so I searched it carefully and found that the passage-way by which I had entered was the only innerwards opening. I next subjected the drawing-room to a thorough search behind the hangings for hidden entrances, but here again there were only two openings, the one by which I had just entered and that leading into the office. From the office, however, there was a third passage-way, and following this I found myself in Abdulla's bedroom.

Like the drawing-room, this room was a completely draped apartment, but was furnished in a somewhat more Spartan style. An ordinary iron bedstead, such as is to be found in many European houses, occupied a somewhat unusual position in the centre of the floor, and against the walls stood two meranti almirahs (neither of which was locked, and both of which, on hasty examination, seemed to contain nothing but the wearing apparel for which they were intended) and a varnished dressing-table made of the same wood, on which stood a mirror, hair-brushes, and a collection of cosmetics which would not have been out of place in the bedroom of a society beauty.

There were one or two chairs and several travelling trunk also standing against the walls, but the general air of the room was one of emptiness. I pulled aside the hangings and examined the walls of this chamber thoroughly, but found no concealed opening, and it seemed to me that if I was right in my surmise regarding a secret entrance, the way to this must lead through the second opening which I had found in the armoury cave; which was the only place I had so far left unexamined.

I therefore returned there and prospected this possibility. From the look of the ground it did not appear that the low winding passage through the rock, in which I now found myself, formed a pathway that had been at all frequently used; small, sharp pieces of stone, which had apparently fallen from the roof, impeded almost every footstep, and it seemed unlikely that if people had been in the habit of using this way they would not have, at any rate, kicked most of them to one side.

Thinking that perhaps this appearance had been deliberately given, and was in the nature of a blind, I pursued my investigations nevertheless. I was led into a veritable maze of inter-connecting caves and passages, none of which presented any appearance of having been frequented by man and, having explored several of these, exercising the greatest care not to lose my way, I decided that, if my path of escape was threaded somewhere through this maze, I would be more likely to lose my way completely in the search and starve to death, than to find it.

Whilst groping about in this hopeless manner, a thought kept fluttering about the back of my mind—like a bat trying to escape from a lighted room. It was a very insistent thought, I knew; and yet so vagrant was it that I could not capture it. It was something suspicious. It was a suspicion I had in my mind. Yes, but of what? Of what? Something suspicious that I had seen. Yes! that was it. But where? At last I was getting hold of it. I must continue to drive it into a corner. I had seen something suspicious somewhere. Now, what was it I had seen? Of what was it suspicious? And where had I seen it? These three questions were at least definite, and I concentrated on them. There sprang into my mind something black and shiny. Black and shiny? Was it a rat snake? No! Of course! Of course!! With a rush I had the errant thought in my hands—Abdulla's bed! Why should the man have his bed standing in the middle of the room? Obviously to conceal something—and that something the entrance to my passage!

I rushed back and studied this strangely disposed sleeping arrangement. Not only was its isolated situation unusual, but the arrangement of the rugs on which it stood was, now I came to study it, itself suspicious. Three rugs lay athwart the bed, the legs at the head standing on one, those at the foot on another, leaving the central rug free for easy removal. A careful look round confirmed the fact that this was the only rug in the room no part of which was held down by some article of furniture or another. Noting all this only took me a second, and dragging aside the rug I found that my suspicions were correct, for under the bed lay a trap-door!

With a sudden shock I realized that time had been slipping by, and that if I did not wish to court discovery I must return at once. I had, at any rate I thought, discovered the entrance to the secret passage, and I must leave further investigation for another occasion. Swiftly spreading the rug again exactly as I had found it, I hurried through the office, and had started to replace the screws in the armoury door when the thought struck me that, as I would have to remove them again when making my escape, it would be as well to prepare to do so as silently as possible; so important did this seem that I risked the extra time necessary and went back with them into Abdulla's bedroom, where I greased them carefully with a mixture of brilliantine and a face cream which were lying on his dressing-table.

When I was again screwing them in, the advisability of having taken this precaution was amply illustrated by the ease and silence with which they screwed firmly home into their dry timber sockets. I carefully rubbed their heads and the surrounding metal, where it had been darkened, with the dry red earth from the floor, removing all signs of the grease I had used and leaving the whole thing looking completely undisturbed. I replaced my parang where it had been lying, amongst the collection of spears and knives on the packing-cases, then climbed to the opening above, finding no more difficulty in walking up the wall, with the stalactite as a support, than I had done in walking down.

Again entering the storeroom, I was dismayed to find that the broom, which I had left standing by the door, had disappeared; also, from the sound of the voices which reached me, it appeared that something unusual was happening in the caves. I crept forward and, on turning the corner of the passage, learnt from what I overheard that the disturbance was on my account! Someone had found my discarded broom, and I had been sent for to be reprimanded for leaving it where I did, but, naturally enough in the circumstances, I could be nowhere discovered outside, and they were now going to search their rooms for me!

This was a very awkward situation for me. I had only a moment in which to make up my mind, but in that moment I darted across the passage in which I stood, and passing through the cave occupied by the Afghan lieutenant, coiled myself up on the floor in the blank end of the corridor which passed it on the other side. Here, in the course of a few minutes I was discovered sound asleep, was soundly kicked, and sounded my sorrow shrilly! I was well beaten both for my laziness and impudence in daring to sleep in these sacrosanct quarters. Needless to say I ran screaming from the cave with every sign of repentant terror. As a matter of fact I thought that I had got off very cheaply from what might have proved a very awkward situation.

Having discovered as much as I had, I felt that the sooner I was able to settle the question of whither the trap-door led the better, and if I was correct in my surmise, escape by it forthwith. Taking it for granted that the trap-door was the entrance to a secret exit, and that I could succeed in making my escape through it, it would be of vital importance that Abdulla should consider its secrecy still inviolate, in order that this means of entrance might be used by the Police who would doubtless be sent to make his arrest when my report had been handed in. I therefore must consider what I would need both to do and to use, in order to completely conceal my having made use of this exit.

During the next day I collected my simple impedimenta—by the ancient method which was known in France as 'winning'. In fact I can be, on occasion, a man of subtly 'winning' ways! Towards the evening I retired discreetly and investigated the secret stores concealed in my quiver; after which I was to be seen busily engaged supplying fresh firewood in the cookhouse. Thus it was that Abdulla's coffee that evening contained a stiff dose of veronal. After having successfully accomplished this slight feat of legerdemain, I had to hurry to the timber pile and proceed with a load of firewood to the staff cave, behind the woodstack in which I had concealed my meagre luggage, during the late afternoon, in anticipation of my successful preparations for the evening.

Seizing an opportunity I concealed myself, I hoped for the last time, in my old position at the back of the alcove. All went well and, starting about midnight, I made my way as quickly as possible by the now familiar route to the armoury cave. My progress was but slightly delayed by the necessity of lifting and lowering my light luggage, on the end of the string, during the climb. Arrived there, I lost no time in taking out my ready-greased screws which, I was pleased to notice, came out wonderfully quietly and easily.

I had my procedure carefully mapped out, so carrying my lighted lamp, I went directly to Abdulla's sleeping apartment. I listened carefully before pulling aside the hangings, and was relieved to hear the heavy, steady breathing of the drugged. Slipping in, I rapidly searched Abdulla's clothing which was lying on a chair, and drew from it his slender bunch of keys, with which I returned to the office. Here

I spent a considerable time in my search, but at last found the large, heavy key of the armoury door, which I had been in search of, locked in a drawer. Turning the bolt of this lock was no quiet matter, try as I might to make it so. The rusty mechanism shrieked its protest to the four corners of heaven, and my heart was in my mouth as I ran to the bedroom entrance and listened—my dose, however, seemed to have been sufficient for Abdulla, who continued to sleep peacefully.

All was now ready for my investigation of the trap-door, and I swiftly replaced the screws and dusted them as before, then, thinking that abstracting one of the automatics and a packet of cartridge clips would be quite safe, as the loss would not be noticed from amongst the many still lying in the already opened case, I took them. All being now ready, I closed the door and locked it from the outside—again to the accompaniment of loud shrieks which, as before, luckily failed to awaken the sleeper. I then replaced the key in the drawer where I had found it, and making sure that all was locked up and that I was leaving no sign of disturbance behind me, I left the office.

My luggage (which now consisted of my quiver, my parang, and my gunny sack, the latter of which was now heavier by the addition of the gun and cartridges) I carried into the bedroom, where my first care was to return Abdulla's keys to their original situation. I then drew aside the rug, and carefully slid back the bolt which held the trap-door.

The great moment had now come, and I gently eased up the trap-door, little by little, till at last I was able to slide the point of my parang through the opening. It had been an awkward lift, working as I was in the confined space under the bed, no part of which I dared risk bumping. However, it was done at last, and judging by the strong draught of cold fresh air which was blowing through the crack, this was undoubtedly to be my way to freedom!

Leaving my parang lying where it did, propping the edge of the trap-door open, I again spread this rug over it across under the bed, then taking the reel of cotton which I had brought with me, I measured off two long lengths of thread. Passing each of these through the fringe at one end of the rug, I drew them through until I had reached midway of their length. I then carefully rolled back the rug from this threaded end rolling the parallel threads with it over the parang and the trap-door, until it rested close behind the hinges of the latter. I then threaded the long ends of the doubled threads through the fringe of the next rug on that side of the room, which was firmly anchored to its position by having an almirah standing on its further end, and bringing the ends back dropped them down the trap-door opening.

All was now ready for my departure, so opening it to the fullest extent possible, I carefully wriggled my feet through the trap-door and found them on the top steps of a flight of stairs. I lowered my simple luggage, piece by piece, and quietly arranged them with my feet; then I passed a fold of my string over the knob of the bolt and, holding this carefully in position with my right hand, lowered myself until the trap-door, supported by my head, was sufficiently closed to lightly grip this string. I could now use both hands, and pulling steadily and equally on my two lengths of doubled thread I felt, and heard, the carpet unrolling itself over my head till at last, by the resistance offered to my pull, I knew that it was lying once more fringe to fringe with its next-door neighbour, as it had been when I first entered the bedroom. Dropping one of the threads from each hand, by now pulling on the other, I withdrew the thread completely from the chamber above me.

The most ticklish part of the business now lay before me, but the weight of the trap-door itself proved sufficient to close it, and pulling strongly on my doubled string I had the satisfaction of hearing the bolt click home. When I had pulled the slack end of the string through the trap-door, I had the satisfaction of knowing that in Abdulla's quarters there was now left no sign of my transit.

As I descended the steps, on which I was equally careful to leave no traces, the roof rose rapidly and the staircase widened. Soon I was on the floor of a large cave, across which a well-trodden track left no doubt as to which direction I should take, and following this I passed through cave after cave, and passage after passage, but always downwards; twisting and turning, past the mouths of caves and the entrances to other passage-ways the path led me, by steep slopes and sometimes by roughly-cut steps, ever further as it seemed, into the centre of the earth. Had the way not been marked for me by the passing of many feet, I would undoubtedly have been as completely lost amongst this jumble of possible routes as I had been in the pathways leading from the armoury above.

The way led sometimes through spacious caverns and sometimes through narrow clefts, and it was whilst descending such a cleft that I heard the sound of running water ahead of me. The way became steeper, until I found myself descending a regularly cut flight of steps. The sound of the water was now very close, and my lamp was flickering wildly in the strong current of fresh air which blew up the stairway, which I descended with the greatest caution from step to step.

Suddenly there was no step, and, kneeling down awkwardly, I lowered my lamp into the black void in which the staircase ended. Beneath me I could see the dark gleam of swirling water—the staircase seemed to lead directly through the roof of a cavern, some six feet above the water!

Tying the string to the handle of my parang, I lowered it to sound the depth of the water, which I found to be only a matter of twelve inches or so over the area I was able to reach with my improvised plummet; evidently the stream was fordable, so I dropped into it. I at once found that the cave I was in was part of the overhanging bank of the river and, as I made my way out of it, I was conscious of the early morning jungle noises around me, so I immediately blew out my lamp. I conjectured that I must now be somewhere near the landing place where stores were delivered, and that there I might find a canoe.

After my eyes had accustomed themselves to the darkness, I prospected carefully both up-stream and down and, in the latter direction, at last found what I was seeking. I would have liked to have made my escape without leaving any indication of which direction I had taken, but as dawn would soon be upon me, and I could put a greater distance between myself and the encampment before that time by stealing a canoe than I possibly could do by other means, I felt that, in spite of the indication given, it was the only thing to be done; so I was soon gliding rapidly down-stream.

As dawn was breaking I drew into the bank, and gave myself a thorough scrub all over with sand to remove as much as possible of the grime which I had allowed to accumulate in my character as a Sakai. I tidied my hair, washed my rags of cloth, and generally smartened myself up so far as was possible with the limited means at my disposal. Even the little I could do made a distinct change in my appearance as I sat in the canoe, for with a cloth twisted turbanwise about my head, another over my shoulders, and the third lying across my knees, I gave to a casual glance the impression of a completely clothed figure. I was to be no longer the Sakai, but was now a peaceful Siamese peasant.

I kept a careful eye on the bank for pathways, and so soon as I saw one, landed there and hurried, to the house from which it led; there, since I was well provided with money, I had no difficulty in providing myself with a more fitting costume for my new character. Whilst making these purchases, I learnt that only three hours down-stream was the large village of Aspore Hina. By paddling with my utmost exertions I came within sight of this village within barely two hours, however, and immediately landed before reaching it. The canoe I sank with several large stones in it, together with the remains of my Sakai belongings, in a deep pool which had been washed out close in to the bank at a curve of the stream.

Here I had no difficulty in purchasing a complete new outfit of clothing, the items of which I need not add were as different as I could make them from those I had purchased earlier in the morning. After a visit to the barber, and attired in my new finery, I had the pleasure of mingling with the crowd on the river bank. These, I found, were answering the anxious questioning of the Siamese lecturer from Abdulla's encampment, who, accompanied by four of the Chinese, left hurriedly down-stream when he learnt that nothing had been seen since daylight of a Sakai in a stolen canoe. It was evident, he said, that the man must have passed Aspore Hina during the night!

With my pursuers, then, in front of me, the continuance of my journey to the coast and thence by way of Bangkok to Singapore and so home, left nothing of sufficient interest to make it worthy of a chronicle of this sort.

* * *

It was not until over two months afterwards that I again found myself in this pleasant village, this time on my way up-stream, where, having been loaned to the Siamese Police, I was acting as their guide to the entrance of the secret passage-way.

By careful timing, the party who broke through the trap-door and collared Mohamet Abdulla as he sprang from his bed, made their capture only four minutes before their confrères appeared demanding admission at the stockade entrance. The synchronization would have been even more exact had the latter party not been delayed by their scrupulous care in avoiding injury to the advance sentry when they noiselessly captured him. At the time these things were happening, however, I was speeding down-stream once more in a fast canoe. My duties had ended at the foot of the stairway, and it would never do for me to appear on the stage in scenes of that sort.

While I was, of course, relieved to be back in civilization once more, yet I found myself taking unkindly to the comparative flatness of routine espionage which formed the greater part of my daily life for a long time after Mohamet Abdulla had been removed—to a 'cell' which I do not suppose he appreciated so much as the one of his own creation!

Chapter 17

JOINING THE CROWD AT FUNERALS, at the races, at weddings. Listening, listening, listening, and reports, reports, reports. How wearisome it all can be, when one returns from a mission on which one has been entirely one's own master!

Although the colour of my skin precluded me from being actually assigned to cases where the subject for investigation was a Tamil or Malayälam, nevertheless my knowledge of the former language had helped me, from time to time, to put my darker-skinned confrères on the right track.

An incident of this sort occurred in the case of Mr. Veerasami Pillay. I was not actually engaged on the case myself, but, like all other members of the detective force, I had been informed that this rich Tamil merchant had been robbed of a collection of gem stones, amounting to many thousands of pounds.

It had been his habit for many years to bank or invest only half his savings, the other half he wished to keep under his hand, and he thought the most convenient way of doing so was to concentrate the money in the form of precious stones. In this way he had gathered together in one casket the fortune which had now disappeared.

I was working as a rickshaw-puller when, as I stood at the counter of a wayside khedai along the Petaling Road drinking tea and passing the time of the day with the Tulacan proprietor, I overheard one of the two Tamils who were sitting on the bench outside mention the words "Rangorara casket". Now this was the name of the ancient Moghul casket which Veerasami had bought, at immense cost, as a fitting house for his treasure, and to hear a Tamil coolie referring to it seemed, on the face of it, to point to suspicious knowledge on his part. So far as I knew the name of this casket had never been divulged—certainly it had not appeared in the meagre notice of the robbery given by the *Malay Mail*, nor in any other paper.

I took it upon myself therefore to shelve the work on which I was engaged, and find out who this knowledgeable individual was. Luckily no one offered to hire my rickshaw, and I was thus able to saunter after the couple when they departed. Before reaching the bridge near Petaling Station they turned off to the left and I realized that, unless they worked on one of the intervening estates or mines, we were bound for either Kajang or Klang. If these two were, indeed, connected with the robbery the latter seemed to be the more likely destination, being practically on the coast. The sooner the jewels were out of the country the better, would be the thieves' natural feeling.

Under the seat of my rickshaw I had my sarong, cap and baju, and I felt that the sooner I could get rid of the vehicle and appear in my natural colours the better. The opportunity presented itself as I toiled up the hill through the strip of jungle near the ninth mile. Choosing a suitable moment at a bend in the road, I hastily pushed the rickshaw well into the undergrowth and, putting my blue cotton trousers and straw hat in their place, I donned my own clothes and proceeded after my suspects.

It was as a quiet Malay once more that I followed them past the Rumah Kapalla Gajah, at Bukit Dinkel, and we came to the turning which would decide whether they were making for the coast or not.

The fact that they were, simplified things for me very considerably, for so soon as I had seen them safely started on the mile-long road across the swamp I made for the nearest telephone, which I knew was in the manager's bungalow on Puchong estate, only a few hundred yards distant. I hurried there and interviewed the Tuan Besar who, having just finished his lunch, lent a kindly ear to my story of the urgent necessity for me to ring up my uncle, who was making the necessary arrangements for a funeral which I would have to attend. Full of sympathy for my bereavement, he gave me permission to use the telephone.

I am quite sure that neither he nor his Tamil *krani* realized that, in the conversation which they then overheard, I was making arrangements which resulted in a Police car from Kuala Lumpur overtaking me before I had reached the bridge over the Klang River, on my way after the two doubtful characters.

Here my connection with the case ended. The chase was continued by others and the jewels recovered as they were being taken on board a boat at Port Swettenham. Neither of my two friends had committed the actual robbery, which was the work of a discharged cook called Manikam, but they had taken an active part in the proceedings of their cousin. They were to be paid their reward for these services when the jewels were safely on the water, and at the time when I had met them they were on their way to witness, and if necessary assist in, this final transaction, and collect their money.

* * *

Bolshevik propaganda efforts seemed to increase and decrease with a surprisingly irregular pulsation. Perhaps this irregularity is not so surprising after all, when one considers the rotten heart which is driving the stream of venom through the pulses. It was at a time when (to change the metaphor) this tide was sweeping in to what appeared to be a spring-tide height, and we were called upon to put forward our utmost effort to stem the flood, that it was decided to make a supreme endeavour to extirpate the local organization which we believed to exist, by digging down, if possible, to the tap-root from which it sprang.

Even as the white ants will kill a rubber tree, so would we, penetrating unseen to the very heart of the movement, kill this noxious weed, the growth of which was befouling the fair face of our land.

Leaving Singapore as a deck passenger to Bangkok, and from thence to Saigon, I made my way, changing my identity from time to time, to Shanghai. There were three of us engaged on the same quest, and each had chosen his own centre and his method of approach to it; it was hoped that by this means at least one of us would be successful. It is not my intention to reveal the secrets of our department, much less those of anyone else's methods, and it is sufficient if I say that the other two agents were native-bred Chinamen, each of whom had therefore that advantage from which to start.

I had decided to appear once again in my character of half-caste; this time a clerk by the name of Loon Ho, a somewhat taller individual than heretofore—thanks to the cork wedges which he wore in the heels of his shoes. On my arrival at Shanghai I lost no time in mixing myself with the self-styled intelligentsia in the native city, where, thanks to judicious free-handedness, Loon Ho speedily became known as a very superior person who, after being educated at the Lycée in Paris, had worked as a clerk in shipping offices in Cardiff and London, where the miserable pittance doled out to him by the bloated capitalists for whom he worked had embittered his spirit; till, shaking the coal-dust of that inhospitable country from his patent-leather shoes, he had determined to seek a wider fortune in his grandfather's native land.

Thanks to the lectures I had involuntarily listened to at Abdulla's school, I was glibly familiar with the shib boleths of the Bolshevik faith, and lost no opportunity when in likely company of expressing my firm belief in the efficacy of this panacea for all the troubles of mankind.

156

Without making too long a story of it, I very soon was thoroughly mixed up with the international gang of plotters who were the accredited representatives of the Soviet Republic, into whose ears I was continually pouring tags and phrases from the "gospel according to Lenin", till in due course I won their complete confidence as being a hardened Communist. There are not too many people in Shanghai who speak Malay, and of those that do there are still fewer who are hardened Communists, so it was probably for these reasons that I was asked to go and join the movement in Singapore. This was, of course, exactly what I wanted to do, so I readily consented; and was duly provided with my passage-money to that port.

Before leaving Shanghai I was given the name of but one Communist in Singapore, to whom I was told to report myself. This was a Tamil gentleman by the name of Ramasami, who was working as a sort of foreman, or *kangani,* in the tannery along Lalang Road. This, of course, was disappointing to a certain extent, as I had half hoped that I would be sent to report to the leader of the movement; but still, it was a start in the right direction, and was in a way better luck than I had had any right to expect.

Not all Communists who set out to form 'cells' are so blatant in their procedure as my late friend Mohamet Abdulla—they are, as a rule, of a shy and retiring nature when it comes to the question of advertising their identity—but, of course, a 'cell' in the wilds of the jungle and one in the centre of a populous city are two widely different questions, and what you can afford to do in the one case would be sheer suicide in the other.

When I arrived at Singapore I took a room for myself in the International Hotel, and then set out to make the distasteful acquaintance of Ramasami. When I discovered this individual he was plying his noxious trade, so, picking my way mincingly across the tanyard, I greeted him and found that he was expecting me, whereupon we made an appointment to meet in the evening. I made the interview as short a one as possible, and hurriedly sought the purer atmosphere of Beach Street.

During the evening's conversation I soon realized that friend Ramasami must be very small fry indeed, for I undoubtedly knew more about Communism than he knew himself. On the other hand, what he lacked in knowledge he certainly made up in enthusiasm.

As we sat in the forecourt of a cafe in Bras Basah Road we were joined by a very different individual, a man of real intelligence. My conversation with the Tamil had been carried on in Malay; the new arrival, however, was a Bengali, a Mr. Tambi Dass, who, after joining

157

in the conversation for some time in the same language, addressed me in English and was, I could see, putting me through a regular examination. He was altogether a well-educated man, and had I not been so well versed as I was, would no doubt have been able to expose me; in meeting him I felt that I had encountered the 'outer guard' of the real Communist nucleus.

From this beginning I slowly but surely increased my circle of acquaintances amongst the more secret workers for the cause, amongst whom was a Chinaman named Ah Yang, with whom I became most friendly. He was a clerk in the Hong Kong and Shanghai Bank, and had promised to use his best endeavours to get me similar employment when a vacancy next occurred. I particularly sought the friendship of this man, as it seemed to me that he was amongst the few who really knew the innermost secrets of the organization, and I hoped through him to learn where I should look, amongst the many business people of Singapore, for the man who was the chief organizer.

With this end in view I entertained Ah Yang fairly lavishly, and I must admit that he did his share in providing for our pleasures. We went motor trips on the mainland and motor boat picnics together, and soon were sufficiently intimate to make a week-end trip to Malacca when a Bank Holiday gave him a long week-end. Things had reached this stage with me, and it was being arranged that I should go to Ipoh to help to spread the gospel of bloodshed from that centre, when disaster almost overtook me.

I was sitting drinking a cup of coffee on the veranda of my hotel, when my attention was caught by a face which I seemed to know; and it was, unfortunately, a few moments before I realized that it was that of a man called Poo Hup, whose arrest I had been instrumental in arranging years ago and who was, I had no doubt, an implacable enemy of mine. Needless to say the instant I remembered who he was, I showed no sign of recognition; and I could only hope that no tell-tale gleam of greeting had momentarily shone from my eyes when I first saw him and so given me away.

In the ordinary way I have little to fear from people recognizing me, since there are few who have the slightest grounds for connecting me with their troubles, and of those few it would be extremely unlikely that I should meet them again in the same guise. In the present case, however, Poo Hup had shown his suspicions of me long before his arrest, and I, moreover, had been in very much the same character that I was now representing when I had had my previous encounter with him. It was also unfortunate that I was sitting when he saw me, as this robbed me of the benefit which my false additional height gave me. He passed on, however, making no sign of recognition, and I hoped that the years which had rolled between had wiped out the recollection of our previous meeting from his mind. After all, it was my business to remember faces, but it was not his, and I hoped that the wrinkles of age which now seam my face had proved a sufficient alteration, as seemed to be the case.

The principal danger in being recognized by this man, however, was not that he knew me to belong to the Police, but that at the time of my previous encounter with him Loon Ho had been, according to his story, in Paris. If his Communistic friends now learned from Poo Hup that, far from being in Paris, he had been in Singapore at that date, his life would not be a very safe investment for an insurance company.

The day had, therefore, been one of potential ill-luck; not so, however, with the day following. It was by the merest good fortune on that day that I decided to have a face massage and so was sitting quietly in the barber's, with my face almost entirely covered with a hot towel, when I saw the reflection of Poo Hup in company with Tambi Dass, come out of the manicure department at the back of the shop. They were in earnest conversation, and as they passed the back of my chair Poo Hup was saying: "There is no doubt my friend. I never forget a face." This seemed to me decisive, and I realized that there had now been such a spoke put in my wheel that my use in the present investigation was finished.

Before leaving Singapore, however, I determined to try to play a little joke on my friends of the Soviet; so, having advised headquarters of my exposure and impending return, I made one or two arrangements and then went round to the bank, where I met my friend Yang as he left for the day. I took him directly over to Johore Bahru, and we commenced a lively evening. Whilst plying him profusely with drink, I managed to merely 'go through the motions' myself, most of my drink finding its way into flower-pots, or elsewhere.

Later on at night we returned to Singapore, and I insisted on Yang coming along to my room for a final drink, which drink, with a little addition I made to it, put him to sleep effectually. I hurriedly dressed him in my pyjamas and put him to bed, then, putting on my Malay costume, I packed my bag, turned out the light, and left the room barefooted, quietly and inconspicuously, by the bathroom entrance, and made my way to the street through the servants' quarters.

I went straight to Fort Canning, where I had arranged to spend the night. I had told the Police that it would be advisable to keep an eye on my late room and arrest anyone who they might see *leaving* it during the night. Early in the morning I was told that two men had been taken up as they were leaving my recently-vacated quarters—a Chinaman called Poo Hup and an Indian named Tambi Dass.

I caught the eight o'clock train back to Kuala Lumpur and it was not until after my arrival there that I learnt how the unfortunate Yang had been found in my bed that morning with his throat slit from ear to ear. Needless to say I felt very glad that I had taken the precaution of making him take my place for the night.

Sudah Habis

Glossary

Almirah	Wardrobe
Atas	Above
Attap	Palm-leaf thatch
Banir	Buttress-like roots
Besar	Big
Bukit	Hill
Chandu	Prepared opium
Chee	An opium weight
Chetti	Money-lender
Chunkol	A hoe-like tool
Churi	To steal
Dato	A chief (lit. grandfather)
Farsi	A Persian
Gajah	Elephant
Hoon	An opium weight
Kampong	Village
Kangani	Foreman
Kangkong	A lettuce-like vegetable
Kapalla	Head, Headman
Khedai	Small shop
Kling	A Tamil
Krani	A clerk
Laut	Sea
Makan	Food
Mandor	Foreman
Mari	Come

Meranti	A mahogany-like wood
Nona	A young female Chinese
Orang	Man
Parang	A large chopping-knife
Pawang	Sorcerer, Medicine-man
Pergi	Go
Plandok	The mouse-deer
Rumah	House
Sakai	Aboriginal Malay
Sampan	A small boat
Sudah Habis	I have finished
Sumpitan	Blow-pipe
Sungei	River
Tuan	Master

Opium Weights

10 *Tee*	1 Hoon
10 *Hoon*	1 Chee
10 *Chee*	1 Tahil